FRACTURED TIES

BOYKOV BRATVA

BETHANY-KRIS

Published by Bethany-Kris

www.bethanykris.com

ISBN: 978-1-989658-21-5

Editor: Nina S. Gooden

Cover Design © London Miller

This is a work of fiction. Names, characters, places, organizations, corporations, locales and so forth are a product of the author's imagination, or if real, used fictitiously. Any resemblance to a person, living or dead, is entirely coincidental.

To all the readers who met these Boykovs years ago and waited patiently to say hello again.

CONTENTS

1.

IF HIS father sent someone to drag his ass out of bed—even if it was a night when he drank half of his body weight in vodka—Kolya couldn't refuse. Especially not when his father was the *Pakhan*.

The stars tattooed on Kolya Boykov's chest meant that regardless if he was drunk or not, Vadim owned his fucking ass for life. Or at least until death.

"Move your ass, Kolya," the man outside his bathroom barked. "You know the boss won't appreciate being made to wait on you again."

Fuck.

Like Kolya needed a reminder, or something.

"I'm trying to take a piss, yeah? Shut that goddamn hole in your face."

"Surly today, no?"

Kolya spat out a laugh that tasted like hatred, bitterness, and vodka on his tongue. *Today*, right. That was a goddamn joke when it was … Kolya glanced down at the Rolex watch adorning his large wrist. Four in the *fucking* morning!

Who called someone at four in the morning?

Jesus.

Tipping his head back to let out another frustrated growl, Kolya finished up his business, and took his sweet time washing his hands, too. The less time he had to spend in his father's presence, the better. He swore Vadim pulled shit like this just because he could—because the bastard got a good rise out of pestering the living hell out of his sons—and nothing else.

The fist banging against the bathroom door all but sent Kolya's blood pressure skyrocketing. "Working on getting my foot shoved up your ass, Anatoly."

The fact the bull had been one of Vadim's best men for longer than Kolya cared to remember didn't really make much of a fucking difference to him at the end of the day. He would still make sure the man knew the taste of pain before Kolya ended his life.

With a smile.

Kolya took that whole *kill them with kindness* thing to another level.

"It's not Anatoly, *brat*," came a new voice.

Kolya's posture softened a bit at Konstantin's—his younger brother by two years—voice. But not very much. Konstantin, depending on the time, day, or his mood, could be just as irritating as anyone else in Kolya's path.

Or shit, maybe it was just Kolya.

1

"When did you get here?"

"Two minutes ago," Konstantin said through the door. "How long are you going to wash your hands?"

Kolya grumbled unintelligibly under his breath—*until I'm decently sober.* At the moment, he was pretty sure if he walked too fast, he would tumble over. Nobody needed to see all six-foot-four, and two-hundred-fifty pounds of him topple over because he wasn't willing to admit he'd drank too much vodka.

That looked good on no man.

But especially not a *vor.*

And definitely not a Russian.

Fuck it.

Kolya shut off the water and ignored the stinging in his hands. The water had been hotter than the devil's ass and turned his hands bright red in the process. Damn—like he needed more proof that he wasn't the least bit up to par for a meeting this early in the goddamn morning with his father.

Vadim Boykov didn't miss a thing.

He ate shit like misdeeds and missteps for breakfast.

Saw them as weaknesses.

And when it came to his sons?

Vadim was *far* worse.

It was as though the man expected ten times from Kolya and Konstantin what he demanded from other men. Anyone else might have to jump when told to, but the Boykov brothers better damn well *fly* when Vadim even suggested it.

Twenty-six years under his father's thumb had taught Kolya one important lesson about life, family, and *vory*: as long as you were a thief, none of the rest meant shit, and the less he expected from his father, the better off he would be.

That was, unless Kolya was expecting something like a slap to the back of his head, or some other form of punishment meant to cut him down a step or two or degrade him enough to humiliate him. Vadim liked to think of that as *teachable moments* for his boys.

Dragging himself from his thoughts, Kolya yanked open the bathroom door and found Konstantin leaning against the wall. Konstantin was peering at the glowing screen of his phone. He didn't even glance up at his brother's entrance.

"Got the call, too, I see," Kolya muttered.

"Yes."

Konstantin's confirmative reply followed Kolya into the bedroom across the hall.

"Where did Anatoly disappear to?"

2

Konstantin tipped his head to the side with one of those looks of his, saying, "Said he wasn't waiting on you anymore, and since I was here …"

Kolya chuckled dryly. "Fucking useless."

"Funny."

"*Izvinee*," Kolya mumbled, "because nothing about this seems fucking funny to me. You like getting your ass up for Papa in the middle of the night, Konstantin? Because I do *not*."

"*Funny*," Konstantin returned, "because Anatoly says the same thing about you."

Yeah, well …

Kolya didn't even bother to respond to that statement, instead he picked up the pace to leave his place. His shitty little apartment in the Heights wasn't much to look at, but it was good enough for him at the moment. It was close to his work, and easy access to everything else. A shitty part of the city, sure, but who the fuck was going to mess with a Boykov in Chicago?

They *owned* this fucking city.

The Boykov Bratva was well-known in the city. Most idiots just referred to them as the Russian mafia, but he attributed that ignorance to the fact that the inner workings of the Bratva and their customs weren't exactly public consumption.

People knew to leave them the fuck alone and stay the hell away. Which was exactly what Kolya enjoyed most about being who he was. He didn't like others, in general—he couldn't even pretend to *try* on most days. His disposition and last name afforded him the sanctuary of people keeping their distance, which meant he rarely needed to bother with anyone else at all.

That was enough for Kolya.

Unless, of course, it was his father.

Because he was *Vadim*.

That was really all Kolya needed to say.

"You need to upgrade from this apartment," Konstantin said, glancing around Kolya's darkened bedroom. "Live up to the standards of your name, no?"

Kolya rolled his eyes and ground his teeth together as he pulled out appropriate clothing for a meeting with his father. No stupid fuck thought to meet Vadim in anything less than a suit, or black clothes that could pass as dressier wear. "Don't take cheap shots at my place, *suka*. Not all of us need to live in a mansion on the hills,"

"I don't live in a fucking mansion on the hills."

"*Yet*," Kolya returned.

He *was* looking at a house in Melrose Park, but buying something like that meant his sister, Viktoria, would probably want to have a housewarming party. And a party for a Boykov meant his father would be invited, and other *people*.

Not Kolya's thing.

At all.

Kolya had already thrown on the black slacks and he left the black dress shirt unbuttoned when he passed by Konstantin on the way out the door. He'd button it up in the car because he had already wasted enough time. Vadim would be worked up enough as it was, without Kolya adding to it.

"You should have splashed some water on your face," Konstantin said. "Showered, yeah? You smell like you bathed in cheap vod—"

He punched his brother hard in the arm, a silent warning for Konstantin to back the fuck off before he got Kolya worked up.

Konstantin bared his teeth. "*Mudak.*"

Kolya laughed darkly as he headed down the dimly lit hallway with his brother on his heels. "Ouch, that hurts my soul."

"Nothing hurts you," Konstantin said when he moved ahead of Kolya to grab the door for him, "I don't think you even have a fucking soul *to* hurt."

"*Nyet.* I have a soul—I just don't own it anymore."

Kolya tossed the keys for his Hummer to Konstantin over his shoulder without even looking back. He heard Konstantin catch the keys, and smirked. Sure, he ribbed his brother a lot, and the two were at each other's throats more often than they weren't.

But at the end of the day?

At the end of *every* single day?

Konstantin was still a Boykov. He was still Kolya's brother, and Vadim hadn't beaten enough lessons into his oldest son yet to make him forget it, either.

It meant something to Kolya.

At least for now.

"You drive," Kolya called. "I'm not legal, *brat.*"

At least he was walking straight, though. That had to count for something. Maybe by the time they made it across the city to where Vadim was waiting with whatever fresh hell he was ready to lay at their feet, he wouldn't look like he just woke up from a night-long bender.

Unlikely.

One could still hope.

Konstantin made a noise in the back of his throat. "Begging for Vadim to throw a fit, Kolya."

Maybe he was.

Maybe he fucking was.

• • •

If there was anything Vadim Boykov loved more than money, and pliable, compliant men in the business of the Bratva, it was his theatrics. Sometimes, those theatrics came in the forms of lessons he liked to teach his men, and other times, they manifested in nothing more than Vadim showing off in a variety of ways.

Kolya never really understood his father's need for those sorts of things, and he rarely found himself surprised by them anymore.

Walking into the Four Seasons hotel room to see two young ladies—likely a couple of years younger than him—dressed in what looked to be only short, white silk robes was nothing uncommon for Vadim. Both young women were draped over the four-poster bed, rolled onto their stomachs with their legs high in the air to give just a peek of their backsides beneath the robes, and overlooking magazines or some other nonsense.

The sheer curtains on the four-poster bed had been pulled as if to shield the girls from the view of the men, but that was only for show, too. Vadim *meant* for the girls to be seen, in the same way he demanded that his men didn't look at them for longer than it took to notice they were actually there.

The women didn't pay the entering men any mind.

Too busy pleasing his father with their *games*, likely. Pretty, young women were a favorite of Vadim's, and he preferred to keep one or two on call for whatever his fancy was on any given day. Back when Kolya was a teenager, seeing this sort of thing had affected him much differently than it did now.

Back then, his mother had still been alive. Cervical cancer was the worst kind of monster because it took without care or concern, caused terrible suffering that couldn't be appeased, and stayed hidden until it was already too late.

God rest my mama's soul.

How someone as wonderful, sweet, and adoring as his mother had fallen for a man like Vadim Boykov was a mystery. Ana couldn't have *not* known Vadim was a philanderer with a half of a dozen *paid* mistresses on call—serial, really. Like it was a disease the man couldn't keep contained. And yet, Ana had never said a thing, nor spoken out against her husband to her three children. Kolya only remembered his mother loving Vadim and keeping his house like a queen should.

Now, though, Kolya barely felt anything at all when he walked in on one of these scenes. He saw them for what they were—another way for his father to show off and extend his power by way of controlling his men in an unusual way.

Look too long at the girls, and a man might lose an eye.

Touch one, and well, maybe you didn't need that hand after all.

Konstantin, on the other hand, was still young enough—or maybe he just hadn't gotten desensitized yet to all of this—that these shows were not as easy for him to swallow like they were for Kolya. Under his breath, in Russian, he said to Kolya, "If this isn't some kind of *shit*. He's got other rooms in here. They could *be* elsewhere."

They *could*.

Vadim wouldn't let them, though.

Kolya's lips twitched with a grin that came out more like a sneer. Probably the closest thing to a smile that he could manage, honestly. He couldn't remember the last time he'd genuinely smiled because something had truly amused him or made him happy.

Unless he was beating the hell out of someone.

Or killing them.

That usually made Kolya happy.

"Relax," Kolya returned to Konstantin at the same quiet level. "Stop letting it piss you off when you know that's something he can—"

"Do you have something to share with the rest of the class, Kolya?"

Kolya's gaze drifted lazily to the man across the room. A good twenty feet from where the women were still pretending like the sheer curtains were doing anything to hide the fact they were still resting on that goddamn bed. Vadim stood next to the windows, haloed in the ray of color the inverted ceiling lights provided over the heavy, dark drapes.

As usual, Vadim kept hold of a glass of vodka that might as well have been his third hand. A man could almost guess by the way Vadim was holding the glass if things would end well for him in a meeting with the man.

Tonight, Vadim kept a light grip on the glass, which meant two things. One, he *was* pissed, and two, the glass could fly into any man's face, should he be brave enough to challenge the man—even without meaning to.

Perfect.

It was only when Vadim kept a tight hold on his glass of vodka that a person should feel safe. It was for only that reason that Kolya decided to tread carefully with his father right then.

He still had a phantom burn in his left eyebrow from the last glass that shattered in his face. It'd taken ten stitches from one of their paid doctors to keep it closed, made more difficult by the fact that Kolya's face was constantly set into some kind of variation of a scowl or frown. It was never relaxed enough not to strain or pull on the stitches.

"Well?" Vadim demanded. "I know you can *speak*, yes? I taught you how."

Actually, his mother probably had.

Kolya didn't correct him.

"I was telling Konstantin that the rug could use a clean."

Vadim's gaze drifted to Konstantin who only shrugged as if to neither confirm, nor deny, and then back to Kolya just as fast. "Hmm."

Once his father's gaze was off him again, Kolya relaxed slightly. Not a whole lot, though. Just being within a visual distance of his father kept him teetering on a very dangerous edge. That's what Vadim wanted—that's what he liked.

Kolya was not an exception to the rule, but rather, an example of it.

Vadim muttered something low to the man in the corner of the room who was using the wall as a leaning post—the only other man besides Kolya, Konstantin, and his father's Sovietnik, Grisha. Anatoly, the bull who had come to drag Kolya out of bed this meeting, was busy glancing at something on his phone, but still seemed to hear whatever it was Vadim said to him.

"*Nyet*, not yet, boss," Anatoly said.

Vadim scowled. "*Blyad*. The *suka* seems determined to test my very gracious patience, no?"

Anatoly only shrugged in response.

Kolya was struck with a heavy jolt of irritation in that moment. He had taken two things from his father, though he hated when people had the audacity and nerve to point them out. One was his father's disposition—reverently distasteful, constantly surly, and almost never pleasant—and the other was his features.

From the dark, short-cropped hair to the sharp line of his jaw, the square-cut chin, and ice-blue eyes. Even the shape of their straight, thick brows—giving them both the gift of a persistently dismissive or disinterested expression—was the same. Even their large, muscular builds were similar, although Kolya had a good inch or two of height on his father now. Right down to the prominent cheekbones, and cleft in his chin, it was all the goddamn same.

Sometimes, he wished it wasn't.

"Not sure *gracious* is the right word to use, yeah," Konstantin muttered low.

Jesus Christ.

The little shit was doing his very best to test Kolya for all he was worth tonight in their father's presence. It took all Kolya's control and effort not to smirk at that statement. He sobered quickly enough when Vadim's sharp eyes turned on them again.

And just like that, the pounding headache from his drunken episode earlier was back, at the idea he was going to have to put on his give-a-fuck suit for his father and act like he gave a shit why he had even been called there in the first place.

"I have a job for the two of you," Vadim started.

One that couldn't wait until a decent time?

Kolya's thoughts were testing his control, too, it seemed.

Konstantin passed Kolya a look, and then went back to his father. "Why are we taking the job?"

Wrong question.

"I *give* jobs to you," Vadim stated, the cold gleam coming into his eye as he spoke, "but you do not get to ask me to justify or explain why I've given you them. Understood?"

"Yeah," Konstantin said, stiffening a bit beside his brother.

"What job?" Kolya asked.

It worked to get his father's attention away from Konstantin for the moment. Soon, the man would be able to go back to petting whichever pussy he preferred on the bed, and maybe he'd be in a better mood tomorrow when they had to meet up again.

But who knew?

"A brigadier has gotten out of hand—owes debts to someone after he'd already been warned on that end. Not only do I need you to *collect* something worthy of satisfying the trouble he's caused ... *again*," Vadim added with a growl, "It would be helpful if you could make his lesson permanent. I'm sure they'll be others around. Nature of his business. It'll be a good reminder for them, too."

Dirty work.

Kolya wasn't even surprised.

"I can't handle the issue personally, since I have the Markovic Bratva arriving this morning, and will need to deal with Vasily."

Kolya could *hear* the disgust in his father's tone. Vadim made a decent effort to play nice with other organizations when the need arose, but that was about as far as it went. He didn't make any effort to pretend to like them, though.

"But back to the brigadier issue, as I will handle the Markovics." Vadim passed him another dismissive glance, adding, "Because you're a captain, he won't think much of you going into his business. I would like it to be done with little fanfare on his end. He isn't aware that I know of his misdeeds and have been keeping track of them for a while, so he won't be expecting this move on my part. Nor will he be suspicious of you, yes?"

His father smiled.

It wasn't *at all* friendly.

"Strip him of his stars while you're at it," Vadim added. "Really drive the point home for me."

The upturned spider tattooed on Kolya's right hand itched a bit, much like the stars on his chest stung at those words. To strip a man of his tattoos—*before* his death, no less—was akin to pissing on his grave while his grieving family looked on. And only another *vor* could do the job when the boss gave an order like that.

"Great," Kolya said.

"Excuse me?"

Kolya checked the attitude that he hadn't meant to let slip out. "It'll be done."

"Who's the mark?" Konstantin asked.

"Ivan Kozlov." Vadim nodded. "Now, get the fuck out of my sight."

• • •

Konstantin was already reaching to shut the door of Kolya's Hummer before he had even finished tugging on his leather gloves. Driving gloves, actually, but Kolya rarely used them for driving.

Killing, yes.

Not driving.

"Good to see you again, Kolya," came a voice across the street.

Kolya eyed the figure leaning against his younger brother's car. "You brought the Markovic shit along?"

Konstantin shrugged. "He was bored."

Yeah, Kolya bet.

Kazimir—or Kaz, as he preferred—was the second oldest son of Vasily Markovic, the one Russian with all the pull in Brighton Beach, New York. Despite being the same age as Kolya, Kaz got on far better with Konstantin than the older Boykov brother. He was a cocky fucking thing—Kaz, but his father, too.

All the Markovics were, really.

Sometimes, Kolya thought it was Kaz's cockiness and attitude that was going to kill him someday. That, or his goddamn mouth.

Kolya did share *one* thing in common with Kaz, although it was rarely ever a topic of conversation between the two whenever they were unlucky enough to have a face-to-face meeting. Kaz, like Kolya, was the son of a Russian mob boss—*the* son, as some liked to say. The one being looked at to move higher in the organization and take over their father's position when the eventual time came for it to happen.

The thought irked Kolya.

It was never a question of *if* he wanted the position, simply a matter of him being given it whether he cared to have it or not. He'd never really given it much thought, but apparently, his thoughts wouldn't make a difference at the end of the day.

Or, that's what he was always told.

"Where's Ruslan?" Kolya asked, referring to Kaz's older brother.

"That's how you greet me," Kaz said, smirking a bit, "by referring to me as shit, and then asking where the fuck Rus is?"

Kolya fixed the straps on his gloves, tightening them until he felt the tell-tale pinch of the metal hooks biting against his flesh. "Ruslan doesn't make me want to beat a lesson into him every time we meet up, *pizda*."

Kaz bared his teeth at that comment.

A warning if Kolya ever saw one.

He knew the *pussy* remark would do it. Kaz fucking hated that shit. Kolya was the type to push a man's buttons, just because he knew the guy had ones that were easy to press, whenever the fuck he felt like it. Also, all in all, Kaz was decent people, and he could give it as well as he took it.

Kolya respected that.

Didn't mean he had to be pleasant.

"Asking to go a round, yeah?" Kaz asked. "Thought the last time when I busted your mouth up taught you something, Kolya."

Little shit.

"Can't say it did, but I'm willing to let you believe that shot was something more than a miracle." Kolya shrugged. "Maybe later, yeah? Business to do, Markovic."

"Lucky you."

"Or lucky *you*," Kolya tossed over his shoulder.

"I get a fucking headache just listening to the two of you," Konstantin grumbled, following to catch up with his brother. "Try to get along, yes?"

Kolya scowled. "This *is* me getting along, Konstantin."

Konstantin tipped his head to the side, bowing to the matter. "Fine."

"Anatoly is already in the place, then."

"According to his last text."

"Would have liked for him to be across the goddamn state."

"Vadim wanted—"

"Vadim wants too fucking much from me," Kolya snapped. "He could bend a bit to shit I ask for when it's not very much to begin with."

Konstantin opted not to reply to that, and instead, stepped up to the warehouse door to open it for his brother and Kazimir who had been quietly following behind the whole time. So was the Markovic way—they listened and soaked it all in so they could use it later.

Smart, really.

"*Blyad.*" Kolya tossed his brother a look, seeing that Konstantin was tight-jawed, shadowed in his features, and his eyes had gone rather dark. It spoke of his irritation—probably at Kolya. "Let's just get this done with, yes?"

"Fine by me, *brat.*"

Situated on the outskirts of the city, the warehouse Ivan Kozlov used for his main business didn't look like very much on the outside. Steel walls, and a tin roof. Very few windows, although the place was certainly large enough to be a good three or four floors high. Kolya knew there were a few windows on the upper floors on the north and east sides of the building, but certainly not low enough for someone to look into and see anything.

Up above the entrance doors—ones Kolya had only walked through maybe twice before, as this wasn't his scene when he much preferred the other side of the Boykov business—a security camera zoned in on his face.

He gave it his best fuck-you smirk.

Complimented by his middle finger.

Inside, the first thing to greet the three men was a long, darkened hallway. The smell coming through the corridor reminded Kolya of dirt, decaying *something*, and rotting hay.

Not surprising, considering …

"What's this place for?" Kaz asked.

"Fights," Konstantin replied.

"Fights?"

"Animals," Kolya uttered low. "Ivan's got a sick thing for that shit. Vadim said nothing because—well, fuck, look at this place, yeah? Tucked away, never been raided, and illegal animal fighting hasn't been touched on in the news cycle in half of a decade."

"Brings in decent money from it, too," Konstantin added.

"Except for lately, I suspect," Kaz put in.

Kolya shot the man a look over his shoulder. "*Da*. The boss says he owes debts, so that money is coming from somewhere."

"Vadim only steps in when it comes from his pocket, or he knows it's going to," Konstantin muttered.

"Quiet."

The two men hushed under Kolya's warning as they neared the door at the far end of the hall. He didn't need for their discussion to be overheard by whoever was watching the first set of inner doors. It was only because of his previous two visits to the warehouse that Kolya knew basically what to expect once he got a little deeper into the place.

Twenty-thousand square feet of *hell*, that was.

The door opened before Kolya could even knock on it. The man waiting on the other side kept a firm grip on an AR-15 like it was going to do something to Kolya if he looked at it the wrong way. It was only once the man actually took a good look at who was standing there that he backed off a bit and dropped his gaze to keep it from meeting a higher-ranking man's. All the security in this place was only used for *after* shit when down. Nobody was ever watching the cameras when the place was opened for business because only certain people even knew this was a place that was opened for business.

"*Kapitan* is in the bar," the man said, clearly referring to Ivan.

Kolya didn't bother to acknowledge or respond to the guy. Instead, he stepped through the door and moving forward with his brother and Kaz close on his heels. Another corridor, although slightly less dark this time, led them to a second set of doors.

This time, Kolya did need to knock.

A slate on the door was opened just long enough for the man to see who was waiting behind it before it was slammed shut, and the trio was ushered in right after. Into the bar section of the warehouse, that was. If someone wanted to call the dirt-floored section a *bar*. Frankly, the only liquor Ivan was known to keep on hand was vodka and spirits. He might occasionally bring in a bottle of wine if someone was bringing a woman of any importance, but even that was a rarity.

Women didn't tend to look kindly upon animals being made to fight to either survive or die.

A couple of old pool tables—although in better condition than the chairs and tables—sat along the far side of the large room. The bare bulbs hanging overhead kept the room just dim enough that someone might be able to pretend they were somewhere else.

With a flick of his wrist in the direction of the pool tables, he sent Konstantin and Kaz off to be on their own. Harmless in their corner as they shot the shit or played a bit of billiards. Kolya knew at least ninety-five percent of his brother's attention would be on him, and he'd be ready to step in when needed.

Regardless of whether Konstantin was pissed off or not.

Some shit never changed.

Kolya found the man of the hour—probably his *last* hour, too—sitting at the far end of the bar talking to another man he recognized. Anatoly and Ivan were what looked to be three-quarters of the way deep into a bottle of vodka, and a discussion they didn't want other people overhearing.

One in Russian, too.

Kolya kept his footsteps light as he approached.

"And what do you plan to do with that fucking *thing*?" Anatoly asked. "You can't keep it *here*, comrade."

"Can't get rid of it, either," Ivan muttered, his Russian slurred a bit from his drink. "Do you know how much money it brings when we take it out of the cage? I'd be fucking stupid to—"

"You recognize then when you're being stupid, no?" Kolya asked, sliding into the stool beside Ivan's. "Hard to believe, all things considered."

The man swung around on his stool to face Kolya with a drunken gaze. At the same time, Kolya waved two fingers over his shoulder for whoever was down the bar to bring him a drink. Or come take a fucking order for one.

Behind Ivan, Anatoly gave a subtle nod.

"Kolya," Ivan greeted, "since when do you make your way to my part of town?"

"Since tonight." Kolya drummed his leather-clad fingertips to the worn bar and gave Ivan a look from the side. "Seems I'm needed down this way, unfortunately."

"Thought you weren't the type to—"

"Could I get you something?"

Kolya stiffened.

That voice.

Soft, and sweet, yet bubbly and friendly.

Not at all what he expected to greet him when the bartender made his—no, shit, apparently *her*—way down to serve him. It was something about the fact there was a woman here … a woman with the softest, sweetest tone he had ever heard … that made him hesitate.

And *tense.*

A knot of stress pulled his shoulder blades together.

Still, he looked at the woman.

Pixie-like in her features, the top of her head would barely reach his chest. He could probably use her fucking head as an arm rest when he was standing beside her. Her tiny button nose accentuated the rest of her dainty features. She had small lips, pink and uncolored by makeup or stain, that smiled even though he found hesitance and uncertainty in her blue eyes.

And *blue.*

Damn, so blue.

Like the ocean right before a storm.

Or a sky on a cloudless summer day.

But her hair was pin-straight hanging over her shoulders, and jet-black.

Like the darkest night.

Like tar.

Like his soul.

She wasn't particularly dressed up, but she wasn't dressed down in her outfit, either. Simple straight-leg, tight jeans and a bohemian-style blouse. It told him she had dressed to look appropriate, but not draw attention.

He didn't blame her.

The only attention a woman like her—delicate, beautiful, and sweet-looking—might find here was the bad kind.

Kind of like him.

Because, yeah, Kolya noticed her.

Something he *didn't* do.

"Maya, stop standing there," Ivan barked, drawing Kolya's attention away from the woman, "and make yourself useful, yes? Go do *anything* else but be near me."

"Sorry," the woman—*Maya*—whispered.

Quickly, she scurried off.

"I wanted a drink," Kolya groused, shooting Ivan a glare.

Really, he just wanted Maya to come back.

So he could tell her to *run*.

Ivan waved a hand and didn't even realize with that action and his next words, he just made Kolya's hesitance to kill him with a woman near null and void altogether. "The cunt will come back—my daughter doesn't know how to *listen*. It's why she belongs in the den with the rest of the mutts."

Oh, yeah.

And the fact that Maya was the man's daughter just made it worse, too. *Beyond fucking dead.*

Kolya's favorite knife—a black obsidian blade his brother had given to him when he turned sixteen—was pulled from the sheath at his ankle in his next breath and sliding along Ivan's throat before the man could protest, or *blink*.

"You asked the wrong questions, *suka*," Kolya murmured, reverting back to the familiar feeling of numbness and nothingness. "You should have asked *why* I came here first, and then I could have let you beg for a bit. Now, you're going to learn *pain*. The boss says hello, in case you wondered, and it's time to pay up."

2.

IVAN DIDN'T even get the chance to give Kolya a proper reaction before the two men he probably hadn't even noticed stepped in his path. Kaz yanked Ivan backwards off the stool by gripping the hair at the base of his skull at the same time Konstantin came to stand behind Kolya.

"I didn't—swear I fucking didn't!"

Ivan's words fell on deaf ears because frankly, Kolya had better shit to do, and orders to throw out. "Konstantin, find something that makes fire, yeah?"

"You got it," Konstantin murmured before he jumped the bar using one hand to propel him over.

"Anatoly—watch the door," Kolya said, not even bothering to give the man the benefit of his attention. "Make sure anybody who might step in knows this is business for the boss. Unless they want the same, they can step the fuck back. Anybody leaves while this goes down, and it's your head. You fucking hear me?"

"I hear you."

He was rather amused by the sight of Kazimir dragging Ivan across the dirt floor toward one of the pool tables. Ivan was fighting and thrashing, but too drunk to make much of a difference. Besides, Kaz had probably fifty pounds and twenty years of youth on Ivan.

He didn't even need Kolya's help getting the foolish man up on the pool table. Kolya still made his way over nice and slow, making sure to give Ivan appropriate time to suffer within the privacy of his mind about what exactly would be going down in the next few minutes.

A person could be their own worse torture device when it came right down to it. Kolya swore a man could imagine the worst kinds of things inside his head—shit that wouldn't even happen—but it terrified a person just the same.

Kolya came up to the side of the pool table, and grabbed a pool stick someone had left sitting on the floor. Or hell, maybe it had gotten knocked off in Kaz's stunt to get Ivan up on top. Who the fuck knew, and what did it matter?

He brought that pool stick down across Ivan's knees hard enough for the wood to splinter, and break. By the looks of the way Ivan's left leg was bent at the knee, Kolya had broken *something*.

Good.

He liked to start off slow.

The scream of pain Ivan let loose made Kolya smile fleetingly—he could only get a *real* smile on his face once he actually got going.

Still, what followed Ivan's shout was silence. Well, for the most part. Kolya grabbed another stick and tossed it to Kaz as he took a quick look around. Kaz used that stick to place up under Ivan's chin, and pull taut against the man's throat. He likely wasn't getting much air and, given the way Kaz was putting as much tension as he could on the stick, he wasn't fucking getting up, either.

For such a little shit, Kaz had brains. Kolya had to give him that. Credit where it was due, and all that good stuff.

"I like it, Kaz."

Kaz shrugged. "Might need a hand once this gets going, no?"

"Konstantin will help."

No doubt.

Speaking of Konstantin …

Kolya's gaze did another sweep of the floor. The few scattered men—given it was still too early for most of Ivan's patrons to be taking part in his *other* offerings—were either looking for a way out, or stuck like statues and staring into their drinks. He recognized a few—at least two bore the same eight-pointed stars under their shirts as he did, which meant Vadim's point would be well-made before this was all over.

They likely hadn't seen something like this go down in here before, but any *vor* or man connected to any kind of mafia business knew this shit was always right around the corner. Men like them lived their lives on a constant precipice of sin, atonement, and answering violence.

It was their only promise.

Next to death.

Anatoly was watching the door like he'd been told. Although, the man didn't particularly look like he cared or that he wanted to be there, given his lazy posture and the way he stared at the lights overhead. But who was Kolya to judge?

He was only here because he'd been told to do so.

Konstantin had a torch in his hand, which perked up Kolya's sour mood, considering Ivan was still blabbering on, albeit now in Russian. Like it made a fucking difference.

"Let me talk to the boss—the boss, please!"

"The boss doesn't give a fuck about you," Kolya said out of the corner of his mouth. "And don't act like you don't already fucking know that, Ivan."

"*Schas po ebalu poluchish, suka, blyad!*"

Kaz's brow shot up as he gave Kolya an amused chuckle. "Shit, now he's going to kill you, Kolya."

16

Kolya passed Ivan a disinterested look. "Looks like it, yeah?"

Ivan's struggle against Kaz's hold gained more strength when Kolya took the now-lit torch Konstantin passed over. It didn't make any difference, really, because Konstantin simply stepped in to hold the man's kicking legs down, and gave Kolya a look like, *Fucking get on with it.*

And to add to his point, Konstantin actually dared to say, "Are we doing this or not?"

Kolya clicked his tongue.

Always ruining his fun.

"You never did appreciate good torture," Kolya muttered.

"Because you would be here *all day*," his brother returned.

"That's the whole point."

Like his own personal brand of therapy.

Konstantin could *do* torture, and was decent at it, but Kolya had a way of taking it to the next level. And honestly, if someone didn't step in to reel him back, he could fucking lose himself in the act, too.

Like an animal.

Baser needs came out to play.

He was the predator.

They were the prey.

Needs that delved into the deepest recesses of his mind—where right and wrong didn't live, and goodness never touched. His moral compass had always been broken to begin with, but when he was in *that* state, he didn't even know words like *morals* existed.

"Just so we're clear," Kolya told Ivan as he aimed the six-inch blue flame toward the man's face, "this is happening because you're a fuck up, and the boss is tired of dealing with your shit, Ivan. I could go on a rant and make a point, but that's what it boils down to. I'm sure you understand, yeah?"

Ivan's instincts made him jerk away from the flame—or *try*. Kaz's hold kept him pinned against the pool table.

"Feel free to watch the show, yes?" Kolya called to the few others in the bar. "I'm sure it'll be … a productive experience."

His gaze swept the people.

He didn't see *her*, though.

The black-haired, blue-eyed sprite of a woman.

Maya.

A part of him was grateful, though he wondered which fucking door she'd darted out of, and *when*. Another part of him was pissed for reasons he didn't even understand.

After all, he'd come here to strip a man of his stars and end his life. That was business as usual for Kolya on any given day when Vadim didn't want him working some deal or overlooking the Compound where their *real* cash was made.

So to speak.

But he'd only decided—like a switch flipping off in his brain—to really make it fucking hurt for Ivan because of the way he'd spoken to his daughter.

Kolya figured it might do the woman some good to see a man answer for his misdeeds of disrespecting her, even if that man was her father.

But what did he know?

Later.

Business right now.

He would deal with the rest later.

Kolya slipped a metal knife from his pocket—he didn't like to heat up his obsidian blade when doing so might compromise the integrity. Flashing the blade at a wide-eyed, shouting Ivan, Kolya sneered as he stuck the blade into the hot flame until it was morbidly red, and ready to use.

It took a quick pull of his hands against Ivan's button-down shirt for it to rip open, and buttons flew everywhere. Not that the goddamn floor would notice the mess, really.

It seemed like only *then* that Ivan really understood what was about to happen to him. "No—*nyet*. Don't you fucking dare take my—"

"*Zatknis*," Kolya said coldly. "You're under some kind of impression that you get a *choice*, Ivan. You don't—*at all*. Lower men than you have taken this punishment and *died* for it without whispering a word. You think just because you were given the stars that they can't be taken from you? You *continue* to earn the right to keep them through your miserable existence, and nothing else."

Kolya laughed, and then spit his disgust to the floor. "*Nepravil'no*. Try again."

"You won't take my stars, you cock—"

"You've got a son, no?" Konstantin asked. "One trying to earn his stars?"

Kolya shot his brother a look and wondered where in the fuck he was going with this. Konstantin didn't pay Kolya any mind, but that wasn't entirely unusual, either. Maybe his brother wasn't in the mood for this tonight, or maybe it was something else altogether. Kolya didn't really have the time, patience, or give-a-fuck to figure it out.

Either way, Ivan's fight fled for a second as he did his best to lift his head and stare at Konstantin still holding down his legs. The two men stayed quiet as they gaged one another before Konstantin was the first to speak up between the two. Kolya decided to let his brother have his moment, if he apparently *needed it*.

"You've got a son," Konstantin repeated, "so you shut up, and you do it for him. You do it so he doesn't have to say that even in punishment and death, his father left him with stains that he's unable to remove or outgrow. *Ponimayu?*"

Kolya did a quiet inventory of his younger brother, then—two years younger, but fuck if Konstantin didn't have the mind of a man twice his age, and the right words to use when the time called for it. He never understood why Vadim looked to *him* as the man to take over when someone else had a far better temperament and the reasoning for the job.

Not the time.

Kolya didn't give Ivan a chance to respond to Konstantin before he laid his cooling blade flat to the man's eight-pointed star below his right clavicle. Ivan roared his pain as he practically lifted himself from the table, but Kolya pressed harder, listened for the sound of burning flesh, and then pulled the blade up.

It took a sizeable chunk of burnt flesh with it. And the smell that accompanied the fresh burn and sizzling skin was unlike anything else.

Damn.

"Fuck you," Ivan spat.

Kolya was already heating up the blade to do the man's remaining star as he turned to his brother. "Don't ruin my fun, Konstantin. I like it when they scream."

A ghost of a smile played at the edges of his brother's lips. "Of course, you do."

Kaz just looked bored and as though maybe he needed a drink. Kolya suspected they all would by the time this was over, frankly.

So was the nature of this business.

Death *was* a bit messy.

Ivan, on the other hand, spat and sobbed his way through Russian curses, and occasionally a few English words slipped through, too. Kolya wasn't even listening to the stupid cocksucker anymore. It wasn't like his pleading or cursing would do him any good, and Kolya wasn't here to offer atonement or redemption.

Unless, of course, the man found that in death.

So be it.

"I was told to do *just* the stars," Kolya said, leaning over Ivan once more with the red-hot blade, "but I'll strip you of all your markings, Ivan, and then you can beg me for death. You've earned it."

And really, so had Kolya.

Then, to Konstantin, he said, "Let him go, and light me a smoke. This is going to take a while."

• • •

Kolya flexed his fingers and watched the dried blood in his knuckles make fissure cracks from the strain. Sitting on the barstool, he took the small roll of medical tape Konstantin had found somewhere beneath Ivan's bar, and began wrapping the small nicks and cuts on his fingers. Usually, he would wait until he was home in private to do this, but he had a moment to spare.

And Konstantin would pester him until he did something about the cuts.

Working with a knife could be tricky sometimes.

"You always cut yourself," Konstantin mused.

Kolya shrugged. "Hazard of the job, no?"

"Or maybe you should lay off the knives."

Maybe.

But maybe not.

"*Napitok*?" Kaz offered, pushing a glass of vodka down the bar toward Kolya. He gave the man a nod but continued his work all the same. His mind was still hyper-focused on the dried blood under his fingernails, and what it all meant. "You know, I'm starting to get it, now, Konstantin."

Kolya's brother grunted under his breath. "Came here to do one thing; end up with him making a fucking game out of it."

"I'm not saying the man didn't *deserve* it."

"Better to keep Kolya on that leash when we can, Kaz."

Kolya heard their words, but he wasn't really listening. Sometimes, his nature of killing and the way he could lose himself in the act was disconcerting for those around him. Sure, they put on a good show when he was in the midst of it all, but it was after when his work was fully on display that he found those around him gave him a second or third look.

Or their stares lingered a bit too long.

They didn't get it.

His mind didn't work like theirs.

And that was okay, too.

"Place is empty—shit, you sent them running once they could leave, Kolya," Anatoly said, coming to slide into the stool beside Kolya's.

Yes, he hadn't missed how fast the few patrons inside of Ivan's warehouse were quick to up and go once he'd hissed out the word *leave*. Of course, he had probably been quite a sight standing next to Ivan's burned and sliced corpse, with a good portion of him soaked in the dead man's blood. It was hard to say—he didn't remember a great deal.

That was usually how it worked.

He hadn't exactly intended to start cutting into Ivan—removing the man's tattoos would have done a good enough job before his death—but once Kolya got started, it was difficult to pull him off. Like a fucking dog with his jaws locked on the body of a victim, he wasn't letting go until someone *made* him, or the prey was dead.

"What's left for the boss?" Anatoly asked.

Kolya wasn't in the mood to speak, and Anatoly already fucking knew what Vadim wanted them to do after Ivan was dead. *Find something worthy of repayment for Ivan's debts.* Anatoly was only talking to hear himself *talk* because like most people, he found Kolya to be disturbing after an event like this. Talking filled the silence.

Talking was better than thinking about what he had seen, or what was running through his mind. Talking about something else—*anything fucking else*—might keep them from needing to talk about all of that instead.

Fuck it.

Kolya didn't care.

"Here, *brat.*"

Kolya took the lit cigarette Konstantin offered. His last one had been tossed because the filter soaked up too much blood from his fingers and started tasting like shit. He liked to smoke while he worked—old habits died fucking hard for him.

"Well?" Anatoly asked again.

"Would you *shut the fuck up?*"

Kolya's voice came out raspy and hoarse. Like his mouth and throat were both dry, and the words dragged their way out of his chest to get out. The force behind his tone was still as clear as day, and it was enough to send silence covering the bar.

Konstantin and Kaz passed a look between one another while Kolya stared at the tip of his cigarette. It burned bright red—hot, and warning. He blew the ash from the coal away, and then stuck the filter between his lips for a hard, long drag.

Smoke filled his lungs.

He held it.

It *burned.*

Inhale.

Exhale.

Finally, after half the cigarette was gone and all Kolya could taste in his mouth was smoke and ash and vodka, he turned to Konstantin and asked, "Where did she go?"

Konstantin blinked. "Who?"

"*Her*—the woman. Behind the bar, Konstantin. Where did she go?"

"I don't—"

"Maya," Anatoly said.

Kolya visibly stiffened on the stool. His shoulders knotted together with a ball of tension, and his hand curled into a tight ball against the bar top. A sure sign he was getting ready to put that fucking fist to use for some kind of violence that was going to *hurt.* It wasn't even Anatoly or his voice that put Kolya on that fast track to thinking about death again, but rather, *her* name coming out of *his* mouth like he had any business saying it.

Like a switch in his head.

On, or off.

On, then off.

Something was fucking flipping that goddamn switch and Kolya didn't know how to fucking *handle* it. Not at all. He didn't even understand why it was happening.

Anatoly didn't notice Kolya's reaction.

Konstantin did. "*Brat.*"

His gaze cut to Konstantin. "Did you see where she went?"

"I barely noticed her at all, Kolya."

That was good for Konstantin.

The whole switch-flipping thing.

Bad for Kolya.

"Went out there," Kaz said, coming into the conversation. Kolya glanced up from the empty glass of vodka he'd finished to see Kaz pointing at a door built in between the two shelving units behind the bar. "After the guy told her to beat it."

Kaz had heard that?

Huh.

"Her father," Anatoly said. "Ivan is her father."

"Was," Kolya corrected roughly.

Throats cleared around him.

"What's that lead to?" he asked after a second.

He posed the question to Anatoly because he was likely the only stupid fuck in the room who had any clue about this place. Sure, Kolya had a few memories of the layout, but shit changed when things called for it.

There were another two doors on the other side of the bar—across from the one they'd first come in through. Kolya remembered those being used to allow guests into the fighting section of the warehouse, while the other one allowed certain people into the spot where some of the animals were held before the fights.

Early betting, so to speak.

They would get a look at the goods before the animals ripped each other to shreds in their terror and instinctual natures. Laugh when they stuck their fingers through too-small cages, and then managed to pull them out just in time to save them from getting bitten off by a terrified dog.

Probably someone's pet they'd stolen from a front yard. Likely starved, beaten, and terrorized until all the animal understood was *survival.*

And *he* was the monster.

Right.

"Are you deaf?" Kolya asked, turning on the stool to face Anatoly.

"What?"

"*Glukhoy*—deaf, you stupid fucker," Kolya uttered before he pointed to the door. "What does that door lead to?"

Anatoly's gaze narrowed, and he swore he saw the man's hand twitch like it was going to come up and smack Kolya.

Try it, he wanted to say. *Give me a fucking reason—I didn't get enough to satisfy me with the first fucker today.*

Anatoly stayed in his spot, and his hand never moved again. Smart, really. Christ.

The guy was still working every nerve Kolya had left.

And that wasn't very goddamn many.

"It leads to the offices," Anatoly spat through his scowling lips. "Mind you, Ivan's got hallways up there leading into everywhere else, too, and a couple of doors that'll lead to the exits at the side of the building."

Kolya didn't want to bring Maya's name up again. He didn't want his brother looking at him in that way again, either—like he had grown a second fucking head.

All because he noticed and asked about a *woman*.

"She likely took off," Anatoly added after a minute. "The woman isn't fucking stupid, despite what her father likes to say about her."

Kolya's cheek twitched. "You think?"

He didn't like that.

He didn't want her *gone*.

"What?"

"That she took off," Kolya muttered.

Konstantin was looking at him in *that way* again.

"You okay?"

"Fuck off, yes," he told his brother. "Mind your own."

Konstantin just nodded.

Asshole.

"If she's smart, she did," Anatoly replied, "but I know Ivan likes to keep her here sometimes, too. Maybe that's why she was around tonight. Who fucking knows?"

Wait, what?

"Why?" Kolya asked, deathly still.

"I don't know, comrade."

Yes, he did.

Kolya could *hear* the lie. He didn't think he would like the answer if he did get one, so Kolya chose not to force out whatever Anatoly was hiding.

At least, not yet.

And, fucking hell …

"I'm not your comrade," Kolya said through thin lips.

Pushing off the stool, he jumped the bar with a quick leap. He headed for the door, and Kaz's voice trailed behind him, as did Konstantin's.

"It's locked," Kaz said.

"What do you want us to do?" Konstantin asked.

Locks never stopped me before.

"Clear the rest of the building, or make sure it is clear," Kolya said.

"There's animals—"

"We know about the fucking animals," Konstantin barked at Anatoly. "Maybe I'll get you to release them while we stay out of the way."

Anatoly blanched.

Konstantin smiled.

"Just kill them," Anatoly said quickly. "The mutts, and the rest."

The rest?

Kolya had better things to do than ask what the fuck Anatoly meant.

"Keep me out of that mess, yes?" Kaz tossed Konstantin a look, adding, "I didn't come to Chicago for any part of that. I'm not helping you dispose of animals."

"We're not doing that at all."

"Then how are you going to handle that mess?" Anatoly asked.

Konstantin was now looking at Kolya and ignoring Anatoly altogether. "What are *you* doing?"

He heard his brother's unspoken question.

Are you going to look for her?

Yes, and no.

Yes, he was going to look for *her*, as useless of an effort as that might be in the end, and despite the fact he didn't have any particular reason why he felt like he needed to do that. Not to mention, he had zero clue about what he would do if he did find her.

What was he going to say—*You caught my attention, but I don't know why. Oh, and I killed your father because of business, but let's ignore the last part, yeah?*

Good fucking plan.

And no, he wasn't telling Konstantin that was his intention.

"I need to find the deed for this place, or something valuable enough to hand over to Vadim for repayment of Ivan's debts," Kolya said. "I'll come find you after."

Then, he kicked the fucking door open.

• • •

"We've got a problem."

Kolya shook his head and didn't even bother to glance up from the papers he had pulled out of Ivan's beaten and worn out filing cabinet. The guy *did* have a safe, but it wasn't a very good one considering Kolya had been able to pry the goddamn thing open with a crowbar hidden under the desk.

"Are you even listening to me?" Konstantin asked. "I said we have a *problem.*"

"I don't want to hear about your problems, Konstantin," Kolya muttered.

He had enough of his own, starting with the fact he hadn't been able to find even a hint of Maya anywhere in his search of the offices, or the rooms he'd been inside. Not a shirt, not a goddamn pair of shoes, and not even a feminine scent.

One of the exit doors on the side had been unlocked, so Kolya figured she'd probably slipped out, and beat it out of Dodge. Which would have been the fucking smart thing to do on her part, considering everything. Still, a part of him had been *hoping.*

Hoping for what, he didn't know.

"No, this is a problem I need your opinion on," Konstantin said.

Nope.

Not interested.

"Handle it yourself, Konstantin."

He was not handling the animals, or anything to do with them. All he needed was the right fucking papers to go along with the other shit he'd found, and that was it, that was all.

He was almost done in this damn place, and then maybe he could salvage the rest of his night in some bar. Scowling in his way and drinking half his body weight in vodka until he was numb. Until he didn't feel so pissed off.

Perpetually unhappy.

That was fucking Kolya Boykov.

"Could you ... just *not* be you for five seconds, yeah? That'd be mighty fucking helpful, Kolya."

Kolya's gaze narrowed as he lifted his head. "Excuse you?"

Konstantin stood in the doorway of the office, not looking one bit bothered or frightened of his brother. Even with Kolya like he currently was—pissed the fuck off, covered in dried blood, and little too goddamn sober for his liking. No, his brother didn't look like he was going to back down at all.

Sometimes, Kolya respected the hell out of Konstantin for his ability to do that with him. Other times, it made him want to snap his brother's neck.

It was a *very* fine line.

"What is it, then?" Kolya snapped. "Spit it out, yeah?"

"It's a ... well, shit, Kolya. It's—"

"Konstantin!"

"Fuck, it's a *bear*, Kolya. A real, live *motherfucking* grizzly bear."

Kolya blinked.

And then blinked again.

"Say what?"

Because surely—*surely*—he had not fucking heard his brother right. Surely not.

Jesus Christ.

"Ivan has a grizzly bear in one of the sections for the animals downstairs. It's in a cage way too fucking small—it's pissed off like nothing else and probably hungry. I don't really know, but it's a problem."

Um.

"And it looks fucking *sad*," Konstantin added, "even though it also looks like it might kill me if I get too close. But it's scarred in a lot of places and bleeding on its head, too. Anatoly said Ivan would put it in the fights chained up with a pack of dogs, and—"

"Konstantin, it's a *bear*," Kolya said, speaking slowly so his brother heard every word.

"Yeah, I know, but—"

"No, it's a *bear*, Konstantin."

"Yeah, but—"

"Konstantin, it's a bear, and you can't *have a fucking bear!*"

Why did he even need to tell his brother that?

Why?

"You live in an apartment in the middle of Chicago," Kolya uttered, "and why in the *fuck* do you even need me to explain the reasons why you can't possibly keep a *bear?*"

Konstantin quieted as he eyed his brother. Kolya stared right back, unbothered.

That was the thing about Konstantin that a lot of people didn't know— he was soft-fucking-hearted in ways he didn't let very many people see. He felt for shit in ways Kolya didn't even think he himself was capable of feeling.

It was what it was.

"Anatoly wants to kill it, and the rest of the animals, too," Konstantin muttered.

Kolya cringed.

A part of him understood that was the better idea—the animals wouldn't suffer more than they already had, and the problem would be cleaned. Another part of him didn't like the idea at all because shit, what had those poor animals done to anybody?

"How many is there?"

"So far," Konstantin said, "there's a hundred, or so. Mostly dogs— aggressive breeds. The bear was picked up as a cub a couple of years back. How the fuck Ivan even kept that quiet, I don't know. I guess he got it from some ranger out west."

"Probably a rescue—untagged."

"Maybe."

Kolya sighed, tossed the files on the desk that'd he'd been looking over, and scrubbed a hand down his jaw. Shit, he needed a shave, shower, and a good drink.

"We *could* release the animals," Konstantin said.

Kolya cleared his throat. "And what about the bear?"

"I know a guy."

He side-eyed his brother. "Like Ivan fucking knew a guy, or no?"

Konstantin glowered. "*Blyad*, Kolya."

Yeah, he deserved that.

"Well, speak," Kolya demanded.

"Like I said, I know a guy. That's all I'm willing to say."

"Then, you've got a day—no more, and no less—to get the bear out of here, Konstantin."

"Two would be better."

"A day is all you have before I need to take this shit to Vadim."

Konstantin glanced at the stacks of cash and papers on the desk. "What'd you find, anyway?"

"A hundred grand, and the slips for this place. Good enough, no?"

"Should be. And—"

"Found her!"

Kolya's head snapped up at the voice filtering into the office from the hallway. The feminine shouts and Russian curses that accompanied Anatoly's victorious declaration made Kolya's heart stop for a split-second.

And then there she was.

There she was.

Being dragged in by Anatoly, there she fucking was.

All five feet of her, pissed off, messy black hair, and her pixie-like face screwed into a mask of indignation and rage.

Anatoly shoved Maya Kozlov further into the room and made her stumble over her own two feet. The sudden swell of rage that washed over Kolya at the sight was unbelievable, and hardly fucking containable. It was also shocking enough to keep him rooted right to the fucking floor.

"Fuck you," she spat at Anatoly.

Anatoly only laughed at her. "*Zatknis*, Maya. You should have run, you stupid girl." Then, to Kolya, and entirely unaware how close to death he was as he moved closer to the window, and further away from the shaking girl, Anatoly added, "There's your payment right there—she's worth four times what anything you've found is worth, Kolya. Vadim would agree, and I know the man Ivan owes money to has been suggesting he'd take the offer of her—or a fucking taste of her—to wipe away the account he had with him."

Kolya's throat tightened.

A bitter taste filled his mouth.

Hatred thickened his blood.

Anatoly, still unaware, continued on with, "We both know Vadim would rather have something like this place to keep *making* him money, comrade. It's a one-time deal with her—this place is a goldmine. Consider it."

"But ... but, no," Maya whispered.

Kolya's gaze drifted to the woman who seemed shell-shocked and suddenly terrified. Like all of the fight she had just shown was gone from her personality just like that.

And the *tears*.

Holy sweet baby Jesus in *heaven* ... the tears.

They welled in her eyes.

Tracked lines down her cheeks.

Touched her *lips*.

The fucking tears!

How dare he fucking make her cry like that?

Kolya wasn't even sure what he was seeing except it was a hell of a lot of red, and the imprint of Maya's crying face stayed firmly in the background when he edged around the desk, and hissed out, "Apologize to her, *now*."

"I—" Anatoly's head snapped in Kolya's direction. "Why the fuck would I apologize? She knows what she's worth, and so did her *father*."

Maya's tears started again.

Kolya saw more red.

Konstantin said his name.

It was a damn good thing the ground had been there to break Anatoly's fall—you know, after Kolya *punched* him, and sent him flying straight out of the window he'd been standing in front of.

Again, to the ground ... three fucking flights down.

"Shit," he heard Konstantin hiss before his brother darted to the window where a breeze was now coming in. Konstantin leaned out while Kolya just flexed his sore, and now-bleeding-again knuckles to shake out the pain a bit. "He's not moving."

My bad.

"Shame," Kolya muttered. "Vadim's favorite dog, too."

"This is bad," Konstantin added.

Yeah.

Maya had stopped crying, though.

So, hey, winning.

3.

MAYA KOZLOV was a lot of things—dumb was not one of them.

Life had taught her to be several things.

Smart.

Quick.

Quiet.

And resourceful.

So, when she watched a man literally get *punched* out of a window after he made her cry because the Russian they kept calling Kolya didn't like the sight of her tears ... well, she sat her ass down on the worn couch in her father's office and shut her mouth.

That seemed like the smart course of action.

All things considered ...

"What happened, Konstantin?"

Maya found a man she had heard the others call Kaz while they were surveying the chained, or caged, animals downstairs. In her attempt to hide, thinking whatever was going on in the bar would pass like most other things did, they passed her by twice in her spot before a rat scared her and sent her running.

Kolya sighed but didn't answer.

Konstantin finally pushed away from the window. "Kolya—that's what."

"Context, Konstantin," Kolya bitched under his breath. "Context always matters, no?"

Kaz looked to Konstantin. "What's he going on about?"

"Oh, nothing big. He just punched Anatoly for making a suggestion, and now he's three floors down on the ground. And he's not moving. Let's safely assume he's dead, but I've got other shit to do before I can go check."

Kaz cringed.

Kolya scowled. "That is *not* the right context. It wasn't because he made a suggestion, *suka*."

"Call me that again, *brat*."

Brothers, then.

The two—Kolya and Konstantin—glowered at one another. Maya could practically feel their irritation wafting from their bodies in waves. She took a moment to survey the two and take in their differences despite the relation.

Sure, they shared some of the same features. Strong, square jaws, the

29

same ice-blue eyes, and their hair was the same dark brown.

That was about as far as it went.

Kolya was muscle and meat while Konstantin was lean and mean. With a torso the size of a barrel, she had little doubt that Kolya was not to be messed with. Yet, Konstantin didn't exactly give off the impression that he should be messed with, either.

Both were incredibly good-looking, although Maya's attention continued to drift back to the bigger of the two—the one that spurred a spark of fear in those around him the same way he seemed to intrigue her.

Kolya.

He *should* fucking terrify her, frankly. Splattered with dried blood, his suit was all but ruined, although he didn't look like it was causing him any discomfort. His bloody, swollen knuckles made her heart clench with what might have happened after she'd left the bar. And the tattoos coloring up the visible parts of his hands?

Those tattoos told her far more than anything else about him did.

She knew bratva tattoos.

She recognized them all too well.

How could she not when this had always been her life?

Kolya had maybe an inch of height on his brother, and something else that made him a little different, too.

A coldness.

Maya could *feel* it.

She'd noticed it from the second he'd looked at her down in the bar. His face was expressionless unless he was scowling, or frowning. Or, it seemed, if she was looking at him.

Yeah, she hadn't missed that.

Not the way his eyes widened, or his pupils blew wide at the sight of her. Not the way he'd lost his words, or his ability to use them when they'd locked gazes. He probably hadn't even realized it, but the stiffness in his shoulders had released, and so had his clenched fist for those quick, few seconds.

His guard had been up.

He saw her …

It dropped.

He'd been sitting around some of the most dangerous men she knew—one, she'd lived with for twenty-one years—and yet, he'd barely blinked an eye at them. They hadn't fazed him at all. Then, Maya had come into his line of vision, and he was … knocked off balance.

Yeah, she saw all of that.

The conversation between the men drew Maya back to the present, and took her gaze away from the towering, massive bull of a man still watching her. He kept doing that—she could still feel him doing it even *now*.

"These are problems I don't need," Kaz told Konstantin in Russian.

Konstantin nodded, but his expression was marred with annoyance. "None of us do, but thank you."

Kolya grunted, making Maya glance his way again, but now his attention was on the other two men in the room. "Nothing happened—nothing important. We'll say it was ... a by-product of the Ivan issue. Who the fuck is going to know any different? Vadim won't."

"And her," Kaz said, tipping his head in Maya's direction, "what do you plan to do with her now?"

"She's fine where she is," Kolya muttered.

Konstantin's head snapped around so he could stare at his brother. "What does *that* mean?"

"Just what I said. She's fine."

"She—"

"She's right here," Maya said in English.

Three pairs of eyes turned on her.

For a second, she almost wanted to shrink into the couch, and act like she hadn't said a thing. It wasn't that people staring at her put her on edge—quite the contrary. Her father often liked to put her on display in his business *because* she drew attention. He liked that she was enough to distract a man, and it gave Ivan an edge.

It was just about the only time he *did* like her.

Any other time, and Maya was just the little bitch who her mother had dropped off on his doorstep one December afternoon. Or, that's how her father had always told the story, anyway. She was his liability and responsibility.

One he didn't want and had never asked for.

She wasn't a *boy*.

Not like her brother.

She wasn't *useful*.

Her father never let her forget it, either. Whether it be with his words, his hand, a belt, or some other form of degradation and humiliation, Ivan Kozlov never once thought it appropriate to let his daughter live down her legacy.

She was the child of a whore.

Abandoned, and unwanted.

To be used where there was a need, and nothing more.

So was her life.

"Well, she knows Russian," Konstantin grumbled.

Maya's cheek twitched when he again spoke like she wasn't in the room. "*She* is right here."

"Stop doing that," Kolya snapped at his brother.

Maya sat a little straighter at the same time Konstantin's brow furrowed when he stared at his brother. What was *happening?*

"You're *not* okay, are you?" Konstantin asked.

"I … fuck off," Kolya grumbled. "Stop looking at me like that."

"Like *what?*"

"Like *that*, Konstantin! Stop looking at me like I've got two fucking heads sprouting out of either side of my goddamn neck."

"Is he usually this … *emotional?*" Maya asked the man still standing in the doorway.

Kaz sucked air through his teeth and rocked back on his heels while the rest of the room went completely silent. "We like to say he's been stuck in a bad mood for a while. It's an easier way to deal with him, yes?"

Kolya cursed roughly. "I am not emotional."

Konstantin cleared his throat, saying quietly, "Okay, *brat.*"

"I am—"

"What happened to my father?" Maya asked suddenly.

All eyes turned on her again.

The silence stretched on.

"Something bad, then," she murmured knowingly.

"We'll handle that later," Konstantin said quickly, refusing to meet her gaze.

"Yes, later," Kaz agreed.

Kolya, on the other hand, tipped his head to the side, and his gaze narrowed on her. "It depends, Maya."

Jesus.

She was pretty sure that was the first time he had said her name. And like everything else that came out of his mouth, he spoke her name roughly, as though it had to be pulled from his lips in the harshest way to even be heard. And yet, everything else he said was delivered with a cold flatness that he clearly didn't care about.

Except her name.

She heard the heat—*felt* the pull that came with it.

As though he wanted to yank her name right back between his lips the moment he let it out because it *didn't* sound like everything else he dared to say out loud.

She blinked.

He kept staring.

"Depends on what?" she dared to ask.

A part of her didn't want to know.

Another part wanted to keep him talking.

"It depends," Kolya murmured, "on how you might feel about him being dead."

Huh.

Well …

"I know you can speak," Kolya said when she stayed quiet. "We've all heard you do it. I don't like being left in suspense, so *talk*."

"You don't have to be rude," Maya mumbled. "Tonight was a lot to take in, okay?"

"*Prosti*, Maya."

His soft-spoken apology all but took every bit of air that was in the room out with it. She didn't know why, but the change in atmosphere was fucking *tangible*. Like something she could actually reach out and feel.

That was the best way she could describe it.

Kolya was still staring at her, sure, but the other two men in the room were gaping like fools at one another.

What just happened?

Did Kolya *not* apologize, or something?

Was it because he spoke softly?

Was it both things?

"He is dead," Kolya added. "Your father, I mean."

Maya glanced down at her hands and nodded. "Thought so."

"You don't sound surprised."

"Luck always runs out, and karma is heavy-handed when it strikes."

Was she supposed to be sad?

Hurting?

Crying, even?

Maya couldn't dredge up more than a pang of resentment in her chest for a man who had spent her whole life calling her names, beating her down physically and emotionally, and even going as far as to make her sleep with dogs because he didn't think she was *worthy*.

At least the dogs were always kind.

They only wanted love, too.

"Where do you live, or stay?" Kolya asked her.

Embarrassment filled Maya instantly. Heat colored her cheeks with a light pink, and she refused to look up so the rest of them could see it. "Why?"

"Because I asked." Kolya cleared his throat, adding, "And I asked *nicely*."

He had.

Still … her pride made her keep quiet.

Apparently, that was not going to be acceptable to Kolya. "Well?"

"I don't have a home," Maya admitted. "My father wouldn't allow me to move out on my own, and so I stayed with him, or he made me stay here."

She did look up then, to see Kolya's gaze had all but narrowed into slits. "And where did you stay when you were *here*?"

That, Maya refused to answer.

Someone else had the answer, anyway. Cutting her with shame even deeper than before.

"I would say with the dogs, considering she had been hiding in the kennels with a blanket and a pillow," Kaz said.

Asshole.

Maya didn't need her horrible life put on display for more people. It was bad enough as it was without adding more pity to her fucking days. That thick, heavy silence was back again.

Kolya broke it first.

"She will go with me," Kolya said.

Maya's head snapped up. "What?"

His sharp gaze turned on her, unapologetic and hard when he repeated, "You will come with me."

She didn't get a chance to respond before Konstantin asked, "Do you think that's a wise fucking idea, *brat?*"

Kolya never glanced away from her while he spoke. "I think she is mine to do with as I wish, and I have what Vadim wanted from Ivan in the form of something else. So, yes, she will come with me."

"You can't *take* me," Maya said, her voice faint.

He raised a single brow. "I can't? Tell me why not. Tell me where you'll go tonight, girl. Your father's home, and his businesses? This place? It all belongs to the Boykov family, now."

Her brother.

She could have said him—Alexei—but she knew better. He was just like their father, but *worse.* He hated her even more than Ivan did, it seemed. Like she was always in the way, or something for him to abuse.

No, she certainly didn't want to go to her brother.

Kolya had her backed into a fucking corner.

"You have *no* home to go to, and you cannot stay here," Kolya said, dragging Maya from her painful thoughts and thrusting her back into a sickening reality. "That, by default, makes you my … responsibility."

Maya's brow knotted together as the two stared at one another. "Responsibility or *property?* I know how the Bratva works, Kolya."

And honestly, Maya had been waiting for a day like this to come along. It had been years in the making, from the first time her father threatened to sell her, or use her in some other way, to further his business, or his status. Then, those threats had not been so empty all of the sudden, and Maya was her father's leverage.

She didn't like to think about that.

She *refused* to.

Apparently, she was only worthless to her father.

To someone else, she could be *gold.*

"I'm staying out of whatever comes of this," Konstantin said, jumping into the conversation. "So we're clear on that, yes?"

Kolya nodded at his brother, but never looked away from Maya.

"Understood."

"Well, which one is it?" Maya asked. "Responsibility or property? At least give me the decency of letting me know what I am now."

"Why aren't you afraid?" he asked her instead.

"Of who—*you?*"

Kolya smiled.

Thin as it was.

Faint as it was.

Cold as it was.

He still *smiled.*

And he smiled for her.

"Yes, girl, of *me.*"

"Why should I be scared of you, Kolya?"

He'd not yet given her a good reason to feel fear.

He only *looked* like fear.

It was not the same.

• • •

"Oh, my God," Maya huffed as Kolya pushed her along the west side of the warehouse. "You were actually *serious.*"

"About you coming with me? Yes."

"But-but—"

"Do you splutter often?" Kolya asked.

"What?"

"You, and the spluttering as you try to figure out your words. Does it happen *often?*"

"I—"

Maya didn't see the fucking rock coming before she tripped over it. She could practically taste the dirt coming for her mouth, and even threw her hands out to catch herself before she hit the ground. And yet the dirt never came, nor did the hard, cold ground.

Kolya's arm saved the day as it easily wrapped around her midsection. He righted Maya to her feet without as much as a word about her tripping like an idiot. He hadn't even missed a step as he'd kept on walking with his hand pressed firmly against her lower back just like it had been before.

She was hyperaware of that hand, too.

Of the warmth that bled through.

Of how rough his palm felt overtop the thin blouse she wore.

Of how he wouldn't seem to *remove it.*

"Now," Kolya said as they waded overgrowth and dead grass, "*but,* what?"

Maya blinked. "Excuse me?"

"You were trying to get something out—to tell me something, no? What was it?"

Oh, yeah.

That.

Not that she figured it was going to make any kind of difference, really. Here he was, and there she was. He had made his stance on this whole thing pretty clear up in the office, and it seemed Maya wasn't going to get much of a choice at all.

"You said I wasn't property," she muttered.

"You're not," he agreed.

"Then why do I still have to go with you?"

"*Nyet.* You're not *coming,* Maya. I am taking you."

His words contrasted brightly against the backdrop of his actions, though. In ways … He posed it like she didn't have a choice, yet refused to label her as property like another man would have in this kind of circumstance. It gave the impression she could come and go, or *leave,* should she want to, but he didn't seem to be giving her that option, either.

So, what was happening?

What was she to expect here?

"Again," she said quietly, "then why do I have to go with—"

The look Kolya shot her had Maya quickly correcting her statement.

"Why are you *taking* me?"

"Because if I don't, then someone else will."

Oh.

That still left her with more questions than answers, though. Maya found that just as confusing and concerning as everything else that had happened tonight.

Maybe this was just going to be her life, now.

"I'm not going to fuck you," Maya blurted out. "If that's what you think you're going to get by taking me home with you, it won't happen. My father handed me around to enough people, like I was a toy for them to pet and use, but I never did it because I wanted to, and I won't start with you."

Maya had been just a step and a half ahead of Kolya in their trek around the side of the warehouse, but in a blink, she found herself spun around until her back hit the cool metal of the building. Everything was nothing more than a blur until it *wasn't.*

Until all she could see was ice-blue eyes locked on hers, dark features drinking her in, and every inch of Kolya Boykov crowding her space to the point she couldn't move. Hell, she couldn't *breathe* like this.

She found he was too close.

And yet, not possibly close enough.

She thought he was kind of beautiful.

But maybe terrifying, too.

Or maybe he can be.

Maya didn't have the first clue of what was going on with her—this man had spent maybe thirty minutes in her direct vicinity, but he was making her body and mind react like a fucking ping pong ball that was out of control.

She just thought she was gaining ground ...

Boom.

He hit her with something else.

"Did he?" Kolya asked.

Maya's exhale came out ragged, and sharp. "What?"

"Your father—did he share you?"

"What does it matter?"

Kolya's lips edged a little higher at the corners in what she thought might be a sneer. It was hard to tell, when his face barely flickered with any emotion at all. "It matters because I asked, that's why."

Maya dropped his gaze because that was *easier*. She wouldn't be able to hide the shame in her voice, but she sure as fuck wasn't going to let him see the shame in her face, too. "If he needed—"

"*Nyet.*"

His negative rebuttal came out harder than she had ever heard someone say the word. It was punctuated by him moving just an inch or two closer. Enough to press his much larger form against hers, and cause them both to push harder into the wall. It was punctuated by his hand coming up to slide under her chin, and then his fingers danced along her throat with a soft touch before they gripped there, too.

He would not be the first man to grab her throat.

He was the first man not to *squeeze*, though.

Still, her natural reaction was to tense, and plead.

"*Ple*—"

"Don't beg unless I ask you to," Kolya murmured, his hand coming up a little higher on her throat to make her head tip back. Now, she was staring at him again, and she was surprised to see the man looking back had real, honest emotion in his gaze. Lost were the coldness and blank irises. Instead, she was staring at the same man who'd shown surprise when he'd turned to see her at the bar, and then rage later on when a man had made her *cry*. "And do not hide your eyes from me; I don't like it."

Maya swallowed hard. "O-okay."

"*Just* okay?"

"Not really sure I get any other choice right now, Kolya."

"You will always have a choice. This is how I'm making sure to give you one."

What did that even mean?

"Now," he added, a thickness coloring his tone, "answer my question."

Yes, about her father.

She couldn't look away now.

Couldn't hide now.

"He did." Her breath caught in her throat when she said, "Not often."

"Enough, yes?"

Maya nodded. "Yeah, it was enough."

Kolya's expression hardened briefly before his fingers tapped a smooth, gentle beat against her throat. She swore she felt the pad of his thumb stroke her pulse point, too, but it was done quicker than it had even begun, and Kolya pushed away to start walking along the building once more.

She was left there with her back against the wall, staring at the black backdrop of an inky sky, and feeling a little too breathless. It was like *he* hadn't been there at all.

Except … he had been.

Every part of her knew it. Like the way her heart raced, and her palms ached from being clenched into tight little balls to keep from reaching out to touch him. Or like the way her skin felt warm to the touch, and a little numb where his hand and fingers had been.

Oh, yeah.

She knew he'd been there.

"Are you trying to get left behind?" she heard him call.

He never even looked over his shoulder or anything. He was still walking away. Maybe, had Maya been a smarter woman, she might have taken the chance right then and there to turn her back on that strangely fascinating— and *confusing*—Russian, and run as fast as she could in the opposite direction.

Something told her that he would let her go.

And yet, she didn't.

She raced to catch up.

Maya swore she saw a ghost of a smile on Kolya's face as she moved into step beside him again. He said nothing, but his warm palm came to rest on her lower back again like it hadn't moved from the spot in the first place. She realized in those seconds that maybe she liked it there a little more than she should, all things considered.

"Watch your step," Kolya murmured.

She didn't get a chance to look for what he was talking about because his hands simply slipped around her waist, grabbed tight to lift her from the ground, and then quickly set her back down two steps later. Glancing over her shoulder, she found a slight divot in the ground that didn't look like much but probably would have rolled her ankle something awful, considering she hadn't seen it in the first place.

"*Spasibo*," Maya said.

"Never thank me—I'm not the type of man who deserves it, no?"

Maya peered up at him.

She doubted that.

Very much so.

They had just rounded the front of the building when the barking started. It was only then that Maya realized the front doors of the warehouse had been opened, and propped to stay that way with cinderblocks that had once been along the eastern wall.

The barking, though?

It was coming from *inside* the place.

And then came the dogs.

Bounding as fast as their legs could take them and terrified. Shaking, with ears pinned back, and growls that came out sharp like warnings for the animal that might get too close. Some of the dogs nipped and snapped at the animal to their left and right as they fought to get out of the doorway first. They stumbled and yelped in their effort.

"You're releasing them?" Maya asked.

Her heart swelled a bit.

"Well, they are," Kolya said, "but it's for the best, either way. Come, get in the truck before one of those dogs takes a bite out of you. It's not like there's very much for them to chew on."

His gaze darkened a bit as it traveled over her.

Maya felt that familiar heat creep into her cheeks. "Enough for you to look at, apparently."

Kolya did smirk that time.

Almost a smile, too.

He didn't look the least bit ashamed.

"You lose that sometimes," he told her. "That bark of yours, Maya. Or maybe you hide it. I wish you wouldn't. I think I like it."

He didn't give her time to ponder his words because he picked her up like she weighed nothing more than a bag of feathers, and tossed her over his shoulder like she was worth about as much, too. He navigated the fighting and running dogs as though they didn't bother him in the least. She didn't realize what was happening until a beep echoed, and then a door was opened.

Maya was placed carefully into the front passenger seat of a Hummer.

She glanced down.

It was *high.*

"How do normal people get in here?"

Kolya chuckled, as dry as it was. "Normal people don't get to drive in my vehicles."

Maya's brow furrowed. "So, what does that make me?"

"I'll let you know when I figure it out."

Special, then.

She heard what he didn't say.

"Is that why we didn't go out the front?" she asked when she noticed the last few dogs trotting out of the front doors. "Because they were letting the dogs out?"

"No. Because I didn't think you would appreciate the sight of your father flayed open on a pool table."

Jesus Christ.

Just like that, he reminded her why she should probably be scared of him.

Then, he slammed the door closed.

Damn.

Maya had a strange urge to peer around the inside of the Hummer and see what she could find, but instead, she looked back out the window. It wasn't Kolya approaching the two men coming around the side of the building that drew her attention, but the small black dog tripping over its own too-big feet at the mouth of the doorway.

Black as night.

Big yellow eyes.

He—or maybe she, Maya didn't know—was skin and fucking bones. The pup was maybe a couple of months old, but possibly older, depending on how malnourished it had been. It could possibly be some breed of pit bull if the look of its short, small ears and stout snout were any indication. It wasn't uncommon for the dogs in the kennels to mate, and then have pups if the female survived the fights.

The pups *rarely* lasted, though.

They were typically killed by the other dogs when they tried to eat, or they starved when their mother died and didn't come back to feed them.

She hated *everything* about this place. Everything her father did—it had not just been to her, after all.

What kind of luck did this pup have to survive this hell?

Maya rolled down the window of the Hummer to call out to Kolya— although he probably wouldn't give a shit about the dog. It wasn't his responsibility, now. She didn't even have to move, apparently.

A final big dog came rushing out of the doorway and ran over the pup in its haste. The pup went head over heels over the threshold. Even inside the Hummer, Maya heard the pups cries for help. A horrifying, heart-clenching yelping that made her sick to her stomach and want to cry.

Kolya had been thoroughly engrossed in his conversation with Konstantin and Kaz, but instantly, his attention sought out the noise. His gaze landed on the black-as-night pup, and Maya swore she saw his shoulders loosen momentarily.

Then, the pup looked up.

Big yellow eyes.

Just like the moon high in the sky.

Kolya stared back.

"*Brat*," Konstantin said. "You're sure that's what you want to do with the Anatoly mess, then?"

Kolya waved a hand at his brother, and Maya wasn't sure if he was agreeing or dismissing. He didn't say a thing as he walked away from the conversation altogether, and moved closer to the little pup still trying to stand up on his wobbly legs.

The pup saw Kolya coming.

He growled.

Or *tried*.

Kolya laughed.

Maya swore she fucking heard it.

He *laughed*.

Bending down in front of the pup, Kolya scooped it up with one big hand, and brought the whining, wiggling dog face-to-face with him.

"*Privet*," he said to the pup. "You wouldn't last a night, hmm?"

The dog growled again in its barely-there way.

Kolya smiled.

Not a sneer.

Not a smirk.

No, a real *smile*.

"Not afraid, either," he said.

Maya couldn't drag her gaze away, but she knew the other two men were probably just as flabbergasted by the scene as she was.

Without saying another thing, Kolya stood, and tucked the dog into his arm as he turned to face the others waiting on him. "I'll call you tomorrow, yes? Make sure this is … done here."

Konstantin glanced down at the pup. "What are you—"

"Mind your own."

Kolya headed for the Hummer with the pup still firmly tucked into his arm, although the dog had stopped wiggling and was now quiet. Even as Kolya climbed inside the driver's side of the Hummer, and set the pup down on the armrest between them, the dog didn't make a peep.

He started the vehicle and pulled away. Maya didn't even think to watch her past grow distant. She was too busy staring at the dog.

It really was *small*.

"It's probably hungry," she said.

Kolya didn't look away from the road. "It's a *he*. I saw what was between his legs."

"Oh. Well, then, he'll need a name."

"He has one."

As though Kolya had picked it the moment he'd laid eyes on the dog. Like there was nothing else for him to say about it.

"What is it, then?" Maya asked.

"*Sumerki.*"

Maya blinked.

She peered back out the window at the sky. Black ink dotted by light stars. A yellow moon hung high.

"Nightfall," she said.

Kolya nodded. "Good things seem to happen to me at that time. It fits, yes?"

4.

THE STREETS of Wicker Park were quiet and dark, only lit by the lamps on the sidewalk. Maya wasn't surprised—this part of the city was a relatively decent area and safer than a lot of others. Chicago's crime rate was through the roof, but here, people could walk their dogs at night and not feel like they should probably carry a weapon with them while they did it.

Then again ...

Maya glanced at the man driving the vehicle and second-guessed that theory of hers. She wondered how safe someone might feel if they realized the man they lived near was a killer, *vor*—a genuine, *real* criminal—and probably a hell of a lot more.

With his eyes firmly on the road in front of them, Kolya seemed somewhat innocuous. Harmless, even, if someone discounted his size and the tattoos coloring up his hands. Like this, a person was only getting a shadowed view of his features, and not a full-on glance at the things Maya had seen earlier—his coldness and calm; his indifference and his flashing bouts of rage.

She'd seen other things, too.

Things that said he *wasn't* all that he appeared.

And Maya didn't know what to do with it.

"Why are you staring?" Kolya asked quietly.

Maya quickly glanced away.

How had he even known that? It wasn't like he was looking at her or anything.

"I was—"

"You're not now, no? You *were*. Just then, before I asked."

"You weren't even looking at me."

"Your point?"

Maya wished he was staring at her then so he could see the dirty look she was sporting, but she let her tone do the talking instead. "Sorry that I find you a little ... confusing and disconcerting. After everything that happened tonight, can't I have a little reflection to absorb it."

Kolya chuckled.

She frowned.

"What is so funny about that?"

"Confusing and disconcerting," Kolya murmured, "is that all?"

"Well ..."

"People tend to have a lot of things to say about me, but I don't think confusing or disconcerting are one of them, Maya."

He'd offered her that statement as though it was bait on a hook, and like the stupid little fish she was, Maya chased after it and bit on—hook, line, and sinker.

"What do people say about you, then?" she asked.

The slow curve forming on Kolya's lips could only be described as a sneer. Nothing more and nothing less. Maya wasn't even sure what to make of it—sure, it made his features darker and even more handsome, if that were possible, but it also chilled.

Her, the vehicle, and the air.

It all felt a little colder.

Was something wrong with her?

Broken, even?

How could her instincts feel the way this man gave off the aura of danger, yet her body and mind remained calm, and collected? No part of her wanted to get away, or try to run. She was perfectly comfortable right where she was.

It was … strange.

Shit, maybe *she* was confusing and disconcerting.

"The things people *whisper* about me would not be something you want to hear this late at night when the streets are quiet and dark," Kolya said, finally glancing her way.

He delivered the words with a cold flatness.

Yet his *eyes*—there, he blazed like a roaring fire.

"You must think I'm some innocent, naive angel," Maya replied, "who frightens easily."

"Quite the opposite."

Maya's brow lifted. "Pardon?"

"You can't be innocent or naive in your position, Maya. You know who and what I am—the same as who and what your father was. I think you've probably seen and heard quite a bit in your lifetime. And instead of begging to be freed when you were found, you fought. Instead of keeping a distance from obvious *vory* at the bar, you approached. Why would I think you *frighten easily*?"

"Then why not tell me what people say?"

Kolya shrugged. "Maybe I don't want you to know what people say about me. Maybe I don't want you to hear it, too."

Oh.

She wasn't sure what to make of that, either.

Kolya quieted then and glanced down at the napping pup on the large armrest between them. Sumerki had curled himself into a tight ball of black fur, with only his short ears occasionally twitching to say he was still alive and heard their voices.

Lifting a hand from the wheel, Kolya placed it on top of the pup's back and stroked Sumerki before leaving his palm to rest on the dog's lower half. His hand was so large, and Sumerki so small, that it practically swallowed half of the pup whole.

The kind act—the fact he even remembered the quiet pup sleeping there—made Maya smile, but at the same time, her gaze was drawn to the ink coloring Kolya's hand and fingers.

The upturned spider—an active thief in a life.

OMYT across his knuckles—her uncle had had that once before he'd died of lung cancer, and he'd laughed when she asked what it meant. *Don't ever try to run, girl, and you won't have to learn.* Her brother clarified later: it was designated to a man who was hard to get away from.

On his pointer finger, a dot inside a circle.

That one didn't make sense to her.

"You're not an orphan," Maya said quietly. "You have a brother."

She didn't miss how Kolya's fingers twitched—a sure sign he understood what she was referring to, and maybe that her forwardness had taken him off guard.

"And a sister," Kolya muttered, "as fucking annoying as she is."

"Why the orphan ring, then?"

"I'm not an orphan, but I do rely only on myself," Kolya replied, "and it works both ways."

"You're missing some rings, aren't you?"

"Or I haven't earned them yet," he countered easily. "Or maybe there's some I don't want at all."

"You didn't seem to have a problem with the ones you have."

Kolya chuckled dryly. "They fit me."

How would she know?

"Which ones don't you want, then?"

She could tell just by the way Kolya's brow dipped and his smirk melted away, that he wasn't comfortable with that question. Still, he surprised her by answering.

"Ones my father would like for me to wear … eventually," he said.

"I don't understand."

Kolya's gaze drifted to her, but just as fast, moved back to the road in front of them. "You don't even realize who you're sitting beside, do you?"

Sure, she did.

A *vor.*

A criminal.

Killer.

A man.

Kolya.

"You," Maya said.

Kolya nodded. "I am a Boykov man—like your father was, too."

"The tattoos are a good indication."

"The difference between the two of us is the fact I actually *own* the Boykov surname, and he only had the privilege of working *under* it, Maya."

It took her a second.

And then *two*.

"Boykov."

Kolya tipped his head subtly. "Keep going."

"You're a Boykov son.*"*

"The oldest, Maya. *Favored*. Context is important."

How had she not realized that?

All of this suddenly made a lot more sense to her—why he had taken her like he could under *his* demand, and not to someone else; why his authority climbed higher than the others around him; why he had been there to do the job he had in the first damn place.

Funnily enough …

She still didn't know what to do about it.

Or him, for that matter.

Kolya made the sign of a large cross on his chest, murmuring, "Besides, my father already put one mark on me that effectively placed me where he felt I should go—that's enough without having to add more for him, yes?"

She had no idea what he was talking about.

None at all.

• • •

Maya only got a peek at the front of the brown Wicker Park townhouse before Kolya's Hummer made a sharp right turn, and disappeared into the opening garage leading into a below-ground port. He said nothing as he parked the vehicle and turned the engine off. He scooped up Sumerki, and the sleepy dog blinked its big yellow eyes and took in his new surroundings while Kolya exited the truck.

"Do you need me to lift you down?" he asked.

Maya shook her head, amused. "I think I have it."

"Your broken ankle."

And there he went again. Like a fucking light switch flicking on or off, his moods and words were just as quick to be kind … or *not*.

Asshole.

"Don't be rude," Maya mumbled, climbing out of the Hummer. Jumping was more like it, really, but she wasn't going to give Kolya that satisfaction. "You did take me tonight, and won't even tell me what you're going to do with me because, apparently, I don't get the right to know. If you're going to do those kinds of things, and not be an asshole all of the time, the least you could do is not give me whiplash, you know?"

Kolya rounded the back of the vehicle with a furrowed brow and a slightly more alert Sumerki hanging over his thick arm. "Was it?"

Maya brushed her hands on her blouse. "What?"

"Rude?"

She stood straighter and eyed Kolya. He seemed genuinely confused, and she didn't know whether to laugh, or feel bad for him. "You're not very kind to people, are you?"

"Should I be?"

"I would think so."

Or rather, when the time called for it. It would probably do him wonders.

Kolya arched one dark brow. "Being *this* way gets me better results, yes?"

"Not with me," Maya mumbled.

Kolya was quiet for a moment.

She didn't even meet his gaze.

"Noted," he finally said. "I'm sure you're tired."

To say the least.

"Today was a lot to take in," she admitted.

"There's two bedrooms here—pick one, and it's yours."

Maya blinked, confused at his statement. She intended to ask him what he meant—didn't *he* already have a bedroom here to sleep in? What if she picked *his* room? Was he going to sleep in the fucking bed with her?

And why did that idea interest her more than it terrified her?

No one is saying he isn't a fine piece of man, Maya.

A man she apparently belonged to now.

Even if he wasn't going to *say* it.

It was the sounds of a beep and a door clicking as it unlatched, that brought Maya from her thoughts, and made her realize Kolya was stepping into the darkness of the townhouse. The garage door closed right after he stepped inside, and Maya rushed to catch up.

So much for asking him anything.

Kolya had already disappeared to somewhere else, anyway. Maya wasn't sure where, because darkness stared back at her, and she wasn't even sure what she was looking at. Then, lights lit up the space, showcasing a hallway and the living room it led into.

The bottom floor of the townhouse had a standard layout of a sitting area, a dining room, and a kitchen. The small front entrance didn't have even a speck of dirt to be found on the mat in front of the door until she kicked her shoes off onto it. The beige walls toted no family pictures and only a few strategically-placed mirrors or pieces of artwork.

There were no coats hanging on the coatrack.

No shoes in the closet.

No dishes in the sink.

And yet, the place was spotless. The dark oak wood floors shined, and barely looked like they had seen any wear at all from people traveling on them. Even the heat had been turned on just enough that the nighttime chill didn't affect the townhouse. The furniture was leather, stylish, and placed as if to make someone comfortable when using it. The kitchen table was large enough to seat ten, at the very least.

Still, the place didn't have that *homey* feel. It didn't seem lived in at all.

She didn't for a second think *anyone* lived here—but especially not Kolya—and yet she found fully-stocked cupboards in the kitchen and a fridge full of food.

"Hungry?"

Maya straightened fast from her position of peering into the fridge and slammed the door. Kolya stood in the kitchen entryway—sans Sumerki, now.

"No, I was just looking around," she said.

"You're free to do that."

Good to know.

"This isn't your house, is it?" she asked.

Kolya's lips edged higher at the corners—a ghost of a smile. "What makes you think that?"

"Because it looks like a showroom, and not a home."

"Perhaps I am impersonal about my space."

No, she doubted that.

"I don't think so," she returned.

Kolya nodded. "It's not my place—it's a ... mutually owned and used house for certain people, should they need it."

She wasn't sure what he meant.

But whatever.

"Why bring me here, then?"

This time, Kolya did smile.

And *laugh*.

The sound was shocking. It wasn't the same kind of laugh he had given to Sumerki earlier, but rather, a deeper bass that made Maya's skin tingle.

Why?

Because he looked so damned good doing it.

"Because, Maya," Kolya said, "my place is one step up from the dog kennels you were going to sleep in tonight, had I not taken you out of there. I figured you might appreciate being comfortable."

Huh.

She had so many questions.

So many things to ask.

To *know*.

Yet she didn't know where to start.

"Good night," Kolya murmured, turning his back to her. "I'm sure you'll find me if you need me, Maya."

"Wait."

His broad back stiffened, and his footsteps hesitated. Still, he didn't turn around.

Maya decided to ask what she figured was the *most* important question she had at the moment. "What's going to happen to me now?"

She didn't expect him to answer.

Or perhaps to give her another vague response that left her with more questions.

And if he *did*, by chance answer, she didn't think she would like it very much. It would probably terrify her, actually.

Kolya surprised her.

Maya wondered if it would be just one of many to come.

"I guess we're going to find out."

• • •

It was warm sunlight that woke Maya first, and then the softness of the bed that lulled her back into a state of semi-consciousness just as fast. Even in her comfort, and with the side of her face buried into the pillow, she still had a nice view of the room and the window. The stream of morning light filtering through the curtains was just long enough to reach the bed and part of her face. As bright as it was, she chose not to move.

It was nice.

Pretty, too.

She couldn't remember the last time she had woken up like this— peaceful, calm, and *relaxed*. Her life had been in some constant state of disarray for longer than she cared to remember. Someone was usually pissed at her or she had to do something she didn't want to. Her father had never been a quiet man, and rarely spoke to her with anything less than contempt or bitterness.

She'd dreaded mornings.

She was accustomed to waking up feeling that dread, too. Of what was to come, and what mood she might find her father in by the time she made it to the kitchen. Worse, too, was when she would find her brother waiting there—Alexei liked to treat Maya as though she were wasted space in his atmosphere.

And that was just her family.

People who were *supposed* to care for her.

Funny how that worked.

Even as the events of the night before began to filter into Maya's consciousness—every strange and terrifying second that lead up to this morning with all the unknowns ahead of her—she couldn't manage to feel even an ounce of that same dread she had once woken up with.

She didn't even know *why*.

The townhouse seemed quiet—at least, from her spot under thick, warm blankets. She stayed like that for another ten minutes before pushing up out of the bed. Until her bladder and hungry stomach both decided to make themselves known at the same time.

Maya was stuck with the same clothes she had worn the night before, but they weren't a total mess. Pulling on the jeans and blouse, she padded to the doorway and peered out into the hall. At first she didn't see anything, and the place was still quiet.

She almost wondered if Kolya was even there.

She had heard Sumerki whimpering on and off throughout the night. Probably not all that unusual for a puppy that was still young and had just been taken from his home. Pups were a lot like babies—needy, messy, and *loud*.

Although, that was about as far as the similarities went.

Maya headed down the hall—for the bathroom she knew was just two doors down. She'd passed it the night before, but had been too tired to even consider the shower she likely would have greatly benefitted from.

Not even paying attention, she swung fast to enter the bathroom and stopped just short of a figure sitting beyond the doorway. She almost tripped over him, for fuck's sake.

It was hard to miss a man like Kolya—considering his size and disposition—but Maya had somehow managed to do just that in her haste to use the bathroom.

Tucked just beyond the opened door, Kolya sat with his knees drawn up to his chest, and his arm resting over his bent legs as a pillow for his head. He still had his bloodstained slacks on from the night before, but he'd lost the ruined shirt and jacket.

Maya found herself distracted by the hard lines of his body that melted into smooth ridges of firm muscle. He was built like a heavyweight boxer, and she had seen the proof to know he could throw a punch like one, too. His arms looked strong enough to crush anything if he held it too long— her included, likely.

She got a peek at one eight-pointed star tattooed just below his clavicle bone, and the epaulette with a shadowed skull design on the background of the piece on his shoulder. She bet he had matching ink on his other side where she couldn't see. He had some kind of phrase tattooed beneath his stars, but she couldn't read it.

She could only see a small peek of the large thieves' cross tattooed across his chest, given his position. She could see that it had no crown—only bosses had a crown on their cross—but from their conversation the night before, she *knew* ... This was the tattoo he'd meant when he'd made a cross over his chest to suggest one had been forced on him to signify his bloodline and the position his father expected him to take in the future.

Still, the sight of him was enough to make her hesitate.

For her breath to catch.

In his sleep, Kolya had lost the perpetual scowl and unhappy disposition that seemed to constantly accompany him. She wouldn't say he looked *boyish*—a man of his size, with the tattoos he'd *earned* and a body like his could not be considered in any way a boy.

Definitely a man.

Too many parts of her seemed to know it, too.

He did look ... calm.

Serene, even.

Maybe that was why she stood there staring at him for so long. He'd not done anything to hurt her directly—yet, anyway. He'd also not offered her any explanation of what she should expect, or what was going to happen to her now.

Maya didn't know what to make of it.

It was only a flash of black hair lifting from Kolya's arm resting in his lap that took Maya's attention away from the sleeping man's face. Sumerki's head popped up, and his yellow eyes blinked from his position tucked safely in Kolya's arm.

Well, the dog *had* stopped whimpering and whining.

She supposed now she knew why.

Sumerki's pink-and-black, speckled tongue lolled out of his mouth in a yawn as he found Maya standing in the doorway. She gave the pup a small smile and decided the bathroom on the main floor would do her just fine.

No need to wake Kolya up.

She suspected he probably hadn't intended for her to find him like that, anyway.

Backing away from the doorway and Kolya, she kept her gaze on him and the pup until she finally turned around. It was amusing because Sumerki didn't take his yellow eyes off her, either, as though he might jump out of Kolya's lap and try to take a bite out of her lest she dare to wake up his master.

Apparently, the dog had found his home.

In a towering, massive bull of a Russian man.

Somehow, Maya just knew ...

Someday, Sumerki was going to match the look and disposition of his master just fine. He wouldn't be a little ball of black fur covering skin and bones for long.

Downstairs, Maya made quick work of freshening up in the bathroom, and was digging through the cupboards when she heard the commotion start upstairs.

Or rather, the *yelling*.

Mostly in Russian.

"I told you *one fucking day*, no?"

Kolya's voice boomed—loud and angry enough to pierce through the walls. She hadn't even heard him wake up and start to move around, even as she had found all the ingredients to make pancakes, but apparently, he had done just that.

His tone and words were enough to tell Maya he was pissed. She didn't need to actually *see* him to confirm it, too.

"What the fuck do you want me to do, *brat?*" Kolya's question was followed by his hard scoff before he added, "Avoid him for you? We agreed, Konstantin."

A beat of silence passed.

Then, Kolya let out a string of curses harsh enough to scare the fucking devil. Yet, Maya found herself unbothered by his rage, even as she started to mix together the dry ingredients to make pancakes. This constant, swinging pendulum of moods seemed to be a regular thing for Kolya.

She'd seen him soft, too.

Almost *sweet*, even.

He'd spoken a single line that made her breath catch, and suggested with a couple of more, he could probably get her wet between her thighs, too.

She'd seen him be tender—with his pup, mostly.

Still, he *could* be.

She'd seen all of that in less than twenty-four hours. She had the distinct feeling other people didn't get to see it at all. Maybe she had seen it because she actually *looked* for it.

That's just who Maya was.

"Tell the fucking ranger to get the goddamn thing gone by tomorrow morning at the latest," Kolya snarled from somewhere in the hallway upstairs, "or someone else will remove it."

The silence only lasted long enough for Kolya to bark out, "That isn't my problem!"

That was it.

Maya glanced up as she listened for more, but heard nothing. She even hesitated on continuing to make the food as she waited for footsteps or some kind of sign Kolya was coming closer to the kitchen. She heard nothing.

So, she went back to cooking.

What else could she do?

Maya was just beginning to pour batter onto a simmering griddle when she felt him behind her—close enough that goosebumps bloomed over the back of her neck. Still, when he spoke, it was enough to make her suck in a sharp breath in surprise.

"Why didn't you run?" he asked quietly.

Maya closed her eyes and swallowed the lump that had formed in her throat. She didn't bother to give Kolya the satisfaction of seeing how much he unsettled her in a multitude of ways, so she continued facing the stove even as she replied with, "I don't know what you mean."

"This morning, no? You could have run, Maya. You had the chance. So, why not?"

She didn't even have to think about it.

Not *really*.

"Wouldn't you have just found me anyway? *Looked* for me until you did?"

Truthfully, she hadn't once thought about running from the time she woke up. It had never even been a blip on her radar.

Kolya didn't reply.

Maya did turn to glance at him, then, if only to see why he hadn't responded. She found a happy looking Sumerki in his arms; the dog licked at his forearm and then nibbled on the same spot. Kolya didn't look bothered by the teething pup in the slightest.

Still, she could tell by the look on his face—in the shadows as he frowned, and in the darkness of his eyes when they met hers—that *yes*, absolutely yes, he would have looked for her until he found her, had she run on him.

Maya forgot about the pancake cooking on the griddle as Kolya inched a little closer to her. Enough to take away any personal space she might have had, which only caused her mind to blank when all she could see was *him* looking at her.

She liked the way he looked at her.

Even impassive and cold.

Something still burned.

Something still warmed her.

He still wasn't wearing a shirt, either. And she could finally see the tattooed phrase beneath his eight-pointed stars.

Momento mori.

"Is that Latin?" she asked.

Kolya seemed to know exactly what she was talking about without asking. "It is."

"What does it mean?"

"Something unpleasant, but not untrue."

"Would you tell me?"

"Would you look at me?"

She did.

Curiosity stared back at her.

"What?" Maya managed to ask.

"It means *remember you will die.*"

"You're right—it's unpleasant."

"But also not untrue."

Maybe so.

She wondered *why* he had gotten something like that tattooed on his body, but didn't get the chance to ask.

Kolya's brow dipped, and he glanced down at the pup as he said, "If Sumerki got away, I would go after him, too. I like him—I want to keep him around."

Maya blinked.

She *thought* she understood what he was not saying.

"Like me, too?"

Kolya shrugged.

Maya frowned. "You just compared me to a *dog*, Kolya."

Unflinchingly, he replied, "That's better than what I compare everyone else to."

He inched closer still—the tilt of the corner of his mouth drawing her gaze to the shape of his lips and the small scar that slit through the cleft in his chin. It was their lack of distance from each other that made it hard for her to think or breathe.

And yet, she wasn't entirely sure she wanted him to move, either.

Something was wrong with her, clearly.

He'd *taken* her. Without care, or concern. Just took her like he had every right. And now, she wasn't even sure what was going to become of her life.

Except here she was, enjoying his closeness a little too much, and what it might mean.

Kolya's head tipped down a bit, and Maya peered up. There was maybe an inch between their lips, but she didn't dare to close the distance.

His smirk deepened into something more sinful when he asked, "Would you want me to find you?"

She didn't speak.

Couldn't speak, really.

Kolya grinned like he didn't need her to, and in a blink, stepped back altogether. Suddenly, there was distance between them again, and her mind was clear.

Holy shit.

"Flip your pancake before it burns, *dushka.*"

Maya hesitated.

"You shouldn't call me that—*dushka*, I mean."

Kolya arched a brow. "Do you not want me to?"

She hadn't said *that*.

But she also knew what it meant.

His soul.

An endearment meant for a person's soul.

She wasn't that at all.

"I will call you what I like unless you ask for something different," Kolya said.

"Didn't I just do that—ask, I mean?"

Kolya chuckled. "No, you said *shouldn't*. And that's a huge step away from *can't*. Finish your breakfast, and then we can go."

Go?

He must have seen her silent question.

"Sumerki needs a vet visit and you need things."

"Oh," Maya said.

Kolya's gaze drifted over her from head to toe—a lingering, heated stare that made the best kind of chill work its way up Maya's spine.

She didn't know what to do with this man.

With *herself*.

With them.

He looked hungry.

A little wild, too.

Jesus.

"I don't like doing anything," Kolya said, "but especially shopping."

"I can be quick."

He shook his head. "I don't think I'll mind very much with you."

5.

KOLYA FOUND over his lifetime that the world tended to treat him better when he didn't engage society like most people did. Normal people enjoyed going out, being seen, and doing *things*. He was not that kind of person.

Hell, he could have everything and anything ordered in should he need something, and the only time he did go out was to work, to handle a problem, or if his tailor wanted an update on his fucking measurements for his suits. Even the clothes he wore right then—clean, as he'd gotten rid of the blood-stained shit from the day before—had been delivered to him by a soldier he'd relatively trusted to be inside his place.

But anything more and people were just asking too fucking much of Kolya.

"You did bring me here," Maya whispered, "you know."

Kolya glanced down at her, momentarily taking his scowl away from the wall he'd been leveling it on at the upscale mid-city boutique. The place was quaint—if that was even the right fucking word—and catered to those with deep enough pockets to afford the brand names hanging on the walls and racks. The place had everything a woman might need or want, it seemed.

A wall lined with designer heels, shoes, and boots in assorted colors, styles, and height. Another covered in leather bags with luxury labels he recognized on the spot. Upstairs in the loft section, he could see fur coats, and lingerie—the bottom floor housed everything in between.

In the back, he could see a sign for dressing rooms.

Modern, stylish, and comfortable. Neutral colors, and a woman who'd asked if they preferred wine or tea when they'd first come in the door. The hardwood floors clearly saw a lot of travel, but it was difficult to tell, with the way they shined under his leather loafers.

It was quite … quaint.

Yes, that *was* the right word.

And Kolya decided he *hated* that fucking word.

"I did bring you here," he said to Maya, "because there are things you need here."

She gave him a pointed look. "Then you could try to be a little happier about it, Kolya."

He blinked.

Somehow, she kept managing to surprise him, although he wasn't quite sure how or why. Despite her words, which suggested he should step in line, she'd delivered the statement with the same sort of bubbly tone she had first greeted him when she'd approached him at the bar.

Before Kolya could say something to Maya, the woman who had approached them shortly after they entered the store, came back down the aisle to greet them with a smile. First, to Maya, and then she lingered a little too long on Kolya for his liking.

"Ah, Viktoria said you were coming today, Kolya," the woman—Trina, Tiffany or some shit like that—said with her same smile. "She said you might seem a little surly, but I promised we would make you feel right at home here."

Kolya was not a stupid man—he may not have liked to be around people as a general rule of thumb, but he wasn't so stuck in the recesses of society that he couldn't recognize when a woman was hitting on him. Or … *trying* to.

He was regretting making that call to his sister to ask Vic about an appropriate place to take a woman for clothing and things.

Seriously fucking regretting it.

"We're not shopping for *me*," Kolya muttered, glancing down at Maya beside him. "Clearly."

This place didn't have anything a man would want.

Except for maybe the pussy inside it.

And he wasn't interested in that, either.

At least not from this woman.

Maya gave him a small smile, and he tried to muster one back for her, although he wasn't quite sure if he succeeded or not. Smiling felt strange and foreign to him—not something he liked or did often enough. Very little made him happy.

Her smile did, though.

Maya's smile, that was.

It was just her happiness alone that made him want to give her whatever in the fuck he could to keep her looking like that for him. This whole goddamn store, and everything in it, should that be the case. The whole fucking block, even.

Did she want him to burn it down?

He would.

For her, Christ, he would.

All because she was smiling, and he wanted to keep her that way. She didn't know that, though. She couldn't possibly know it. Hell, even he didn't understand why she made him feel like this. It shouldn't be like this, should it? He'd taken a woman simply because he *could*, and she interested him.

She could have run from him—she hadn't.

She could have fought him—she hadn't.

She should be terrified of him—she *wasn't*.

Kolya was borderline obsessed with these facts about Maya, and how much they *pleased* him. It was going to be a problem for him—he knew it already.

"Whatever you want in here," Kolya told a still-smiling Maya, "and it's yours. Point and say, I'm paying."

"You don't—"

"I do. *Now.*"

His unspoken words quieted her from saying anything else. She was his to do with as he wanted—and he wanted for her to be treated well and happy. Didn't that include having nice things?

"Okay," Maya said

Kolya nodded.

"And just how much does she *need?*" the sale's woman asked.

Kolya saw the flash of hurt in Maya's gaze and readied to snap at the woman simply because she'd offered her words with an air of arrogance. A person couldn't miss that—he knew when someone felt better than him just by their tone of voice.

Maya saved him the trouble when she turned to the woman, and her ice-blue eyes seemed colder as all of her pleasant joy seemed to bleed out of her expression and tone in a blink. Especially when she said, "My measurements are thirty-two, twenty-two, thirty-two. Size six shoe."

"I'm sure—"

"And what's your name?" Maya asked.

"Trisha."

Trisha.

That was it.

Kolya reminded himself to tell Viktoria to give the woman hell the next time she came around.

"And *Trisha*," Maya added, her tone twisting the woman's name with a false saccharine sweetness, "anything but black; we don't all need to look like we're going to a funeral."

Kolya smirked.

Trisha was in black.

Head to toe.

Out of the corner of his eye, Kolya saw the woman glance at him again, but when he didn't even bother to look her way, she quickly nodded and headed off. Maya's tense shoulders loosened a little bit, and when she turned to stare at him, he was already looking at her.

"I really won't need very much," she said.

"I don't like that," he told her.

Maya frowned. "What?"

"When you do that—you're happy and smiling, and then you snarl at a woman for dismissing you, but then you go back to this …" Kolya waved at her with one inked hand, and shrugged, saying, "Shell of who you occasionally let come out to play. That's the reason I noticed you, Maya. At the bar, no? You sounded so *bubbly*. It was strange and interesting to me."

For a long while, the two continued staring at each other in silence. Kolya wasn't sure how much time had passed, but the buzzing of his phone in his pocket broke their daze. Likely the vet giving an update on Sumerki—Kolya's *demand*.

Still, he didn't reach for the phone.

He had other things to do right now.

Maya cleared her throat. "So, if I stay like this—"

"Quiet, timid, and *meek*."

"Yes, that—then what would happen? Would you lose interest and send me on my way?"

Kolya barely had to think about it and his answer was already on the tip of his tongue as he shook his head. "No, I would just see how much pushing and bending and prodding it would take to break you of it. I'm told that I am good at that—breaking people, I mean."

He didn't miss the widening of her eyes.

The way her throat clenched.

Her parting lips.

None of it.

He saw it all.

"And what does *that* mean?" Maya asked.

"Probably nothing good." Kolya chuckled, adding, "Who's to say it wouldn't be different for you, no?"

"I—"

"Let's go find you beautiful things, Maya. You deserve beautiful things."

Kolya didn't give her a chance to argue or asking something else. Instead, he pressed his hand to her lower back, and moved her further into the store. He didn't miss the warmth from her body soaking into his palm, or the shiver that worked its way up her spine.

Oh, she did well to hide it.

But he knew, too.

Kolya wasn't going to have to force this woman to do anything— certainly not to get her into his bed. She was going to come there willingly once she got her feelings all sorted out about this strange situation of theirs.

It was almost comical how settled he was in what he had done to Maya—taking her like he had, and still without regret. He was fine with waiting on her, too. He didn't mind letting her come to the same conclusion he already knew even if it *was* only brought on by nothing more than his spark of interest, and the fact he took her with him without giving her a choice.

She was his.

And he was going to enjoy every second he had to wait for her to figure it out, too.

It was what she did with it that might make all the difference.

• • •

Konstantin stepped into the townhouse a week later, not looking any worse for wear considering his last conversation with Kolya had been his brother bitching at him. Then again, maybe Konstantin was used to that, considering how most of their conversations ended up going.

Who was he to say?

"You handled that issue, then?" Kolya asked.

He headed for the living room where his favorite baseball team was losing by five runs. Konstantin followed behind, although, not silently.

"The bear is in his new home—a sanctuary out west."

Kolya didn't care about details.

Just that it was *handled*.

"*Khorosho,*" he said gruffly as he dropped onto the couch.

Konstantin took a seat closer to the window. "Since when you do you use one of the safehouses?"

"Mind your own."

"You could *attempt* to have a real conversation, *brat.*"

"I could," Kolya agreed.

He left it at that.

"The good news for you," Kolya added, his gaze firmly stuck on the television where the bases were now loaded, and the best hitter on the team was coming up to bat, "is that Vadim has been too fucking distracted with his latest guests in the city to notice I was avoiding him."

Out of the corner of his eye, he saw Konstantin lift a brow.

"Not even a call?" he asked.

Kolya shook his head. "Not one—*yet.*"

It would happen, though.

Soon, likely.

"That's about to run out, then," Konstantin stated, shrugging when Kolya looked to him for explanation. "Kaz headed back to New York today. Suggested his father was staying behind for a bit."

Kolya scowled. "Vasily works every one of Vadim's nerves."

The two Pakhans put on a good show, though.

They managed that.

At least.

He fully expected his father would be in some kind of state—mood-

60

wise—for the next little while. Or for however long it took for Vadim to get Vasily Markovic the hell out of his city.

"He still thinks Vasily is trying to make a move on the counterfeit business," Konstantin muttered.

Yes, the bread and butter of the Boykov Bratva's criminal dealings. Oh, sure, they had their hand in just about every pot, but their most and *best* dirty money was made in their counterfeit cash making business. It was a tradition, really. Passed down through their organization for generations and generations. Some called it an art form, and Kolya would tend to agree.

It was the part of business he liked the most, anyway.

Next to killing.

"That's because Vasily *is* trying to move in on it, Konstantin."

"You think?"

"Vadim won't even give Vasily the satisfaction of a dollar bill to look at, never mind allowing him to enter the Compound because he knows Vasily only wants those things to have someone replicate our process. Vadim is a paranoid fucker, yes? He's not a stupid one, though."

"There's no honor amongst thieves," Konstantin murmured, glancing out the window.

"Not in this lifetime, anyway."

"Huh."

Kolya glanced over at his brother, but Konstantin's gaze was stuck on something just outside the window. From his position, he couldn't see what it was, though.

"Problem?"

Konstantin shook his head, and turned back to his brother. "No, I just thought—"

It was the front door of the townhouse opening and closing that cut off whatever his brother was about to say. Kolya figured he didn't need Konstantin's confirmation because he now knew exactly what had caught Konstantin's attention.

Maya coming back from her walk.

With Sumerki.

She'd taken on the task—Kolya didn't see the harm.

"Kept them both, did you?" Konstantin asked as the sound of footsteps neared the living room. "That's cute, Kolya. You've found two new pets to take care of, yes?"

Kolya dead-stared his brother until Konstantin grinned back in that smug fucking way of his. Sure, he had heard the joking tone of Konstantin's voice, but it still rubbed him wrong all the same. He might have snapped something right back at his brother—nature of his beast, and their competitive relationship—had Maya not come to stand in the doorway of the living room.

She made him check himself.

Attitude and all.

Maya didn't even seem to notice Konstantin sitting in the corner as she bent down to unclip Sumerki's leash from his new spike-studded collar. Something Maya had convinced him to buy at a pet store when she'd also suggested the pup might like some toys.

To chew on, or some shit.

Kolya figured Sumerki chewed on him enough for *him* to be the dog's toy, but who was he to fucking say? Apparently, puppies teethed like human babies.

And one could quickly spend a small fortune on their pets, too.

Kolya smiled at the way Maya seemed far more comfortable into her new situation with him. Time could make all the difference for a person—he suspected her life was a hell of a lot better *now* than it had ever been before.

As long as she kept smiling.

He was good.

"Oh, *privet*," Maya greeted, not unkindly, although still a little stiff, when she stood up straight and finally noticed Konstantin sitting in the corner. "Konstantin, right?"

Konstantin flashed his teeth in a rueful smile. "That's right, Maya."

Kolya gave his brother a passing glance.

A warning, if you would.

Konstantin acted like he didn't even see it. "You're looking … well, yes? I assume my brother has been staying in line, then."

Maya's gaze darted to Kolya, and then back to Konstantin before she cocked an eyebrow and smiled widely. "You could say that."

Sumerki decided *that* was the time he was done with nibbling on the end of his tail, and his yellow eyes landed on Kolya. Full steam ahead, the pup bounded across the floor—all legs and paws because his body wasn't quite filled out just yet. Kolya bent down just in time to catch Sumerki in his hands after the dog went head over paws with a yelp.

Setting the pup back to his feet with a chuckle, Kolya placed Sumerki at his boots, and kept one hand on the dog's head.

Training started now.

Sumerki stayed—quietly. The chewing on Kolya's boots couldn't really be helped, though. He didn't do that to *Maya's* things.

Kolya looked back at Maya. "*Spasibo.*"

She nodded. "Sure."

"Get something nice on. We're going to dinner."

"Are we?"

Konstantin was all but forgotten, then.

"It's a nice place—pick a dress," he told her.

Maya nodded once more, and then gave Konstantin one last look. "Nice to see you, Konstantin."

His brother smiled in kind. "And you, Maya."

Kolya's attention went back to the game playing on the television as Maya disappeared and her footsteps faded into the upstairs. Konstantin said nothing for a while, too, although Kolya could practically feel the questions burning on the tip of his brother's tongue.

"How hard are you going to chew on whatever you want to say?" Kolya asked.

Konstantin hummed under his breath. "I remember myself saying I wanted to stay clear of this, so as to not cause myself any trouble by the mess you might find yourself in."

"You did say that. Wise, no?"

"No one has ever called me wise."

That they did not.

Kolya looked to his brother. "What?"

"She looks happy."

"Good. I intend for her to—she deserves that."

Konstantin's brow lifted subtly. "Are you fucking her?"

"*Nyet.*"

"Yeah, yeah. Mind my own. I know, but—"

"No," Kolya interjected, "the answer to your question is *no*. But yes, mind your own. That will get you a hell of a lot farther in this life when you pay less attention to the private business of the men around you."

"On the contrary, *brat*, that's what very well might save me someday."

Well …

Damn.

He focused his chaotic thoughts by glancing down at his still-chewing pup and scratching behind the dog's ears. The good thing about Sumerki was he liked to learn, and he was quick at it. Only one mess in the house after that first night, but the chewing couldn't be contained.

Win some, lose some.

"Kolya," Konstantin murmured.

Kolya didn't even look up. "*Kakiye*—just say it, yes?"

"I think she's going to be a problem for you, although it's the *how* or the *what* I don't have an answer to right now."

"Do tell what makes you think that," Kolya replied dryly. "How do you figure?"

"You didn't stop smiling from the time she opened the front door. You only stopped after she left your space. You took her like that was your right—yet, you're not doing *anything* with her."

"Should I?"

Konstantin stiffened. "What?"

"Should I do something with her—*to* her?" Kolya asked. "Force her into something she doesn't want, or whatever the case may be. Drag her to my bed or brand her skin to make a claim. I don't see the point in any of those things when what I did was more than enough to state my right and purpose."

His brother let out a harsh sigh before he dragged his hand down his unshaven jaw. "I mean … at least, Kolya, the girl belongs to her family, or what might be left of it. At most, she belongs to the organization—to the *Boykovs*. That's how this has always worked."

Kolya nodded. "And I am a Boykov, no?"

And that was why he'd taken her. He saw her, and he'd wanted to have her. He had never wanted anything before—not like that, not so fast, and not with such intensity. He had every ability to make the call, and so he had. Besides, had he not taken Maya, someone else would have . Which was exactly what Konstantin was saying in a roundabout way.

Kolya continued with, "*The* son Vadim wants to take his place, and be his next king on the chess board. I think that—and the cross he demanded be put on my chest three years ago—has given me this … privilege. What good is having privilege if I never use it, *brat*?"

It was hard to miss the clenching in his brother's jaw at his words. It wasn't that Kolya meant to poke Konstantin's only nerve because he didn't. And God knew Konstantin did his very best to hide how much that one particular thing bothered him.

Vadim's dismissal of Konstantin.

Vadim's choice in *Kolya*.

Hell, Konstantin still didn't have his stars—something Kolya *had* been given by his brother's age, although he suspected it would happen soon for Konstantin. It didn't matter because both brothers knew what the real, honest-to-God truth was when it came to their father.

Right now, Vadim had what he wanted in Kolya.

He was not going to look for it in Konstantin.

Shame, really.

Everything Vadim wanted was staring back at Kolya in his brother. From Konstantin's calm, cold disposition or his immaculate control and appearance—he could be every inch a little boss in waiting. He never stepped out of line directly, but he knew when to push just enough to bend it and get what he wanted, too. Their father was such a fucking asshole that he was too caught up in his own desires to see it.

"I meant," Konstantin said, taking careful effort to keep his tone level, "that she belongs to *Vadim*."

Kolya's rage simmered on low. Like someone had shot him with fire straight to his goddamn heart.

Somehow, he hid it.

Like Konstantin hid his anger, too.

The two of them were good like that.

Trained like that, really.

They could both thank Vadim for this.

Standing from his seat, Kolya shoved his hands into his pockets. Sumerki hustled to get up to his paws, too, always wanting to follow along with his master, now. That pup was the second-best decision Kolya had ever made, next to taking Maya. "Nice visit, *brat*, but that's quite enough for the day, no? Time to go."

Konstantin didn't even argue.

• • •

Kolya occasionally glanced over his shoulder as he quietly climbed the stairs to the second level of the townhouse, and even as he headed down the hallway to where the bedroom was that he'd been using for their stay. Sumerki trailed behind a few paces, although it took him time to navigate the stairs.

Still, it amused Kolya.

Without even needing to be told, the pup followed. He wanted to *please*.

Coming to his doorway while still peering back at the pup, Kolya didn't notice his room wasn't empty. When he did see Maya inside, he turned into a statue. She stood in front of the full-length mirror—her room didn't have one—and held a dress up against the front of her body. Another handful of dresses had been tossed on the bed.

Discarded or not yet tried, likely.

He didn't care about those.

Or that she was in his room.

Or that Sumerki ambled his way into Maya's room farther down the hall even though Kolya was supposed to be making the dog stay with him.

No, what he cared about was the ample view he got of Maya's peach-shaped ass being tightly hugged in pale lavender lace. His gaze drifted from the black heels on her feet—compliments of that terrible store he hated, much like the lace bralette and panty set she had on—all the way up to where her pin-straight black hair fell halfway down her back.

She had an hour-glass figure, although, smaller given her height. Still, she had soft curves in all the right places, and they were more than enough to make his cock perk and press against the zipper of his pants. It was all of that pale, creamy skin of hers that made him linger for a little bit longer.

Just enough to know she was sexy, and perfect, and beauti—

"Are you finished staring?" Maya asked softly.

She hadn't even looked at him. She was still subjugating that dress to her scrutiny. Frankly, he thought a goddamn potato sack would look fine, too.

She'd be wearing it, after all.

"Sorry, I'll lea—"

Maya's gaze lifted in the mirror to stare at him straight-on. "You don't have to leave. It is *your* room. I just needed the mirror. You said a dress—I have to pick one. It's a process."

Really?

Because he just threw shit on and hoped for the best.

His whole life in a nutshell.

"Did you find a favorite?" he asked.

Maya smiled a little. "What, a dress or an undergarment set? I like the lavender."

"It does look nice against your skin."

To say the least.

He was being civil.

It was his thoughts that were horrifyingly dirty.

He refused to entertain them right now. Wasn't it bad enough that they were screaming loud enough in his ears that he couldn't even hear his own blood rushing?

Damn, he could *feel* that, though.

It didn't help that every word she spoke was soft and almost demure. That she had stopped meeting his gaze, but he could still see the pink climbing in her cheeks to warm them. Maybe he hadn't tried to hide his staring very much, but the sight of her like that said she was just as affected by him as he was of her.

And he *liked it.*

Too much, maybe.

"What good is any of this, anyway?" Maya asked, flicking a hand at the satin and lace delicates next to the dresses. "It's only made for a woman to look good for a man."

Kolya hadn't realized it until he was right beside Maya, but he'd closed that distance between them in a fucking *breath.* Each word she spoke drew him closer like a magnet he couldn't control. He couldn't decide if he cared, or not.

"The better question is *do you*, Maya."

Her gaze darted to his in the mirror again. "Do I what?"

"Want to look good for a man?"

Maya's tongue peeked out to wet her lips as her stare darted down to his mouth, and any and all control Kolya had maintained in those few seconds were gone. It snapped with the lowering of her lashes, and the sexy little smile curving her lips.

Shit, he bet that smile would look good wrapped around his cock.

Later.

Oh, that would be coming later.

Like him.

And *her*.

He barely thought about what it might mean when he fisted his hand into the back of her lavender lace bralette and pulled hard enough to bring her into his chest. Her spine and ass melded against his hard lines, and she turned her head just enough for him to catch her lips with his own.

His first thoughts weren't soft, or slow, or sweet.

No, he just wanted to *taste*.

His kiss was bruising—rough. And yet, she didn't shy away. Her lips parted for him at the first stroke of his tongue, and he found a teasing wet heat inside her mouth that only made his cock pound harder against his pants to be released.

To find *relief*.

His phone rang instead.

Just like that, Kolya's daze was shattered. He stepped back away from Maya with two larges paces as he fished the phone from his pocket. He didn't miss the way her brow furrowed and her gaze darkened.

A silent question stared back at him, asking, *Why?*

He had to answer that call.

He always had to answer *that* call.

"Vadim," Kolya said coolly when he finally put the ringing phone to his ear. "What can I do for you?"

"The Kozlov issue," his father barked, not even waiting a second before he was spitting his rage into the phone, "why haven't you updated me or brought me what I asked for? Time is running out for me to make amends here, Kolya."

Vadim didn't even give him time to make up an excuse. "Tomorrow morning—*be at the Compound*. And have *everything*. Do you understand?"

"I could bring it tonight," Kolya returned.

"No. Vasily Markovic is making his presence known tonight, and you know how I feel about that bastard when he's in my city."

The call promptly hung up.

That was that.

Kolya glanced back at Maya, but she was already slipping the purple dress down over her head. Covering her skin and curves from his view. Their moment was over, and *damn*, he'd been so close. Not that it mattered, now.

There was nothing quite like his father to make his dick go soft.

"I heard what you said to your brother after I came upstairs," she said quietly.

Kolya's brow dipped. "Pardon?"

"That it was your right to take me—for me to be passed on or kept by you."

He swallowed hard. It was impossible to miss the heat in her words.

"What about it, Maya?"

"Why won't you just say what I am—*property*?"

"Because you don't want me to."

She'd asked, sure, but that wasn't the same thing as wanting it. Who would want something like that?

Maya blinked.

Kolya stayed stone-still, too.

"But I'm not free, Kolya. Not now. Maybe I don't want that, either."

"You're free as long as you're with me."

It was the best he could offer.

It was *all* he could offer.

6.

THE *COMPOUND*, as the Boykovs had affectionately dubbed the section of warehouses they'd connected by small, portable buildings was just a well-guarded section of storage facilities. And one old factory. Located in the lower portion of Chicago's shipping district, it was in the perfect spot for business.

So much shit came in and out of the place that it wasn't all that unusual for people to miss anything that might not be on the up and up, when it came to the law. And if they *did* happen to see something, they were also the kind of people who were willing to take a bribe to keep their mouths shut about it.

Kolya wasn't sure how long the Boykovs had owned the Compound, but it was long before his fucking time on this earth. Probably long before their organization had even been known as the Boykov Bratva, for that matter, but he wasn't too keen on asking his father for details. That might appear to Vadim like his oldest son was interested in something, and there was no need to go ahead and encourage that nonsense.

Still, a great sense of nostalgia thickened Kolya's blood as he moved through the Compound's many hallways and sections without as much as the slightest of hesitation about his direction. The layout was familiar to him—as familiar as the back of his own hand, really. Unlike many who would get lost at the first corridor after the entrance to the main warehouse, Kolya could navigate this place with his eyes closed.

He could remember chasing after his grandfather—now dead from smoking two packs a day for three-quarters of his life—down this very corridor when he had been just old enough to walk. It was one of his earliest memories. It was quickly chased away when he passed a room they now used for storage.

He'd once hidden in the room with Konstantin when they'd come along with their father. Kolya hadn't been quite a pre-teen in age. Bad shit went down between a meeting of *vory*, someone died, someone else got shot, and the rest was history.

Boys in this life learned *young*.

No doubt about that.

The main offices—ones used by the Boykov brothers, and their father when Vadim actually wanted to do work *in* here—were right in the heart of the Compound. The very middle building, with the most protection of any of their properties.

And for good reason.

Kolya opened up the two large metal doors, and barely felt their substantial weight under his palm when they slammed closed behind him. Already, he could smell the heady scent of ink clinging to the air, and hear the swoosh of paper as it was shuffled through the printers.

Next to the sound of sex first thing in the morning, or a man's last breath under his hand, Kolya thought the Compound's presses had to be one of the best things he'd ever heard in his life. He was pretty damn sure he could fall asleep to that noise and only dream of dollar signs.

That's how much he liked it.

And it did sound like that, too—like money being made.

Because that's exactly what was happening.

Counterfeit money, sure, but given their skills in the trade and the knowledge they possessed about faking cash, no average fucker, or store clerk, for that matter, was going to notice the bill in their hand wasn't real. The paper was the same and so was the ink. Or … it looked that way on the surface.

Everything about their process nearly matched the official process but for one tiny detail—the Boykov signature on every bill.

It was a tradition in the trade.

Every counterfeiter had a signature.

Kolya had a good mind to go and check on the presses and the men working them today, as it had been a while since he'd spent any time in the Compound to actually work, but he didn't have time. Before his need kicked in too much, he made a sharp right and headed down the spiral staircases that led to the one and only office downstairs, below the presses.

His and Konstantin's offices were upstairs.

Vadim kept his downstairs.

His father's patience was clearly thin enough, given his unwanted guest in the city, and whatever else Vadim wasn't telling Kolya. It wasn't unusual for Vadim to keep problems quiet until he couldn't anymore. Then he simply sent someone in to deal with the issue for him.

Boss's right, no?

Or that's what his father liked to say.

Kolya found his father's office was closed as he rounded the final steps, but it wasn't uncommon. The unknown man posted directly outside the door, dressed in all black, was a new sight. The man barely spared Kolya a glance and he didn't even speak as he came closer.

Reaching over, Kolya knocked with two knuckles against his father's office door, although that wasn't really necessary. It was a matter of semantics—respect, and nothing more. Vadim had known Kolya was on the property from the moment he'd pulled up, and definitely had eyes on him right then, considering the camera positioned right above the arch of the doorway.

The door stayed closed. Given it was six inches thick of pure steel, and with walls just as thick and well-insulated, there wasn't a peep coming out of the office.

"A meeting?" Kolya asked the unknown man.

The guy nodded.

Nothing else.

All right.

Stepping back, Kolya leaned against the wall, and waited whatever was happening behind closed doors out. Vadim had been specific about the time he wanted Kolya to show up, so the meeting had to be important for him to change plans.

Vadim didn't *change plans.*

Not if he could help it.

It was another ten minutes before the heavy office door was opened, and out stepped a man Kolya certainly hadn't expected to see. Even if Kolya didn't know his name, his scarred face was well-known in Chicago, and a fair warning to anyone who thought to cross him.

Or his family.

Idriz Gashi.

Brother to the boss of the Albanian mob, and second in command. The thick, discolored scar that ran down the left side of his face was a grisly sight, but Idriz rarely acted like he noticed it at all. Kolya couldn't remember a time when he hadn't seen that scar on the man, either, but then again ... he didn't particularly know him all that well.

And he didn't know why the fuck he was *here.*

Vadim was a lot of things.

Moody.

Difficult.

Territorial.

The last one was *most* prominent when it came to his father. It could be considered a virtue as much as it was a fucking flaw, really.

Vadim had his rules—the Compound was theirs, and he didn't tend to do a lot of business with other organizations inside its walls. Sure, they fulfilled business deals here, but they didn't typically make them here, as well.

Idriz allowed the door to close behind him without as much as a look over his shoulder, and glanced quickly at the man still standing at his post.

"Tomor."

The ... solider, guard ... whatever the fuck he was, gave Idriz a nod.

"I'll be going," Idriz said.

The other man replied in a language Kolya couldn't understand, and the two moved in the same time to leave. It was only then that Idriz caught sight of Kolya leaning against the far wall. In his dark, three-piece suit and towering at over six feet in height, it wasn't surprising to Kolya that a great deal of people found this man to be intimidating.

The stories of the Gashi brothers were widely spread and well-known. Likely much to their pleasure, as there was always a bit of truth to every rumor. Every man wanted his disposition and demands clear before he ever entered a room.

Less bloodshed that way.

Vicious and volatile, people said. The Gashis were not to be crossed. *Blood debts.*

A lot like the Boykovs.

Kolya suspected it was all true.

He still wasn't bothered or concerned by Idriz, even as the Albanian's gaze lingered on him for a beat in time as though he were sizing him up. Just as quickly, Idriz nodded at Kolya without as much as a greeting and strolled down the hall with his man on his heels.

It was only when Kolya couldn't hear echoing footsteps that he crossed the space, and knocked on his father's office again, even though Vadim could have just used his fucking speaker to allow his son entrance. He didn't bother to wait for his father to grant him access to the office, instead just opened the door and walked on in.

Vadim sat behind his large oak desk with his back to Kolya and a phone pressed to his ear. In the corner, his father's right-hand man, Grisha, overlooked papers in a file and didn't even glance up at Kolya's entrance.

"I will see what we can do to *try* and make that happen, Vasily," Vadim said, still turned around in his chair, "but I make no promises, comrade."

Kolya cleared his throat, but his father only lifted a single hand in response as if to shush him from saying or asking anything else.

"It's the best I can do," Vadim said after a beat of silence. "I'm sure you'll come up with a suitable counteroffer, no? I'll wait for it."

Vadim said nothing else as he turned in his chair—giving Kolya the perfect view of his father's annoyed expression—before he pressed a button on the phone's base and then set the phone on the cradle.

"Still trying to work a deal on an order?" Grisha asked from the corner, never looking up from his work.

"You know how Vasily Markovic is," Vadim returned.

Grisha nodded, but said nothing.

Vadim's sharp gaze fell on Kolya. "Since when have you forgotten how to wait after you knock?"

"I assumed your non-reply was my okay."

"You assumed *wrong.*"

"My mistake."

Vadim scowled. "Don't make too many of those. I would have to start correcting them, Kolya."

That thinly veiled threat barely even brushed Kolya's shoulders with tension. His father's lessons had been coming for him ever since he'd learned to talk back. They'd only become harder and more brutal as he aged.

Vadim had always been a heavy-handed man.

At least, to his boys.

"Are we doing business with the Albanians?" Kolya asked.

Vadim leaned back in his large chair, and steepled his fingers together as he eyed Kolya. "In a sense, yes."

"And what sense is that? Separation of church and state, as you like to say. We don't usually do very much business with other Chicago families, unless it's absolutely necessary. Tends to keep the peace in the city."

Sure, they did the occasional small deal with the Albanians should they run short on something for their own streets. The Albanians were heavy into the drug trade, and while the Boykovs had their own connections and shops set up to cultivate what they could, they still needed to stock up in certain cases. The Albanians were close in that way. When the time called for it.

That was about the extent of their business relationship, however. It certainly wasn't enough for Vadim to be inviting the second in command for the Albanians into the Compound.

"And then perhaps this is *necessary*, no?" Vadim finally returned, raising one straight, thick brow as if to ask Kolya to question him one more time. "We have a small deal coming up that they brokered for someone else— something *they* approached me with a while ago. I need to keep the peace with them long enough to see it through."

Kolya wasn't entirely sure what his father was going on about, but he also didn't like the sounds of it. At the same time, he had gotten one of Vadim's looks and it was more than enough to keep him from questioning his father on the topic more.

Vadim hated to be questioned.

Through the exchange, Grisha remained quiet in his seat as he flipped through whatever papers were in that folder. Vadim waited long enough for Grisha to find something in the folder, which he brought over to his boss and then took his seat once more. Vadim didn't give the paper a second look; his gaze was firmly on Kolya.

"Well?" he asked. "Where is it?"

He didn't even need to ask what his father meant. It was the whole reason he had been called in, after all.

Kolya dropped the small, black duffle he'd been carrying to the floor and opened it up. Pulling out the documents he'd retrieved from Ivan's Kozlov's property, he grabbed hold of the bag as well, before stepping forward to set both items on his father's desk.

Pointing to the bag, he said, "A little over one-hundred grand in assorted bills—*not* ours, either. Actual cash. And the paperwork to his warehouse, home, and whatever other properties he had a hand in. I assume they'll make a decent profit when liquidated, or in the case of the businesses, they'll continue to *be* profitable, yes?"

Vadim's gaze drifted over the papers, and then the duffle before he came back to Kolya. "Is that all?"

"For this."

"And the run-down on what happened two weeks ago?"

Yeah, *shit.*

He'd been hoping to avoid all those details, but Vadim wasn't the type to skip or skim. He liked to know it all, regardless.

"All in all," Kolya said, keeping his tone level, "it went well. There were just enough faces we recognized in the warehouse to make sure word made the rounds that the Boykovs doled out appropriate punishment. As you wanted."

Vadim's gaze narrowed. "*And?*"

"Anatoly happened to step in the way when a bit of the business was going down, and shit happened. The issue was cleaned up and it's gone."

His father quieted at that. "Stepped in *how?*"

Here, Kolya had to lie. He wasn't about to explain the real reason why Anatoly died because that would lead into the discussion of Maya, and *no.*

"An incident between him and Ivan," Kolya offered simply.

Vadim seemed to take that as gospel, but frankly, he wouldn't have anything else to go on to call Kolya out on his lie. And after all these years under his father's thumb, Kolya had learned how to hide his tells from his father when he did lie.

Not that it happened very often.

Vadim stuck a hand in the duffle to pull out a wad of cash and flicked through the bills as he asked, "And what about the animals? I know he had enough to make a small army."

"All taken care of."

"Meaning?"

"They're not there."

He didn't think details were important on that end. Hell, who knew? Maybe some of those poor animals found their way to animal shelters that might even reunite them with their previous families—unlikely, but one could hope.

Hope.

He wasn't the type for that.

Where had that come from?

Vadim didn't allow for Kolya's thoughts to wander for too long before his voice brought him out of his mind with a bang as he said, "There's nothing else, then."

"*Nyet.*"

"No?"

Kolya simply stared at his father.

Vadim stared back.

Finally, Vadim broke the silence by telling Grisha, "Leave us for a moment, yes?"

Grisha didn't think twice about lifting his old bones—he had a good ten years on Vadim—out of the chair when the Pakhan spoke, and doing what he had been told. The door didn't even make a sound when it closed behind him as he left.

"That's for show," Kolya said unbothered. "Because we all know Grisha is made aware of everything."

Vadim's expression remained unchanged as he stared down his son. "One more time—is there anything else you want to tell me?"

"I said what needed to be said."

Therein lies the difference.

Apparently, not to Vadim.

"You are deliberately leaving information out, yes? Why?"

Kolya stayed quiet.

He wasn't giving this up unless Vadim forced it out of him. And frankly, that was very likely, knowing his father.

Vadim's calm veneer slipped in the face of Kolya's stubborn silence. His jaw tightened in his frustration as he leaned back and waved a finger at his son, saying, "The Kozlov daughter—and no, don't even *think* to pretend like you don't know exactly who I am talking about."

"I won't pretend."

Now that he knew Maya, he couldn't possibly act like he *didn't.*

"I was fit and fine to allow you whatever time you needed before you came *to me* with the fact that you had the girl, but you didn't seem to want to do that."

Kolya stayed like a statue—silent, tall, and unmovable. He knew how his father worked, and right then, the truth was simple. Vadim wanted to rant and talk and go on like he did, but he wasn't actually looking for a response from his son. That would only piss him off more, likely.

"I knew you had her from that very first night," Vadim continued. "Do you really think *anyone* enters one of my safehouses without me knowing about it?"

Kolya cocked a brow but refused to speak. That was good information to know—although he suspected Vadim kept up on his security at their various places, he'd never thought to actually ask for details. Maybe he should have.

"And I had someone go over to check—she walks the pup occasionally, and *without* someone watching her, I might add."

"Why does she need someone watching her to walk the dog?"

"Might she not *come back?*" Vadim questioned.

"That hasn't been a problem yet, no?"

His father leaned forward and his hands curled tightly around the edge of the desk. "Why were you hiding the girl, Kolya?"

"I wasn't hiding her. I *took* her. She has no reason to be gallivanting around the fucking city. She doesn't seem to want to do that, anyway."

The thing about Vadim Boykov—and it was as clear as the fucking sky was blue—was that the man could keep his expression as blank as a white sheet of paper no matter the circumstance. It was only when his anger became damn near uncontrollable that he truly slipped, and the mask cracked enough to show the violence that was about to come someone's way.

It was the tick in his jaw.

The narrowing of his eyes.

The white in his knuckles.

All of that told Kolya that Vadim was about to snap.

"I had already gathered what you needed and asked for where Ivan's debt was concerned when they stumbled upon Maya," Kolya started to say.

"And *what?*"

"Circumstances and rules are clear—she became Boykov property. I didn't see the harm in taking her, considering *my* status."

Vadim relaxed a bit, but his sharp gaze drifted over Kolya's face as though he was trying to read whatever he could from his son's expression. "You wanted her, no?"

Kolya hesitated on that answer—it was an obvious *yes*, but that wasn't why he thought before he spoke. It was how Vadim posed the question, as though he was genuinely interested in the answer. But why?

"The debt would be cleared, and everything was taken care of except for her. Not every girl needs to go to the whorehouses," Kolya settled on saying.

"So, you took her."

"I said that, yes."

"Because you wanted her."

Jesus.

He was not going to let that go.

"You could say that," Kolya settled on saying.

Vadim nodded, and relaxed into his chair a little more. "Well, that's going to be a problem, then."

Kolya blinked. "Why would it be a—"

"Idriz—the Albanian who just left. I am sure you don't need me to explain who he is, or who his brother is, for that matter. He was here *because* of your slave."

Fucking hell.

That word—*slave*—raked along every one of Kolya's nerves. He didn't like it being used to describe Maya, but he forced himself to stay quiet yet again. This was another one of those situations where Vadim was clearly not looking for a response.

"Valbon Gashi—ring a bell?" his father asked.

"A distant one."

Vadim waved a hand, saying, "Figures. He's a cousin to Idriz, and thus, to the boss as well—*Saban*. He is also the one Ivan Kozlov owed the debt to. I have come to learn that debt was more than what was just on the surface—it was a running *tab*."

Kolya swallowed down the discomfort starting to settle in his stomach. "And what does that mean?"

"Valbon had an arrangement of sorts with Ivan ... or he had come to one after a spell had passed between them. Maya, that is. The girl."

"Woman," Kolya corrected before he could think better of it. "She's beyond old enough to be called a woman."

Vadim scowled. "I bet."

He only shrugged.

"Be that as it may, Valbon took an interest, and Ivan gave in to the man's request. Debt was paid then."

"Clearly not," Kolya countered, "as he still owed."

His gaze drifted to the documents and money on the table he had needed to find in order to pay back that debt. Not to mention the man had lost his life because of it.

Vadim drummed his fingers to the desk. "Ivan ended up back in Valbon's debt—not that the details matter this time around, as it won't happen again. Point being, I have been told that the two came to a similar agreement as before. Only this time, the *woman* was to go to Valbon."

Kolya stiffened.

His father likely didn't miss it.

"Permanently," Vadim added after a stretch of silence.

Kolya didn't even have to think about an adequate response, really. "The deal is void with them—Ivan is dead."

"Mmm, but not her brother," Vadim replied, wagging that fucking finger of his again. "This ... *Maya* ... seems to be in hot demand, all things considered. I've gotten word her brother—Alexei—was approached to inherit his father's debt from the Albanians. They do tend to take their debts seriously, yes?"

Vadim gestured at the papers and duffle of money on the desk. "Now, *I* can handle my side of this easily enough, Kolya. I have the means and that's really all I need to do … but it seems this brother of hers is willing to trade Maya for a variety of reasons. None of which I give a damn about at the end of the day, but here we are. It would save me a—"

"That's going to be a problem," Kolya interrupted.

It was risky to do that to his father.

Vadim didn't have a glass close enough to throw, though, so he took the chance.

"How so?" Vadim asked, reverting back to that calm state again.

A dangerous state, really.

"Her position—status—is clear," Kolya murmured, refusing to budge and entirely unaffected. "She is mine to do with as I want, and I am not handing her over to a man who hasn't even earned his stars to pay for the debt of a man who never should have had his rank to begin with."

"Those are strong words."

"I mean them."

Vadim sighed. "Kolya, if it's a slave you want, there is a whorehouse in The Heights full of them that I own. Go *pick one*, and she can be yours. This slave can fix a whole host of issues, simply by transferring her to a new set of hands, yes? See, *easy*."

The visceral reaction at Maya yet again being called a slave was not something Kolya was able to hide at all. His shoulders stiffened, and his hands fisted into tight balls at his side. He heard the crunch of his molars, and his usual scowl sharpened into a glare.

He couldn't hide it.

Vadim didn't miss it.

"Ah," his father murmured.

"What?"

"You can't have the girl to love or marry. She's neither appropriate for your status, nor would I approve of her for you, given her circumstances. You should already know this—why the defensiveness and anger?"

"Who said anything about love or marriage?"

Vadim cocked a brow in challenge.

Kolya refused to rise to greet it.

Clearly knowing he was not going to get what he wanted, Vadim tipped his chin up to almost appear as though he were looking down on his son as he said, "Brand her properly for status if you're so serious about this *keeping* her thing, although why, I don't know. She's a dime a dozen. Do know that any problems that come from this can and will be easily solved. I cannot control what the Albanians want or do when their expectation falls short."

The statement was offered *freely*.

Flippantly.

And yet, it irked Kolya like nothing else.

"Is that a threat?" he asked his father.

The change in atmosphere was damn near instant. Tension so thick it could be cut with a fucking knife. And yet, Kolya didn't take back the words as he probably should. No, he let them hang out there just as freely as his father had given his, and let Vadim make of it what he wanted.

Vadim stood from his desk slowly. "The Albanians had a deal worked out on this—what they chose to do from here on out is their decision, and you are to step back."

"Can't do that."

"Try that again, yes?"

Kolya shook his head. "Won't do it, no."

"I gave you a chance, remember that." His father reached over and pressed a green button on the side of the desk. Speakers crackled in the room before a ringing echoed. "Grisha?"

"Yes, boss?"

"Give Idriz a call and let him know his man may remove the girl."

"Calling now."

Vadim pushed the red button on the same base and never took his gaze away from Kolya as he said, "You have forgotten your place and lessons—a reminder is always good."

Kolya barely heard him; he was already turning to leave.

He did hear someone else, though.

"I have one of those, too, comrade," Vasily Markovic said. "A son who makes me want to choke the fucking life out of him."

"I've spoiled him," Vadim replied. "We always spoil the boys, no?"

Fuck.

The man had been listening on speaker the entire time, when Kolya thought his father had actually hung up the phone when he first came in.

What did it matter?

He had other problems to handle.

Maya. Maya. Maya.

7.

MAYA FOUND time passed a lot faster when someone had something cute to keep them distracted—something like a small, black puppy with big, yellow eyes. Kolya hadn't said much when he'd taken off early that morning, but it was closing in on noon and he still hadn't returned.

She wasn't sure if that meant good things, or not. She was still wrapped up in the way his lips had felt pressed against hers the night before, and the confusing mess her life currently was, all because of Kolya fucking Boykov.

Why did he have to be the way he was?

Interesting.

Dark.

Different.

Kind.

Frightening.

Entirely fucking confusing.

It would be so much easier to deal with Kolya if he could just stick to being the emotionless, expressionless block of ice he sometimes reverted back to. Then, she wouldn't have to also tie that same man to the one who'd spent hours upon hours with his pup, or the same man who had stared at her like she was the most amazing thing he had ever seen when he thought she wasn't looking.

Because, yeah … she'd seen that, too. She watched him, too, and she didn't know what to make of it.

Still, even as she had made a simple breakfast that morning and then after, gotten Sumerki ready for his morning walk, her mind drifted to Kolya. The blank expression he had worn as he'd readied to leave the house, and his flat tone when he said goodbye.

Whatever he was going to do, he hadn't *wanted* to.

Vadim, she heard him say on the phone the night before. His father. Was that where he had to go, and *why* did he clearly not want to?

And there Maya went, right back to concerning herself over a man she probably had no business doing anything for. She was more bothered by the fact she worried at all. And what exactly that might mean.

Instead of letting her thoughts drift to the troubling Russian who had decided to keep, house, and feed—not to mention *kiss*—her, she paid attention to what was at the end of the navy-blue, leather leash. Sumerki, that was. Maya was keeping a tight grip on the leash because God only knew what Kolya would do if he got home, and found out the dog had taken off, or worse, ended up hurt. Sumerki chuffed along at her side.

Every so often, the pup would find a new spot to sniff or mark his territory, and there the two would be, stuck for five minutes while the dog did his business. She didn't really mind—it was cute to see Sumerki get himself all worked up over a blade of grass that some stray cat had probably walked over during the night.

Each day, it never failed, Sumerki was walked at least three times. Kolya's demand.

Maya didn't *have* to walk him because Kolya was more than fine with doing it himself, and often came on the walks with her, but she liked to do it. And every single walk, Sumerki pulled the same kind of tricks—pissing on the same spots over and over again, and sniffing the exact same patches of grass.

She could bet on it, now.

"Are you just about done?" she asked the pup.

Sumerki's tiny, pointed ear on the right side flicked as if to say he heard her speak, but he didn't take his attention away from the patch of grass he was currently sniffing, circling, and every so often, dragging his paw through like he was considering digging.

"Don't you dare," Maya warned. "No digging."

Despite how the pup liked to pretend as though he didn't hear anything he was told, he did actually listen. He was smart, and liked to please. She supposed that was why Kolya had little to no trouble at all when it came to training Sumerki.

Hell, the dog hadn't messed in the house since the first couple of times. He'd already mastered sitting, keeling, staying, and coming when directed. His little tail would wag faster when he finally got his praise for doing something properly.

Sumerki chuffed under his breath, circled once more, and then *finally* did his business after five minutes of playing with the damn spot. Then, he looked up at her with those big, yellow eyes as if to silently ask, *Well, are you ready to go?*

Maya smiled to herself.

"What, you want to go back home?" she asked.

Sumerki's tail wagged.

"Kolya probably isn't back yet."

The dog clearly didn't understand what she said, but at just the mention of *Kolya*, a word which Sumerki absolutely did recognize, his tail picked up speed. So much so, that his whole hind end swayed with the motion.

People who didn't have dogs were missing out, as far as she was concerned. Humans didn't deserve these animals—all innocent, eager to please and loving.

"Let's go, then," Maya said, turning to head down the quiet back alley that would lead them to the townhouse. She preferred walking back here because there was little traffic, and people mostly used it to park their cars. Sumerki was quick to join her and his attention then became laser-focused on the sidewalk ahead. Like he just knew he was on his way home and the thing he wanted most was there waiting for him.

Kolya, that was.

Or so he thought.

Maya was still chatting along to the pup, like he understood and could respond back to her with big eyes and tail wags, as she came to the steps leading up to the backdoor of the townhouse. It was only when she moved to climb the first cement step, and Sumerki pulled back as if to refuse to go along with her that she noticed something was wrong.

The way Sumerki stopped.

How he sniffed like something was different.

And then …

The back door of the townhouse was cracked open. Not a lot—barely noticeable at all, really. Maya probably wouldn't even have noticed it until she tried to put the key in the lock to open the door. She knew just by how meticulous and careful Kolya was about the rules when it came to coming and going from the townhouse that it wasn't him who had left the door open.

And she sure as hell had *not*.

Instinct made Maya step back. A life of knowing something bad was always right around the corner made her aware this wasn't *right*. Sumerki pulling hard on the leash in retreat made her glance back to calm the dog so he didn't hurt himself in the process.

"It's okay—"

"I believe it's Maya, yes?"

Maya stiffened all over, and a cold spike of fear stabbed deep into her spine. She kept a tight grip on Sumeki's leash, even as she searched for the familiar—although *barely*—voice saying her name. She found him standing in the now-open doorway.

Tall.

Dark.

Domineering.

Terrifying.

Dressed in all black from head to toe—including the leather gloves on his hands—the man flashed Maya a cold, flippant grin. As though he didn't have a care in the world, and like he might be able to actually taste her fucking fear.

Tomor.

She was sure that was his name.

Maya had only seen the Albanian once or twice with her father—he'd come with the other Albanian who her father had regularly owed debts to. So much so, that Maya had once been used as a way to *pay it off*.

The thought made her want to be sick.

The possible reason why *Tomor* was here made her want to fucking bolt.

She'd once seen this man stab a man in the eye with a pen because the guy had said something offhandedly while they'd sat at her father's bar. Ivan had laughed it off, but it was clear her father had been uncomfortable.

But what could Ivan do or say?

He *owed* the Albanians.

He always fucking owned them.

"Valbon misses you," Tomor said, his sly grin deepening a bit. "He wanted me to tell you that. I'm sure you haven't forgotten your last meeting with him—he looks forward to repeating that when I return you to him tonight."

Just a few words.

Three simple sentences.

Complete terror for her.

Maya shuddered.

All over.

No, she hadn't forgotten that last meeting. *And no, no, no* … it would not be happening again. Maya didn't even think about what she was going to do next—all she knew was that she needed to get away, and fast. She spun on her heel and bent down to grab Sumerki up from the ground. No doubt, he wouldn't be able to keep up with her.

Grabbing the dog was a mistake. Hesitating that long was her second error.

She would never regret it, though. She would never have forgiven herself had she hurt Sumerki in her haste to get away, or worse, dropped his leash and run.

Maya didn't even make it two steps away from the townhouse before Tomor was right behind her. His fist slammed into the back of her head, sending a cry of pain and shock shooting from her lips. *He'd hit her.* It wasn't the first time a man had hit her, but it was the first time one had punched her with a closed fist in the back of her fucking head when she couldn't even fight back.

The force alone sent her flying to the ground, and in her desire to protect a growling Sumerki, she couldn't catch her fall. Not when she was too busy keeping him wrapped in her arms. Her cheek scraped against the pavement, and blood bloomed in her mouth.

Tomor laughed darkly, and then grabbed Maya by her hair to pull her up from the ground like she was nothing more than a ragdoll. Instinct made her arms fly out to claw at his arms, but all that did was make Sumerki fall to the ground.

The poor pup yelped as he hit the ground on his side, and rolled to his back before getting on all fours again. Maya cried out for Sumerki, even as Tomor yanked her back by her hair and started dragging her down the sidewalk. It didn't matter how much she fought or shouted—no one was on the street to help, and her struggle didn't bother Tomor in the least.

"The less you fight," Tomor said, "the easier this will be, girl."

"Fuck—"

Pop.

Maya had only seen the hazy form through her tear-filled eyes as he came down the street in their direction. She hadn't even gotten a clear view of him before the soft noise. Tomor fell away from Maya with a morbid crack as his head hit the pavement.

Wide, dead eyes stared up.

Blood puddled under his body.

Then, Tomor blinked, a thick groan falling from his lips as his gaze swung in her direction from where he lay on the ground.

Okay, so not *dead.*

Maya inched away from the Albanian.

"You okay?"

Maya blinked, still staring at Tomor. She knew what just happened—that unmistakable pop of a gun firing with a silencer attached. And yet, her brain didn't want to *process.*

"Are. You. Okay?"

That voice . . .

"You talk, no? Answer me, Maya."

She glanced up as Konstantin Boykov came to a stop only a foot away from her. He was keeping his gun carefully aimed at Tomor on the ground, while he pulled out a phone from his pocket with the other. He had the phone pressed to his ear in a flash, and his Russian came out smooth, and quick.

"I need a cleaner at the safehouse in Wicker," he said, "and it'll be in the back alley next to the property. He's not to be killed; do not let him die. Less than twenty—make it happen."

Then, Konstantin hung up the phone, and looked at Maya again.

"Well, are you okay?"

She blinked again.

Unsure.

Wary as hell.

Still breathing, though.

"I'm okay," she said. "Now."

But she wasn't okay, though.

Not at all.

"Lucky for Kolya that I was nearby," Konstantin muttered, giving the Albanian on the ground a disdainful look. "This breed is always causing us trouble."

Something soft, furry, and warm rubbed against Maya's leg. She shrieked and jumped—her heart damn near leaping into her throat at the same fucking time. In her fear, she spun around and made a move to bolt away again.

Hands were on her shoulders in an instant. Warm, but not familiar. A soft touch, but not the one she wanted.

Konstantin held firm, turned her around, and didn't let her run. "It's the *dog*, Maya. The dog, yes?"

He said it again—a third time.

She nodded.

Sure enough, Sumerki sat his furry backside right down on her shoe and stared up at her. His leash still dangled limply from his collar.

"He didn't even run," she whispered.

Konstantin sighed. "Listen, my car is down the way. I have to keep a watch on this fool until someone comes to pick him up. Do you think you can *quietly* make your way to my car, and not move?"

Maya nodded again.

"Good—get going, then."

She didn't need to be told twice.

• • •

"Are you usually this quiet?"

Maya glanced away from the passing buildings that were nothing more than a blur in her vision. She heard Konstantin pose the question, but she wasn't really listening. Or maybe … she was still trying to figure out what exactly had happened, and how they'd gotten here. Or rather, how she'd gotten in this car, driving down these streets, and—

"Are you listening?"

"Is this why Kolya is snappy with you?" Maya asked.

Konstantin took his eyes away from the road to pass her a look. "What?"

"Because you pester people, I mean. People just want to be quiet and alone with their thoughts, but you can't let them be. Is that why he's snappy with you—do you pester him, too?"

"First, everybody pesters Kolya … they just have to be in his presence." Konstantin raised his brows as if to dare her to challenge his statement. "Second, he's snappy with everyone. I don't get to be a special case there, Maya."

Her brow dipped, and she peered down at a sleeping Sumerki in her lap as she said quietly, "He's not snappy with me."

Konstantin stilled, and gave the road his full attention once more. "At all?"

Why did he sound as though that was the strangest thing he had ever heard?

"It can't be a foreign concept, no?" Maya asked. "Kolya can be—"

"Difficult. Moody. Perpetually pissed off. Violent. I can continue," Konstantin said, shrugging one shoulder, "if you would like me to. He owns a whole list of adjectives that are not necessarily to his favor."

Not particularly.

The urge to defend Kolya, or even, protect him in some way rose up strong and fast in Maya's gut. Like a punch of heat had come to slam right into her stomach, and the words fell out of her scowling lips before she could stop them.

Nobody said Kolya was perfect, but he wasn't some monster, either. Maya knew that firsthand. She couldn't help that Konstantin—Kolya's own brother—didn't look hard enough to see the things she did.

She could correct it, though.

"He's also soft-spoken when he's being thoughtful and soft-handed when comfort is needed. He's mindful and careful. Sure, he has his moments, but I bet you do, too. Just like everyone does."

Konstantin blinked and arched one brow as though he were considering Maya's words. He said nothing as he took an exit ramp onto the freeway, and merged onto the semi-congested road.

"Huh," he finally muttered.

To himself, sure.

It didn't sound like it was for her.

Maya still asked, "What?"

She didn't mean it to come out so sharply, and yet, it still had. Konstantin didn't miss it, if his answering chuckle was any indication.

"It's just ..." Konstantin trailed off, and frowned before saying, "Kolya's *moments*, as you said, happen more often than not when it comes to those around him. He's not exactly the pleasant one of the family, and people tend to keep their distance because he's usually given them a reason—or more than one—to do so, yes? If you get my drift."

"Not to me," Maya replied, not unkindly.

Oh, sure, she had absolutely *seen* Kolya's moments. She had witnessed his moods shift, and his darker nature come out to play. She had been right there to see how, in a breath, he could easily switch to violence to answer someone.

And yet, never to her.

Never *against* her.

"And that's where the *huh* comes in," Konstantin said, the corner of his lips tilting up in a half-smile. "Never thought there would be a day when my *brat* found a woman he cared enough about to keep around—never mind a woman actually caring about him."

Maya blinked.

She quieted.

So, that was it, then.

Someone else saw it, too.

Someone else knew, too.

Someone else confirmed it, too.

She cared about Kolya—through no real choice of her own, and for no real reason beyond the fact Kolya had been kind to her, when every action he'd made seemed like it could possibly hurt her. And yet, he'd never once hurt her.

It just ... was.

Konstantin's gaze drifted from the road to Maya again where she sat in the passenger seat. "And there you go being quiet again."

"I think I've given myself a complex," Maya admitted.

To say the least.

The man driving cleared his throat, and didn't even bother to hide his amused grin. "About my brother, no?"

"You could say that."

"Mmhmm, Kolya does have a way of giving people who care about him a complex," Konstantin returned almost flippantly. "See, it would be easy for me to *hate* Kolya for a lot of reasons, and for just as many elsewhere, I often find myself competing with him even when he's not trying to have the spotlight, and yet ... he's my brother, and I know who made him the way he is. How could I hate him when I know all that?"

Maya didn't know what to say to that and so she chose not to say anything at all. It seemed like the right choice at the moment.

Instead, Maya asked something else that had been lingering in the back of her mind ever since she'd watched from the inside of Konstantin's car as a vehicle drove up, and the Albanian who attacked her was stuffed into the trunk before whoever it was took off. He'd looked like he was still alive, then, too.

Although, *barely.*

"Why did they take Tomor—and *where?*" Maya asked.

"Who?"

"The Albanian. The one you shot—his name is Tomor."

"How do you know that?" he asked.

"His name?"

"Don't play stupid, Maya."

She glared.

Konstantin acted like he didn't see it.

Asshole.

"I know his name because that's not my first run-in with him," she confessed. "And don't ask more; I won't tell."

"All right," Konstantin said gruffly. "To answer your question, he was taken because Kolya requested it, if he was still alive, and you don't need to know where. That's not important."

"I asked, though."

"My answer remains the same."

"That's—"

The ringing that suddenly came through the speakers of the car quieted her entirely. Konstantin passed a glance at the number and name that lit up the touchscreen stereo, and then said, "Answer call."

"Where are you?" came a dark, growled demand.

"Hello, Vadim. I'm good—the roads aren't too bad. Things are great. How are you, yeah?"

Maya passed Konstantin a look, knowing by the name he used that he was talking to his and Kolya's father, but all she saw reflected back in the man's profile was a stiffness in his jaw, and a hardness in his gaze.

"I'm sorry," Vadim said, "do you need me to start every phone conversation with pleasantries that you know I don't give a goddamn about?"

"It would be asking a bit much, no?"

"I beg your pardon?"

Konstantin sighed. "What can I do for you?"

"I can't get ahold of your brother."

"Funny—I was just talking to him a half hour ago. You know, when I had to run in and save the day. Or rather, save his newest thing from getting hurt by a crazy Albanian who'd broken into the safehouse."

Vadim made a noise on the other end of the call—one Maya couldn't decipher. "Is that so?"

"Was I not supposed to do that?"

Konstantin asked the question so innocently one wouldn't think he was fucking grinning like the Cheshire cat watching a mouse scuttle across the floor right in front of him. He looked mighty fucking pleased with himself.

God save the poor woman who thinks to play games with this man.

Vadim didn't answer Konstantin's question, instead asking, "The girl is safe then, no?"

"*Maya*, you mean?"

"Whatever her name is—the Kozlov woman, Konstantin. Stop with your word games."

"She's okay."

Vadim made another one of those noises. "Kolya will be pleased, I'm sure."

"I would think—"

"For now," Vadim added before Konstantin could finish. "He forgets his place; the place I *gave* him."

Konstantin said nothing.

Vadim continued on anyway, asking, "And what of the Albanian?"

"He's dead."

"Shame," the man on the other end of the call murmured. "That's going to be a problem."

Vadim hung up the call before Konstantin could finish. It took another five minutes of driving in a tense, uncomfortable silence before Konstantin started to relax a little. He'd been holding onto the steering wheel so tightly that his knuckles were white, and his muscles strained against the sleeve of his dress shirt.

"You lied to him," Maya said softly. "About Tomor."

Konstantin nodded but never looked away from the road. "I did."

"Why?"

"You're not the only one with a complex where Kolya is concerned. I told you that. He's good at a lot of things, my brother, and this is definitely one of those."

It had to be more than that, though.

Had to be.

She heard it in his tone and saw it on his face when he spoke to his father. A lot like she saw and heard it from Kolya when he had to talk about the man.

"You and Kolya … you have a strange relationship with your father, don't you?" she asked.

Konstantin took a second. His reply wasn't particularly ground-breaking. "You could say that," he murmured.

And then, all Maya saw was a flash of black in her mirror before Konstantin cussed, cut the wheel sharply, and realized too late that he hadn't reacted quickly enough. The car sliding against the side of theirs at high speeds while Konstantin tried to swerve to avoid the accident was more than enough force to send them rolling as the wheels hit gravel.

She could hear something else, too. Even over the crunch of metal and the shattering of glass. Even over her rushing blood in her ears and the racing of her heart. Everything slowed in her vision and she could *hear* it.

The *pop, pop, pop.*

Gunshots.

8.

"OUCH."

Maya's quiet exclamation was followed by her hiss when the doctor patted her cheek with an alcohol-soaked cotton ball. In her lap, Sumerki—already a tense ball of fur like a spring ready to come uncoiled—growled under his breath. He was getting better at the whole growling thing. At least, now he didn't sound so squeaky.

It was still kind of cute.

"Sorry," the doctor muttered, being extra gentle with his next swipe at the scratches on her cheek, "but I wouldn't want to risk these getting infected if I didn't clean them."

Maya nodded. "I understand. Thank you."

The man smiled kindly. "Either way, I'll be careful. Wouldn't want your puppy to bite me." His joke made Maya laugh, and she petted Sumerki just to try and ease some of his tension. "Or your other … friend," the doctor added.

He couldn't see Konstantin, what with his back being turned to the Russian on the other side of the room, but Maya could see him just fine over the doctor's shoulder. He'd needed attending to first when they'd finally arrived at the clinic after being pulled out of the wrecked car by men Konstantin called. After all, he'd had a bullet graze his shoulder, and according to the doctor, a broken rib.

One wouldn't guess that was the case by looking at Konstantin. Other than the bloodstain on the sleeve of his shirt, he looked perfectly fine leaning against the far wall of the room. With his arms folded over his chest and his gaze trained firmly on Maya and the doctor, he seemed cool and calm.

Strangely so, really.

No one would think by Konstantin's easy posture and unbothered demeanor that just one hour before they had been run off the road, and shot at before their unknown attacker sped away to leave them to save themselves.

Maya, on the other hand, was still shaking. The doctor had suggested a Valium to calm her, but she'd refused. She'd almost vomited all over the shoes of the man who'd pulled her out of the wreckage of the car. She still didn't think she would be able to look the guy in the eyes when she left the room, considering he and the other man who'd come to help them were still keeping guard outside the office.

"He's not so much a friend as … well, not a friend," Maya said.

Konstantin's lips twitched like he was fighting a smile at that statement, proving to her that he absolutely could hear their conversation, despite how quiet they were being.

The doctor glanced over his shoulder and looked right at Konstantin then, asking, "Oh, have you found yourself something *more* than a friend, Konstantin? Wouldn't have taken you for the type, all things considered."

Just how well did this doctor know the Boykovs? If it was quite well, as the doctor's statement suggested, Maya supposed it made sense now why Konstantin demanded they be taken to this clinic instead of a closer hospital. Not to mention why the doctor had come in like he was on call for Konstantin.

"Not *my* anything," Konstantin countered. "Try Kolya, no?"

The doctor tensed, glanced back at Maya warily, and then quickly back to Konstantin. "Seriously?"

Konstantin shrugged one shoulder, but otherwise didn't move another muscle or speak. No, simply a shrug as his confirmation, and nothing else. Maya didn't quite know what to make of that, really.

"Well, then," the doctor said as his attention came back to Maya and he began cleaning her scratches again. Although now, his voice was a little more hesitant than before, she noticed. "Let's just worry about getting you—"

It was a crash outside the closed door that stopped the doctor from saying anything more. Well, that and a familiar voice shouting at someone else.

"*Zatknis!* Move, right now."

"What is your problem, Kolya?"

"Get the fuck out of my way before I *force* you out of it."

Nothing more was said, instead the door crashed open with a bang as Kolya barreled into the room. Towering over six feet, his shoulders wide enough to fill the door frame, and cold blue eyes zoning straight in on Maya the second he could see her. It was like he didn't see anything else, didn't check for anyone else, and didn't care about a thing but *her.*

She blinked.

And he was still there.

Still staring at her.

Still moving closer.

Still ignoring the world around him.

Silently, the doctor stepped aside when Kolya reached the middle of the room. He had all the medical supplies on the bed quickly scooped up before Kolya even came to stand in front of Maya, and moved entirely away from the line of fire without as much as a word of hello.

And then there was Kolya.

Eyes full of storms.

Stiffness in his jaw.

Rage in the set of his frown.

Softness in his hands.

He reached for her without asking, and she didn't mind a bit. He cupped her face in his two large palms with careful hands, and she couldn't help but smile a little when his thumbs stroked her cheeks but only ghosted over the scratches. She saw fury flash in his gaze when his eyes drifted toward the bruise above her left eye.

He was *harsh*.

His stance.

His aura.

Him.

He was cold, and firm, and unmoved.

And yet, his touch was soft, and sweet, and *warm*.

"I'm okay," Maya said. "I *am*."

She was a lot better now that he was there.

Kolya made a noise in the back of his throat that sounded like a noncommittal grunt—as though he neither agreed nor disagreed with her statement and he didn't trust himself to speak. Maya didn't know where to begin or end with this man.

Maybe that was the problem.

He couldn't *be* figured out.

He wasn't meant to be understood.

He simply *was*.

Konstantin cleared his throat loudly, saying, "If we're all done making others feel awkward, yeah, a quick chat would be nice."

Kolya's jaw stiffened, but he was quick to toss over his shoulder, "Speak, then."

Even as he spoke to his brother, Kolya didn't let go of Maya or look away from her. It was almost like he thought if he did let her go or look away, circumstances would change. She wouldn't be *okay* or she would be gone entirely. She could practically feel that fear vibrating from his very person, yet she kept quiet.

"The run down, then," Konstantin said. "I took care of the one Albanian—Tomor, no?"

Maya nodded at the question. "Yeah, that one."

Kolya's scowl deepened. "He was the guard with the Albanian that Vadim was meeting with earlier when I got to the Compound."

He was looking at her.

But he spoke to Konstantin.

Across the room, Maya saw Konstantin nod at the statement before he replied with, "My apologies on getting there a little bit late, yeah?"

Kolya's gaze dragged its way over Maya's scrapes and bruises again, and not for one single second did she think his rage was in any way quelled over it. "Move on, *brat*."

Konstantin cleared his throat. "And speaking of the Compound—I pulled some strings and asked for a favor."

"How so?"

Kolya's question was quiet, tight, and dark.

"That's where Tomor is." Konstantin let out a dry laugh. "Still alive, for now."

A slow, cold smile spread over Kolya's lips. The sight of it alone was enough to make a shiver crawl up Maya's spine. She had only seen him wear that kind of smile once before—right before he attacked her father.

"Good," Kolya murmured. "And then?"

"We were on our way to a different spot after the Tomor thing when we were attacked on the highway. Run off the road and shot at. I'm thinking the Albanians, likely. Considering I doubt Tomor had gone alone to grab Maya, and maybe they were answering me back for their man being downed by my hand. You know how the Albanians are when you kill or attack one of them."

Silence echoed for a long while—long enough to make Maya uncomfortable, even if the warmth of Kolya's hands holding onto her was soothing in some ways. She didn't know why Kolya had suddenly turned into a statue after his brother spoke.

Kolya stiffened. His mouth opened like he was going to reply, but he hesitated. Konstantin didn't miss it from across the room.

"What is it, Kolya?"

"I don't think—"

Kolya didn't get the chance to finish his statement before a man walked right into the clinic's private room without as much as knocking or even announcing his presence with a hello. His gaze drifted to the doctor working quietly in the corner, and then to Konstantin leaning against the wall before moving to Kolya, too.

A second man came in right after him.

Maya didn't care as much about the second man—he didn't look nearly as pissed off or as angry as the first man did. He didn't give off the promise of violence with just his presence alone like the first man was able to simply by strolling into the room.

"Vadim," Konstantin greeted.

Kolya *finally* glanced over his shoulder, and Maya felt how his hands instinctively tightened their hold on her in an instant. "Vadim."

The brothers' greeting was not rude, nor unkind. And yet, their tones held little warmth or affection.

Even had Konstantin *not* said the man's name right away, Maya still thought she would have known this was Kolya's father simply by looking at the man. They shared the same strong features and ice-blue eyes. The square jaws and cut cheekbones were the same. Their statures were both large and tall, although Vadim looked as though some of his had migrated to his middle over the years.

Still, it was enough.

Their familiarities were clear.

"We had this handled," Konstantin said to his father.

"Is that what you call this?" Vadim barked, gesturing at the wound his son sported. "And what in the *hell* were you thinking, no? You had no business stepping in on something that had nothing to do with you. You shouldn't need to be told that. Getting in the middle of your brother's fucking *problem*. You know better, Konstantin."

"A problem you helped along," Kolya said darkly.

Vadim's head swung back in Kolya's direction instantly. "Excuse me?"

Kolya said nothing, but he did turn around to face his father. Slowly, and with the grace of a sure predator unafraid of what might be waiting for him, he turned. Although, he made sure to stay close enough that Maya—even sitting on the bed—was practically swallowed by his size in front of her.

Like a wall between her and the danger.

His back was tense. His spine—ramrod straight.

She fisted the back of his shirt for reasons she didn't even know. To keep him close maybe because some part of her just *knew* he wanted to jump the gun and bolt forward straight for whatever he felt was threatening her. Another part just wanted to feel him right then—maybe she could keep him calm. It seemed she was the hot button for Kolya. Or so Maya was learning.

All someone needed to do was suggest they were going to be some kind of problem for her, and Kolya was quick to flip his fucking switch on them. Violence and hell and pain all rolled into one and coming for whatever threat he saw as real.

It was terrifying.

Confusing.

And *enthralling*.

Vadim seemed entirely unaware of Kolya's rigid stance or the thick tension in the room as he ranted on, unaffected. "You were *told*, Kolya! Step back, no? Let the Albanians have what they want and let the issue go. You were told—don't deny it!"

"I—"

"And for *what*?" Vadim snarled, his gaze finally drifting to Maya over Kolya's shoulder. Those eyes of his bore hard into Maya—pensive and yet dismissive at the same time. Cold, indifferent, and distant. Like he had seen something just like her before, and she was nothing fucking new or interesting to him. "For *that*? A woman, Kolya? All of this for *her*? There are a dozen just like her!"

Silence answered Vadim back at first.

Tense.

Long.

And sharp.

So sharp, that Maya swore the silence dragged along her skin, and burrowed in deep enough under her skin to reach her fucking nerves. In all her years being abused and used by her father and brother, she had never felt quite as uncomfortable as she did in this moment, staring down Vadim Boykov.

And yet, she refused to look away.

Not when he glared.

Not when his gaze narrowed.

Not even when he inched closer.

She could practically hear him screaming at her inside his head for her to *back down*, to look away, or do something other than challenge him like she was, simply by looking at him. She suspected Vadim was the kind of man who only needed to look at someone to get his point across, and yet, she *refused*.

She would not back down.

Would *not* look away.

He didn't know her—he didn't know her person or her life. And he did not get to decide she was useless, trash, or unworthy simply by looking at her, and nothing else. She would give no man that satisfaction. They could say it and act as if they felt that way, but she would not sit there and *let* someone dismiss her.

She couldn't.

"For *this* woman," Vadim repeated, his voice dropping to a dangerous murmur.

"Yes," Kolya replied at the same level. "For this woman."

Vadim barked out a laugh. "Stupid *boy*."

Maya flinched at that one.

Kolya didn't even *move*.

"You're stupid, no?" Vadim shook his head and pointed a wagging finger at Kolya. "You think this makes a difference? It *doesn't*. The Albanians are going to come for this and want answers. And I plan to—"

"Make the Boykovs look weak and easily manipulated by handing her over after they nearly killed your son?" Konstantin asked quietly.

For the most part, he'd watched the exchange between his brother and father in silence and without stepping in up until that point. He'd remained statue-like leaning against the wall—an expressionless form without an opinion or care.

Until now.

"Because that's what giving the woman to the Albanians will do when they come with demands and threats." Konstantin shrugged and pushed off the wall before grabbing his discarded jacket from the back of the doctor's chair against the small desk. "If you give her over after they *attacked* me—knowing who I was—you will do nothing more than make us a target, Vadim. And not to just the Albanians, no. You will make us a target to any organization who thinks a simple attack, threats, and demands will make us bend to their wants. So, go ahead … give her over. Let's see where that gets us, hmm?"

More silence answered Konstantin back.

He didn't seem bothered by it.

Finally, the man who had remained silent the whole time even though he'd come in with Vadim spoke up. "He makes a good point, Vadim. You should consider it."

"I know that, *Grisha.*"

"I'm just—"

Vadim swung on Kolya again. "You've put us in a terrible position."

Kolya cleared his throat. "I don't see how."

Vadim glanced at Maya. "Of course you don't."

"Also, I was … mistaken when you called. My apologies," Konstantin said, taking his father's attention away from her for the moment. She was grateful and starting to think he was doing that purposely. "The Albanian who attacked us the first time isn't dead—he survived with a little help and was delivered to the Compound."

Vadim's gaze turned into slits. "Is that so?"

Konstantin shrugged. "Seems so."

"*Mistaken*, you say."

"It happens occasionally."

Vadim let out a slow, heavy stream of air. "Send the Albanians a message using their man, then. Make it clear the attack on you was unacceptable, and we won't bend to anything they want after tonight."

Vadim didn't give anyone the chance to respond before he headed for the door and disappeared. His voice trailed behind him when he growled out, "At least Vasily will be gone from the city by morning. That's *one* less problem for me."

Grisha was quick to follow behind the boss, but not before giving the two brothers a pointed look. He didn't even bother to give Maya any of his attention.

Not that she minded.

The door slammed behind him.

Only then did Kolya soften his stance.

Only then did his shoulders drop.

Only then did he relax.

He didn't turn around, though.

"*Spasibo*," he murmured.

Konstantin's head tipped up a bit, and he nodded once. "Don't mention it, but you're treading very thin ice, *brat*."

"I know."

"Be careful not to fall in."

"Kind of hard for a man my size, no?"

Maya stiffened, and Konstantin smiled.

Had Kolya just made a *joke*?

A dry, dark humored, *real* joke?

"You're so fucked," Konstantin said.

"Certainly," Kolya agreed and then gestured at the quiet man still pretending to shuffle papers in the corner as he had through the entire exchange. "Pay the doctor, yes?"

Konstantin nodded. "Will do."

• • •

"And I fucking *swear*," Kolya threatened, "if you as much as bring him back to me with even one goddamn hair gone, I will rip yours from your skull."

The man in the hotel doorway nodded quickly.

"*Don't* let them take him out of your sights."

"I won't, and—"

"I didn't ask for you to *talk*," Kolya snapped.

"Kolya, be nice," Maya said quietly from deeper in the room. She was still trying to unload her bag and get her shoes off. They hadn't even been there for more than five minutes, and already he was in one of his moods— threatening to kill people or do them harm. It was second nature for Kolya, she believed. That was just how the man communicated. "Let him take Sumerki to see the emergency vet."

"*I* should take him," Kolya said, not unkindly. And yet still, a heat lingered in his words. She could hear the struggle.

"Then, let me stay with …" Maya gestured at the man in the doorway with a furry, sleeping Sumerki in his arms. The pup was *fine*—maybe a little shook up over everything that had happened, but he wasn't injured visibly. Didn't matter; Kolya wanted him checked, too. "Whatever his name is there."

"Anton," the man said.

Maya smiled. "Nice to meet you."

Kolya, on the other hand, scowled. "He's not important, Maya."

More heat.

More darkness.

She gave him a look. "Stop that."

"I—"

"Stop it. Either take Sumerki and leave me here, or let Anton take the pup to the vet. This isn't hard, Kolya."

He made a noise in the back of his throat and then glanced sideways at the sleeping pup before that cutting gaze of his drifted back to Anton. "Let him out of your sights, and you will *die*. I'll know you did it, yes? Don't even try to lie to me."

Anton swallowed hard. "*Da*, Kolya. I got it."

"Good—get gone." Kolya swung the door closed in the man's face but caught it just as fast. He opened it wide, and leaned out to shout into the hallway, "And I want a fucking call the second you're done!"

"*Kolya*," Maya said.

His back stiffened, but he didn't turn around. She could see he was gesturing something at Anton, but not exactly what.

"Stop being horrible, Kolya," Maya told him.

That did it.

He was quick to spin around to face her and slam the door closed at the same time. There was something dark in his eyes—a wildness shining back from him that she hadn't seen before. Even as he came closer, and her instincts screamed at her to move, Maya refused. She stood still and firm, refusing to budge even an inch.

"You don't *get* it," Kolya said, passing her by.

Maya blinked, surprise flitting through her. "What don't I *get*—that you worried; that your mood gets worse *because* you worry?"

"Both, and neither."

She nodded and watched him raid the wet bar on the other side of the hotel room. He only seemed satisfied once he'd poured an entire glass of vodka. Not just a shot, no. The whole fucking glass, which was a quarter of the bottle.

"Oh, I'm sorry," Maya murmured, "I should have said when you worry about *me*."

Kolya stiffened with his back turned to her. "We don't have to talk *details*, no?"

"Why, do feelings get in your head and make you feel icky?"

She knew damn well that she was poking at a monster—pushing Kolya's already thin nerves to the limit and waiting for them to snap. She didn't know exactly what would happen once they did snap, but she wasn't afraid.

This man had taught her something.

It was important.

He wouldn't hurt her.

Never.

"They don't make me feel ... what is wrong with you?" he asked, spinning on his heel to face her again with a deeper scowl than before. "You can see I'm in a bad mood, yes?" He waved one hand at her, and said, "Go do something else and stop pestering me."

"No, I'm good."

Kolya sipped from the vodka, and arched a brow. "Maya—"

"You don't get to be an asshole to me just because you're scared."

He blinked. "You think I'm *scared?*"

Maya shrugged. "That's what it is, right? Otherwise, I can't come up with any other reason why you behave the way you do when I'm put into a bad situation. You react from fear, even if you don't want to say it."

"I ... really just want a drink," he mumbled, tipping the glass up again.

"If you really want me to leave you alone, then you could at least give me the decency of telling me the truth as to *why.*"

Maya stayed right where she was standing and refused to move or look away from Kolya, even as the silence stretched on and the awkwardness turned into a tension she wasn't used to feeling around this man. She hoped her point was clear, though. She wasn't doing anything until he gave her something to go on.

Simple as that.

Finally, Kolya's intense gaze slid away from Maya, leaving her feeling both relieved and lonely at the same time. She liked when he stared at her— especially when he thought she wasn't looking back, but she also found when he stared at her like *this*, she didn't know how to feel about it, or him, at all.

"It's too much," he uttered.

Maya tangled her fingers together in an effort to release some of her jitteriness as she asked, "What is?"

"Here," he said, pointing a finger at his head, and then down to his chest before adding, "And here, too. It's too much."

Maya abused her bottom lip with her teeth and tried to understand his words. "Me, you mean?"

Kolya nodded. "I don't know how to handle it. So, I do so badly. I would rather you not be in the crossfire, Maya, that's all."

"Okay," she whispered.

He looked back at her. "Okay?"

"You react from fear, Kolya."

His jaw stiffened as he said, "For *you.*"

He almost sounded bitter about it. And yet, confused too, but also ... satisfied. Maybe she understood then what he meant by it being all a little too much for him to deal with inside his head, and his heart.

99

"I'm sorry that scares you."

It scared her, too.

He let out a heavy sigh, and turned away from her. "You don't scare me—the rest does."

Same difference.

Wasn't it?

• • •

Maya peered up at the inky sky, but failed to find the stars she liked so much. On the veranda attached to their hotel room, she was only four stories above the busy street. Despite it being dark, and well past midnight, there were still a few people strolling the streets.

Not all savory people, either.

Tucking her legs up to her chest, Maya held tight to her cup of tea in an effort to force herself to relax. It didn't work.

Nothing was.

She felt Kolya's presence behind her long before he made himself known—his hand came to rest overtop her shoulder, warm and calloused. Comforting, and yet still rough. He said nothing as his fingertips glided over her skin, and then his hand moved to gently cup the side of her throat.

Her heart raced.

Thump, thump, thump.

Faster than she was used to.

A beat of betrayal, really.

He had to be able to feel her heartbeat, touching her like he was. So he would know just by that alone how much his presence affected her. Maya wasn't sure if she liked that or not. This whole fucking thing between them—whatever it was—was one big conundrum for her.

She felt his fingertips press into her pulse point, and then just as quickly, released the pressure without a word. Yet, his hand remained right where it was, and Maya didn't really mind all that much.

"I'm a ... a *mudak*," he said gruffly.

Maya tipped her head back and stared up at him, although she found he was staring straight out over the balcony of the veranda. "An asshole, I know."

Kolya's lips twitched at the corners like he was considering smiling. How much effort did it take, she wondered, to keep one's self from smiling when a person felt the need? And how sad was it that she noticed he did that very thing all too often for her liking?

"I don't mean to be an asshole." Kolya's lip curled back in a half-sneer and he glanced down at her to add, "At least, not to you, *dushka*."

"Again with *that*," she said shaking her head.

Kolya did smile that time—slow, and sly. "And yet, you still are."

"Hmm?"

"*My* dushka. I'm sorry for earlier."

Maya nodded.

What else could she do?

"Anton called—Sumerki will be back in a half hour or so."

Maya smiled. "He's okay, then?"

"Maybe I overreacted about him."

"*Maybe?*"

"You're not getting more than that."

She laughed and patted his hand on her neck. "It's okay to be scared, Kolya."

"It isn't, actually. Not in my business or family. I don't expect you to understand, Maya, and I hope you don't have to learn, either."

He turned to head back inside through the sliding doors, but Maya grabbed tightly to Kolya's hand still grazing her neck before he could stop touching her entirely. His next step hesitated, and he looked back at her. Maya was already staring up at him.

"Kolya?"

"Yes, *dushka?*"

He wasn't going to let that go.

She didn't mind so much.

"*Spasibo,*" she whispered.

"What are you thanking me for?"

Maya squeezed her smaller fingers around his much larger hand. "For letting me come to you, Kolya."

He quirked one brow high.

She shrugged.

She pulled on his hand to urge him down, and he did just that. He bent down until the two of them were eye-level, and he was all she could see. The busy street down below no longer existed, and neither did the inky sky.

Just this man.

And the blues of his eyes.

There was really only one thing she wanted.

One thing to *do*.

Maya kissed him.

9.

KOLYA DIDN'T know how it happened—one second, Maya was in the wicker chair on the veranda pulling him in for a kiss, and in the next blink, she was stripped down nearly bare on the bed as he hovered above her.

Oh, sure, he remembered that *kiss*.

That fucking kiss and the way she tasted. Her sly little smile against his mouth like she was teasing him as her tongue flicked against his lips. Her sparkling blue eyes turned darker when he reached for her ... and then *this*.

Maya on her back.

Legs spread.

Black hair spread wide on a pillow.

His fist was gripped tightly around the waistband of her cotton panties and he was *seconds* away from yanking them down her creamy, smooth legs. The girl was short as hell, and yet, her legs didn't lack in expanse or shape.

Christ.

He liked that a lot.

"Kolya?" Maya asked.

She sounded fucking airless.

Soft.

Sweet.

Waiting.

Hot, too.

He blinked and his gaze drifted to hers. He was still trying to figure out how they had gone from the veranda with a kiss, to Maya on a bed with barely anything on at all. Just these goddamn cotton panties in his way—separating him from a pussy he'd been dreaming about for *weeks*.

He didn't chase pussy.

Didn't think about it.

Work for it.

Or need it.

Sex was just another irritation for Kolya—something that came up once in a blue fucking moon—and he took care of the urge when it happened. Nothing more, and nothing less. Maybe that's why this woman had taken him entirely off balance in too many ways to name, because nothing was as it should be with her.

Not his feelings.

Not his needs.

Not his *wants*.

No, this wasn't a position he found himself in very fucking often, and yet, more than anything in the world right then in that moment … he wanted her. Whatever she was going to give him, and anything she might offer, he was the starving man ready and willing to get on his knees and *beg her for it*.

Maybe that was why a kiss on the veranda turned into a blink, and Maya was suddenly nearly naked and on her back underneath him. Kolya very rarely found things he wanted, but when he did—and when he was given those things—he was lost to the baser nature he did well to keep hidden.

Except …

He didn't want to do that right now.

He didn't want to lose himself right now.

Not with her.

"Hey," Maya whispered.

Soft fingertips grazed his jawline—a ghost of a touch, really. Like angel wings sweeping over his skin and touching every single one of his nerves all at once. His gaze cut to hers again, and he found that she was smiling at him.

"Don't freeze up on me *now*," Maya said.

She sounded so serious and so damn soft, too. And yet, at the same time, he heard the note of fear underlying her tone, too. Like she was scared she'd made a mistake, and he was second-guessing this.

Jesus.

Didn't she know?

He wanted this.

So badly.

Too much, maybe.

The longer Kolya was quiet, the more Maya fidgeted. Her gaze darted away from his and he saw the way her throat constricted with a nervous swallow. That hand of hers that had touched him was quick to rest over her chest, and hide the swells of her small breasts at the same time.

Like she didn't want him to look.

Like she didn't want to be seen.

What was she doing that for?

Why?

"Maya," Kolya said gruffly.

Her teeth abused her bottom lip as she said, "Hmm?"

Still, she wouldn't look at him.

That couldn't be had.

That was a shame.

"*Dushka*," he rumbled, "stop hiding from me."

He saw her blink and her tension softened a bit under his weight. Still, though, she chewed on her bottom lip and wouldn't look at him. He'd had enough of that—he used the tip of his thumb to gently tug her lip out from the abuse of her teeth. Then, though she put up no resistance to his urging, he turned her head so she was looking at him again.

"That's better, Maya."

"I don't know what happened. You were good, and then you—"

"Woke up," Kolya interjected.

Maya flinched. "Oh."

"No, not *woke up* bad." Kolya felt the edge of his lips curve upward, and at the sight of his half-smirk, Maya traced the edge of his mouth with her fingertips. "Woke up, *dushka*, because why would I want to miss this?"

Her fingertips froze and her gaze slammed back into his again.

Hot.

Heavy.

Sure.

And he was present—not lost, or gone, or anything that took him away from this moment right here and *now*. Because sweet mother Mary in Heaven—didn't she *know*?

"Look at you," Kolya murmured thickly. His hands started at her jaw, stroked down her throat, over her chest, and then came to rest on her side for a brief moment before sliding lower again. Her tight, warm stomach was small enough that his large hands practically covered every inch of skin when he laid them across her body. All unmarked, creamy skin covered in goosebumps and shivering with every little movement he made. "Oh, my God—*look at you*."

Maya sucked in a ragged breath before her tongue peeked out to sweep her bottom lip. "Here I am."

"Yeah."

And it was fucking wonderful.

She was *perfect*.

"Don't hide from me," he repeated. "Don't look away or … just don't. Just *be*, okay?"

Maya nodded. "Okay."

Her hands worked at the buttons on his dress shirt, but Kolya was still stuck just staring at her and taking her in. The way she looked underneath him, and the way those cotton panties melded against her body's soft curves. She smelled like sugar and vanilla—sweet and pure, and made just for him.

How could she not be?

It was only Maya's palm sliding in under his now-opened shirt and resting flat against the thieves' cross on his chest that snapped Kolya back into reality again.

That one action spurred him onto what he wanted—to taste and fuck and feel this woman for as long as he possibly could. To imprint every inch of her—every single curve and line and dip—of her body into his memories.

To *know* her.

God, he wanted to know her like this.

That mouth of hers called his name in a whisper, and with her hand still pressed flat against his chest, the control he'd been maintaining slipped. Not that Kolya minded. Maya didn't seem to care either when he pushed forward, grabbed hold of her face, and pulled her in for a bruising kiss.

Christ.

This woman was a lot of things.

She looked so innocent with those big eyes and quiet demeanor.

Her kiss said something else entirely. From the way she pulled him in for more, to her tongue warring with his the second he was given entrance to the wet heat of her mouth … this woman came *alive*.

Every inch of her hummed.

Anticipated.

The last thing he wanted to do was pull away from her, but *damn*, he needed more. So did she. It was clear in the way her hips lifted and grinded against him—making his raging erection harder still. Painfully fucking hard, really. His cock was about to punch its way out of his slacks, surely.

His mouth found her throat—his teeth biting into the softest part of her neck, where her heart thundered right under the skin with a beat that drove him crazy. He fisted those panties of hers, and yanked them down as his mouth traveled lower.

Salt and sex and sweetness.

That's what she tasted like.

And all her sounds?

Those gasps …

Her voice …

The *moans* …

"Fuck," Kolya grunted against her stomach as he finally got those panties off entirely and tossed somewhere else in the room. "Widen up for me."

Her legs were already spread, but fuck him if she didn't open wider just like he told her to. He found her watching him through lowered, thick lashes with a pink flush crawling up her neck and cheeks as he shifted his body lower so he could be between her thighs.

Heaven stared back at him.

If heaven was her cunt.

Wet already.

Sleek as hell.

Pink.

Bare.

Beautiful.

Kolya's hands grabbed tight to Maya's inner thighs as he came closer to her sex—his nose skimmed the soft skin of her leg while his fingers dug in deep against her muscles. He felt her jump under that hold, but otherwise, she didn't move an inch.

"Tell me how this sounds, *dushka*," Kolya murmured, letting his hand slip down her thigh so that his thumb could slide through the wet lips of her cunt. "You get a hand down here and show me how you like to play while I eat up every drop from that pussy while I wait for you to come. Hmm?"

Maya shuddered.

Kolya grinned.

"Play?"

"That's what I said."

Her shyness was gone, and Jesus, he was grateful. He needed her to be comfortable, but he also wanted her to feel *good*.

It was only going to get better from here.

She just needed to figure it out, too.

"Hurry up," he urged darkly.

Maya was quick to get her hand between her thighs. Kolya couldn't help but lick his lips and chuckle when the first thing she did was sink two of those fingers deep into her cunt, and bring them right back out again before holding them out to him.

Like a fucking *offering.*

"Taste?" she asked.

She didn't even need to *ask.*

He took her soaked fingers into his mouth, and sucked her clean. The taste of her—tart and heady on his tongue—bloomed over his taste buds. That baser urge beat hard against his chest again, and his cock *ached.*

He could feel the tremor working its way through her fingers as his tongue slid between the digits to make sure he hadn't missed a drop.

"Oh, my God," Maya whispered.

Whined, really.

He let her go from his mouth, but he wasn't done. He needed so much more—more of that taste in his mouth, and far more of her sounds.

His gruff order to, "*Play*," was all she got before his head was buried between her thighs. He found that taste he wanted so badly, and that she was wetter than he'd even realized when his tongue burrowed into her sex. He could feel her fingers working against her clit as he sucked, licked, and took every drop of her arousal that her body had to give.

It was never going to be enough.

He felt the hot score of her fingernails rake lines down his shoulder, but it was secondary to everything else.

To the way she *begged*.

How she moved and whimpered.

To the shaking and her legs squeezing around his head.

"Right there, oh, my God—*Kolya*."

She was bent hard off the bed and tense all over. He quite liked the sight of her like that, with her mouth opened in a perfect O shape and her eyes squeezed tightly shut. Even if he would have preferred her to be looking at him—this was damn good, too.

She was wild.

Out of control.

No shame that she was playing with her pussy while he licked her cunt, and grinded his lower half against the bed for some kind of relief. *Shit*, maybe it was him who didn't have any shame right then.

She was so close.

Almost there.

He needed her to be there *now*.

Kolya yanked her hand away from her pussy as his mouth encased her clit, and he sucked hard. Two of his fingers slid into her pussy, and found that soft, fleshy spot on the inside of her walls that was sure to get her soaking the damn bedsheets.

He wasn't wrong.

All it took was his mouth, that trick with her G-spot, and Maya came *hard*. The sound that came out of him when she finally came was primal because, *yeah*, he got what he fucking wanted.

And there had never been anything more beautiful.

Nothing that sounded more perfect.

Christ.

Maya was already begging—that alone was enough to make him jizz in his pants like a teenaged boy who'd just gotten his first taste of pussy— before her trembling had even stopped. Her voice, all airless and hot, soaked into his senses and was the only thing to pull his attention away from the heaven between her thighs.

"Please," she mumbled, needy and ragged with every breath. "Please fuck me. *Please.*"

He was back up her body and kissing her before she could get another word out. He thought her kiss was a little wilder now—all teeth, and tongue, and lips warring with his, and never giving him an inch. His hand curved tightly around her throat as she worked those pants of his off, and shoved them down around his hips.

He should have thought about a condom—where he would have found one, he didn't fucking know. He should have *cared* that he didn't have one, but it wasn't even a blip on his radar.

But he heard, "I'm safe—I'm *good.*"

He heard those words—felt them whispered against his mouth. And then her hand was tight around his dick, and stroking him alive all over again. Firm, smooth pulls that had his hips jerking into her hand with every tug on his cock.

"*Please, please, pl—*"

She already had the head of his cock rubbing up and down her wet slit, and it only took one well-aimed flex of his hips to bury his length deep in her cunt. She tensed all around him—just a brief second where her body froze, and then the tension released with a long exhale. Relief, he knew. It sounded like relief, and he fucking felt it, too.

That relief was hot, and tight, and wet all around him. Sucking him in and holding him there like she wasn't going to let go. Her pussy was one thing to taste—quite another thing to *fuck.*

"Fucking killing me," he grunted against her mouth. "Didn't I tell you once not to beg unless I *asked* you to?"

Maya's blue eyes were wide and locked on his. Those pupils of hers were blown out and fiery with lust. "Don't you want me to beg?"

His fingers tightened on her throat.

She *laughed.*

Sweet, and teasing, and *coy.*

"Be careful, woman," he warned. "You don't know—"

He was going to say, *Who you're fucking with.*

But he thought ... maybe she did know.

He knew she did when Maya said, "I'll let you know when I'm made of glass, but right now isn't it, Kolya."

It was the hot rake of her fingernails down his chest, and her teeth cutting into his jaw when she pretended like she was going to kiss the spot, that had him pressing her hard into the bed, and he started pounding into her. Those sweet whines and sounds of hers came out a little more desperate than before—harsher and louder and *better.*

Every snap of his hips was answered by her dragging those fingernails over his body, and her pussy clamping harder around his dick. She was wetter than a lake, and nothing urged him on more than the sounds her cunt made every time he thrust back in.

But hell, she could take him.

Every inch—thick and long—she took him.

Begging, and pretty, and *sinful.*

Her skin was pink, and slick. Her teeth were clenched and bared.

"Holy fuck, *don't stop,*" she gasped.

How could he, really?

His balls were already tight.

His back, tense as fuck.

He was going to come.

And then he was going to bend her over and fuck her again.

That much he knew.

That was all he wanted to know.

Reality could swing back around to kick him in the ass later. Kolya wasn't here for it tonight. Not while he had Maya like this, anyway.

• • •

Kolya drifted his fingers over the soft expanse of Maya's bare shoulder and ignored the buzzing phone in his pocket. The caller, and business, could wait—they were still going to be there once he was done here.

Maya slept peacefully.

Entirely unaware.

Content.

Kolya would much rather crawl back into the bed with her than what he had to do, especially if that meant he could wake her up while he was between her thighs ... but business called. Someone needed to die, and he hated to make them wait.

One last stroke of his fingertips against Maya's shoulder and Kolya turned away. He was quiet as he slipped out of the hotel room, and locked the door behind him. He found Anton sitting on the roof of his car as Sumerki sniffed around the dark, quiet parking lot.

At the sight of Kolya coming across the lot, Anton was quick to jump off the car. "Sorry, but he didn't want to be held any—"

"I can see he's fine." Kolya held up a hand. "*Idi syuda, Sumerki.*"

At the quiet order, the black pup stopped his search of the ground and headed for Kolya, even as his master spun on his heel and headed for the Hummer.

"What about me?" Anton called after him.

"Watch Maya's door."

"How long are you going to be?"

"As long as it takes."

Kolya hit the unlock button on the fob and opened the passenger door. Sumerki had already put on a few inches and some pounds, but he was still *feet away* from being able to climb inside the tall vehicle himself. Kolya was quick to scoop him up under his furry belly with one hand, and let the pup waddle into the passenger seat where Sumerki sat down happily.

"You be good, yeah," Kolya said to the pup, reaching in to run his palm over the dog's head. "We've got shit to do tonight, and you need to behave or else I won't be able to bring you anymore—this is a good teaching moment for you. Be *good*."

Sumerki's ear flicked.

Good enough for Kolya.

He closed the door, rounded the Hummer, and climbed inside the driver's side. His tires squealed against the pavement as he left the lot— probably not the best idea, considering he was *trying* to stay under the radar for the night, but what could you do?

He was a little impatient.

He'd put this off *only* because Maya had distracted him and, frankly, fucking her was a hell of a lot more fun than listening to a man scream until he was dead. Then again … maybe they were both things he liked to do, just for entirely different reasons.

Yes, that sounded much better.

Sumerki perked in the passenger seat and climbed onto the middle section between the seats when Kolya pulled onto the freeway. He swore it was like the dog just knew where they were going because of the direction Kolya took and nothing else. He glanced over at the pup, and smiled.

"Be good," he murmured again.

Sumerki peered back at him, and his tail wagged.

"You can't be *excitable*," he told the dog. "You have to listen and mind. Stay in your *spot*. *Vashe mesto*, Sumerki. Yes?"

The dog seemed to be hearing him, but Kolya would soon find out if the pup actually understood. He listened, for the most part—he was a quick learner, really. Tonight was really going to test that, though.

Maybe it was for the better.

If Sumerki was there … Kolya might not get so entirely fucked up in the act of taking a life that he forgot his own name.

But who was to say?

It was another thirty minutes before Kolya pulled into the Compound, and fifteen minutes of walking corridors and taking a flight of stairs, before he finally set Sumerki to his four paws on the floor again.

"You walk from here," he said to the pup just outside the door. In his other hand, he'd brought along a fleece blanket from the back of the truck. "And then you stay in your *spot*."

Peering up at him, Sumerki flicked his ear again.

"All right," Kolya murmured.

In the basement of one of the Compound's many warehouses, he took note of how chilly it seemed. And *damp*. Fuck, he hated dampness. It clung to everything and soaked right through a man's bones.

Kolya knocked once on the two steel doors and stepped back to wait. A slate on the door was slid to the side, closed just as quickly, and then the locks clicked. The doors were opened for Kolya, and he was quick to step in beyond the threshold with Sumerki on his heels.

He didn't bother to glance around—he didn't care who was there or what kind of greeting they had for him. Sure, he still took in his brother in the corner, the soaking wet man tied to a chair with live booster cables resting at his feet, and the guy who'd opened the door for Kolya.

They called that man *Zhatka.*

Reaper.

He was the one who kept the chambers down here clean, or watched over a problem while someone else was busy. More often than not, he was the one keeping a man alive by any means while the man waited for his torturer to arrive. He was the one who listened to them beg and said *nothing.*

Kolya didn't even know his real name. As far as he knew, the guy rarely left the Compound, and if he did, it was by order of Vadim to do ... *something.* The guy never spoke, not to them, or to the men he was tasked with holding in one of the chambers until it was their time. He didn't even know if the guy saw the daylight on a regular basis, but probably not.

"You brought the dog?" Konstantin asked. "Why?"

Kolya passed his brother a look and then dropped the blanket on the middle of the floor. He pointed to the fleece square with one finger, and Sumerki was quick to clamber into the middle where he sat his little ass down and watched Kolya.

Bending down to one knee, Kolya pointed between his eyes, and Sumerki. It was yet to be determined how well Sumerki would do, all things considered. It was probably going to get loud, and a little scary for the pup, once Kolya really got going on the passed-out Albanian tied to the chair in the middle of the room.

Kolya figured it would take a couple of times for the dog to get the point when they had to do something like this, but he was hoping for the best tonight.

"*Your spot.* Be good; behave, yes?"

Another ear flick from Sumerki.

Good enough.

He stood and turned back to Konstantin with a nod. "He's learning—don't touch him."

"Learn—"

"That's what I said," Kolya interjected gruffly. "Stop asking questions and let me get to the killing portion of my evening. *Spasibo.*"

He didn't miss the way Konstantin rolled his eyes but Kolya's attention was laser focused on something else, now. Or rather, *someone* else. He tugged the leather driving gloves out of his back pocket and slipped them on as he came closer to the unconscious man tied to a chair. Undoing the buttons on his dress shirt—he thought it might get in the way or bloodstained—Kolya discarded the item as he came to stand in front of the man.

A bucket of cold water rested at Tomor's feet. Kolya picked the bucket up and dumped it over the man's head. Tomor woke up with a gagged shout—*thank you, Zhatka*—and wide, angry eyes.

Oh, good.

He wasn't broken yet.

Kolya liked them better when he was the one who got to break them.

Tomor took a minute to adjust but as soon as his gaze landed on Kolya, his rage became all the more apparent. He pulled and jerked in the chair, spitting words at Kolya in a language he wouldn't have understood even if the gag wasn't tight around his mouth.

"You look angry," Kolya said. "Shame, no?"

Tomor jerked in the chair again, his teeth baring over the gag.

"Oh, scary."

"Don't play with your prey," Konstantin grumbled. "You always do this."

Kolya waved a hand over his shoulder, saying, "I don't remember asking you."

To be honest, Kolya *was* a little bored. Maybe it was because all of his baser urges had been thoroughly satisfied earlier by Maya ... but it was hard to say. He was still raging fucking pissed that this man had thought to put his hands on what didn't belong to him. He was going to hurt for *that*.

Kolya snatched up the live jumper cables from the floor and checked to make sure they would snap loudly when he touched the two clamps together. Sure enough, they crackled and sparked with all the pretty colors of live electricity.

Lowering the cables, he smiled at the wide-eyed Albanian who suddenly couldn't stop looking away from the items in Kolya's hands.

"I love a good electrocution," Kolya said.

Tomor's gaze skipped to him. A lot of his fire and fight was draining right before Kolya's eyes.

"Here's how this is going to go," Kolya said, taking a step forward.

Even as Tomor fought to move away from Kolya, he still managed to clamp one of the cables to the side of the man's neck. The cables had been wired into a two-forty plug putting out forty amps, and would certainly kill a man within seconds.

A little touch of the other cable to the man's stomach though, and—Tomor snapped back, went stiff, his eyes rolled back, and a gagged garble of unintelligible noise slipped from his mouth before Kolya pulled the cable back fast. It took Tomor a few seconds to regain his senses, and then another minute more before Kolya felt comfortable pulling the man's gag down.

Tomor's speech was slurred.

Slowed.

Confused.

Kolya reached out and smacked the man on his forehead. *"Look at me, no?"*

The Albanian did.

"I don't want information from you," Kolya said. "I know why you did what you did. I am just here to make you hurt for what you did to her. And because you enjoy putting your hands on other people, without their permission, once I am done hurting you, I will cut yours off, put them in a box, and mail them to your closest relative. A parting gift, we'll say. Your boss will get the rest of you—my boss's order. A message, if you will."

Tomor's eyes darkened with rage again. "He's going to keep coming for her, Russian. Until he gets ger."

Kolya nodded. "He can try."

• • •

Kolya kneeled down beside a stiff Sumerki as the noise from the other side of the room picked up. He'd quickly gotten tired of the Albanian. The Reaper was there to step in and finish business when Kolya asked.

Sumerki's big, yellow eyes watched Kolya, but quickly darted back to where the sounds of blood dripping and sawing echoed from the middle of the room.

"Come here," he murmured, scooping the pup from his blanket.

He'd done *well.*

Stayed right in his spot.

Stayed *quiet.*

"Good boy," Kolya said, running his hand down Sumerki's back. The pup relaxed a bit—it was quite a bit of noise. "Someday, just you sitting there will be enough to make a man spill his fucking secrets, won't it?"

"I thought he was going to bolt once," Konstantin said, coming closer. The first time he'd left his position at the wall all evening.

"I thought he would, too," Kolya admitted. "Also, we have an issue."

Konstantin frowned. "What is that?"

"The second attack—the one on *you* and Maya—wasn't the Albanians."

"Why would you think—"

"Valbon … he wants Maya. There was at least three minutes where you had no consciousness. You admitted it yourself. After the car rolled, no? Whoever it was had every chance to take her and they didn't, Konstantin. It couldn't be the Albanians. They have one purpose—they want *her.* The second attack wasn't about her."

113

Understanding dawned in Konstantin's eyes. "You're saying we have someone else after the Boykovs, *besides* the Albanians."

Kolya nodded. "*Da.*"

"When did you know that?"

"I suspected it at the clinic when we were talking," Kolya replied, "but I didn't think for sure until about a half hour ago."

Konstantin cleared his throat, and glanced away. "And you didn't think to tell Vadim that he has someone else to worry about?"

"No."

"Kolya—"

"Two issues are one too many for Vadim," Kolya said, his grip on Sumerki tightening a bit. "And if he can get rid of one issue by simply handing Maya over, even if it will make him look a bit weaker to another organization so that his focus can be on the *unknown* coming at him from behind, then he will do that. I can't let him do that."

"That's a dangerous game to play."

"I'm aware."

Konstantin's gaze darted back to his brother. "You've really got something going on with that girl, no?"

Kolya shrugged. "Something."

"Yeah, I can tell by the mess your back is. You should have kept your shirt on—those scratches look like they sting, Kolya."

"Mind your own."

He said it like a warning.

He still smirked, though.

Konstantin sighed. "Hey, at least one of us got to be buried in pussy tonight, no? That's worth something."

Kolya chuckled dryly. "You've still got time to go out and find yourself something to keep your interest for a few hours."

His brother made a noise in the back of his throat and glanced at the dead body in the corner. "Not tonight—you gave me something to consider. Not even pussy is going to make me forget that."

"Now, that's a shame."

"Tell me about it."

10.

"BRAND HER properly."

Kolya grabbed the hot water valve and turned it higher. The temperature of the water stung as it beat against his skin, but he didn't care. It was the only thing he could think to do in order to get out of his fucking head, and away from those words of his father.

A call from Vadim first thing in the morning was never a good thing. It typically meant his father wanted or needed something, and Kolya was highest on Vadim's shit list so the task was delegated to him.

This time, there was no *task*.

Just an order.

A simple demand.

Brand her.

Maya, he meant.

"Brand her properly," his father had said while Kolya's mind was still thick with sleep, and Maya slept comfortably and naked under the sheets with him. "Brand her, and make it clear where she belongs. It has to be done, otherwise, she'll be free game to anyone. I am *trying* to make a statement to the Albanians about her—they cannot have what doesn't belong to them. You'll have her branded, Kolya, and you'll have it done soon."

Fuck Vadim.

Fuck his father straight to hell.

Fuck him for being *right*, in a way, but also asking something of Kolya that made him want to put his fists through the ceramic tiles of the shower's wall. Vadim had a damn good point—with no visible mark to label her safe under the protection of the Boykovs, and no *real* status like a wife or a daughter might have ... she was no one.

To everyone else, anyway.

To Kolya ... he was learning she was quite a lot of things to him.

Even if it fucked him up sideways.

"Are you even listening to me?"

Konstantin's voice drifted through Kolya's haze and the constant downpour of the shower. He glanced at the screen of his phone that he'd set on the edge of the shower where the water couldn't touch it.

"No," he admitted. "I'm not."

"Wait—are you in the fucking *shower?*"

115

"You called *me.*"

"You didn't have to answer, no?"

Kolya leaned forward until his forehead pressed against the cold tile. It did very little to soothe the ache beating in his skull, not to mention the stress tightening his shoulders. He would give anything to go back to when he woke up just so he *wouldn't* pick up that goddamn phone call from his father.

Brand her.

"Do you just wake up in a bad mood?" Konstantin asked.

"I woke up to *Vadim.*"

His brother made a harsh noise in the back of his throat. "That'll do it."

Kolya let out a hard breath and smacked his head against the wall once or twice. "He told me to do something."

"He tells us to do lots of things. Be specific."

"Brand her—he said to *brand* her."

Konstantin's silence answered Kolya back but he wasn't offended. His brother was probably trying to come up with something appropriate to say, but really, there was fucking nothing. Kolya had been trying to come up with something, too—he was going to have to tell *Maya*, after all.

And he had nada.

Not a fucking thing.

"Is that *exactly* what he said?" Konstantin asked after a long pause.

"Yes."

"Just—"

"Brand her, yeah."

"Nothing else?"

"*Konstantin.*"

"Don't get fucking snappy with me—this is important, but I can let you fucking handle it yourself, if you want to play that game with me, *brat.*"

Kolya scowled at the wall, and then slid his gaze to the phone. "I don't see any other way out of this. The boss gave an order—all things considered, I have to follow through if I don't want to be killed for disobeying him."

"He just said *brand her.*"

"Jesus Christ, Kon—"

"Yes or *no?*"

"Yes, that was it. Nothing else."

"It makes sense, no?" Konstantin asked. "Protection and status, that's what a brand gives."

"Yes, the status of *property.* Boykov property. A slave to be bought or sold, if I or *he* fucking chose to do that."

"But he just said brand her," his brother pointed out.

Kolya's brow dipped. "And obviously, he meant—"

"To brand her, yeah, I got that. So, do that, no? Give her your stars—that's a *brand*. A proper brand that labels what she is, to *whom* she belongs, and the status and protection she has because of it. It's a brand that can't be argued or disputed."

"It's not what he means."

"But he didn't specify." Konstantin waited a beat in time, then asked, "Right?"

"Yeah, no, he didn't specify."

And Kolya was thinking, now.

Considering.

It was dangerous and probably stupid. Women didn't *get* the stars of a Vor put on their body just because. And yet, Konstantin was right. Vadim hadn't specified, and Kolya could make of that what he wanted. Even if he did understand exactly what his father had actually meant when he ordered for Maya to be branded.

It was a loophole.

A loophole on fire, sure.

But one nonetheless.

Maya needed to be protected.

From the Albanians.

From anyone else who wanted her.

From Vadim, likely.

Kolya was going to do just that.

"Who did Vadim say to do the brand?" Konstantin asked.

Kolya was already reaching for the water valves to turn them off as he answered with, "Viktoria and I have to go."

"Wait a second, yeah?"

"What?"

"Be kind and give Maya a warning, then, before you take her to Vik. You know how she is, that's all."

Yeah, calling their younger sister a bitch would be *nice*. And it would probably make Viktoria Boykov smile like a happy cat. One with claws already sharpened and coming for your throat. People said Kolya was perpetually pissed off. Well, his sister could put him to shame.

"Planned on it," Kolya said. "Now, *bye*."

He scooped his phone up and hit the end call button. At the same time, he grabbed the towel hanging from a hook. He made quick work of running the towel through his hair, and wiping the water from his body. He stepped out of the bathroom to find Maya was finally awake, and resting on her side on the bed as she stared out the hotel window where the light was filtering in.

Kolya tightened the towel around his waist as he took a moment to appreciate the sight of the woman in front of him. Content and sweet.

Naked under white sheets, but showing off her delicate shoulders and pert breasts with the way she was resting.

His arrival didn't go unnoticed—she turned her head just slightly to blind him with a brilliant, happy smile.

He adored that. He'd had her in this hotel for a week—ever since that night when she was attacked by the Albanians, and then … whoever else tried to run her and Konstantin off the road later. And all week, she'd been like this.

Happy.

Pleased.

Eager.

Soft.

Joyful.

Bubbly.

He'd never been around anyone who seemed to be as constantly upbeat and pleasant as Maya was, day in and day out. It didn't affect his personality all that much—he was still a scowling fucker on his good days, but he did find the days passed by easier and faster when this woman was smiling at him.

How was he supposed to let that—let *her*—go?

He enjoyed it as much as it killed him in that moment. Her smile felt like the softest kiss against his skin—something she did often, and frequently, without warning him first as though she liked the reaction she got. Her smile also felt like a knife twisting in his chest because of two simple words.

Brand her.

Kolya still had to tell her somehow. It might not be the brand that Vadim wanted, but it was still a label. Still black ink on silky, creamy skin. Something she hadn't asked for at all.

"Come here," Maya said, holding a small, delicate hand out as if to reach for him. "Watch the clouds with me, Kolya."

He lifted a brow, but crossed the room. "You're watching clouds, *dushka?*"

"They're big and fluffy this morning."

"Oh?"

"Mmhmm. Come see."

The smallest things made this woman happy—it was both strange and enthralling to Kolya. He could make her smile, simply by looking at her or even stroking her cheek with his thumb. And *clouds* could make her happy, too.

Kolya came to stand next to where Maya was reclined on the side of the bed. She was quick to push up into a sitting position and then pull him down to sit between her legs as she moved to her knees. Between her legs, with his back tucked firmly against her chest, Maya hovered a bit higher than him when he tipped his head back to look at her.

"You're supposed to be looking at the *clouds*."

He managed a smile—for her, it was easy.

"You're nicer to look at."

She grinned slyly. "Oh?"

"Yes."

Maya pressed a kiss to his forehead, and whispered, "Well, thank you."

God, this woman.

She was going to kill him.

Kolya was sure of it.

"Where's Sumerki?" she asked.

"The hotel's concierge took him for a walk."

"Oh—speaking of the hotel."

"Hmm, what?"

"We can't stay here forever," Maya said, dropping another kiss to his forehead. "Even if I do like the bed and the man sharing it with me."

Kolya let out a laugh.

Maya shrugged. "Seriously, though. I know you said your place isn't—"

"It's a dive, Maya."

"Still, we can't stay here forever."

"That's debatable—I can afford to do exactly that, if I want."

"Okay, well, *I* don't want to."

Fair enough.

"I will figure something out," he murmured. "You should know, yeah, that the point of us being here was to lie low while the message was delivered to the Albanians for what they did, and to answer back on their demand to take you. It's about *keeping you safe*."

Maya stiffened behind him.

"You'll let me do that, won't you?"

"What—keep me safe?"

Kolya, still keeping his head tipped back, met Maya's gaze and held it firm. "Exactly that. You'll let me protect you, won't you?"

"But what does that mean?"

"It means whatever it takes, Maya, as long as you're safe."

Maya smiled. "And happy, too?"

"Are you happy right now?"

"With you, I am."

"Then, happy, too, yes."

• • •

A bell above the tattoo shop's door chimed when Kolya pushed it open—it wasn't like his sister to work in a shop. Viktoria preferred to be anywhere and everywhere *but* contained. Some might say she had a wandering soul. Kolya just figured his sister was too restless for her own good. But according to Vik, that wasn't any of his goddamn business.

So, he said nothing.

Kolya held the door open wider for Maya to slip in behind him, and only let it close once she was safely inside, with little Sumerki at her side. She scanned the place, and he did the same. Walls filled with artwork. A counter toward the back of the entrance filled with glass pipes, and different piercing jewelry. Clean floors. Bright lights.

All standard things for a tattoo shop.

"Why are we here?" Maya asked.

"Stars."

She peered over her shoulder at him. The sweetest little knot indented in her brow. "Stars?"

"Mmm, two of them, *dushka.*" Kolya stepped closer to her and reached up to let his fingers graze the back of her neck. "Just below your neckline here, I think. Where not *everyone* can see all the time, but they will when it counts."

He didn't miss the shiver that raced across her skin at his touch. That knot in her brow hadn't disappeared either.

"Wait, *I'm* getting the stars?"

"They'll match mine," he murmured, a smile spreading his lips. "And you like mine, don't you?"

Maya's gaze drifted down to his chest, and then back up to his face just as quickly. "I like all your tattoos, actually."

"I wish I could say the same."

She frowned. "Don't say that."

Kolya shrugged. "Enough about me—this is about *you.*"

"Yes, and putting a permanent mark on my body."

"You need them," he admitted. "They'll protect you more than a man with a gun in some situations, no? They're *important.*"

Maya quieted for a long while before she asked, "You think so?"

"Know so, my girl."

She scrunched her nose up. "Is this like … a property thing? A *brand?*"

Kolya's jaw clenched so hard that he heard his teeth crunch from the action. Maya didn't miss it, if her flinch was any indication. She was quick to spin around, and her hand came up to press soft fingertips into his cheek.

He was here for *her.*

He was trying to reassure *her.*

And there she was, turning the tables on him.

Funny how that worked.

"Is that what it is?" she asked. "A brand?"

Kolya had to force his jaw to unlock so he could speak. "Not in this context. It's more important, and it has more meaning. They'll match my stars—they'll be specific to me."

"So it means—"

"You're mine."

And given who he was—a Boykov, and not just *any* Boykov, the Boykov heir—those stars would make Maya untouchable in most cases. Sure, there were those who wouldn't respect the mark, but that would likely be out of ignorance. Anyone who knew what would happen to a person who messed with someone who was marked ... well, it was far from pleasant.

To say the least.

Maya's gaze jumped back up to his in an instant. "You don't seem bothered to say that at all—like it's second nature to you or something."

He knew exactly what she meant.

"You feel like mine. Why wouldn't you be?"

It seemed simple enough to him.

Kolya was a very *black-and-white* kind of person. He may have lived his life in shades of gray—on the edges of what society saw as wrong—but he wasn't that complex. Things either were or they were not to him. He felt something or he didn't.

He wasn't about to color it up with *bullshit*.

Maya sighed. "Like *that*."

Kolya smiled faintly. "You did say this morning that I could do whatever I needed to keep you safe."

"That wasn't exactly—"

"That's how I took it."

Maya rolled her pretty blue eyes. "You're insufferable."

"It'll be two very small stars—it'll barely hurt at all, no?"

"*Lies.*"

Kolya chuckled. "Scout's honor, Maya."

"And you're not even close to a scout, thank you."

"But you'll do this for me, won't you?"

She gave him a look. "I will because you asked me to."

Kolya nodded. "That's my girl."

He didn't miss the way she smiled at that, either, even if she did try to hide it by spinning around to show him her back.

"What is *that* doing in here?"

Oh, good.

His sister had finally come out from the backrooms.

A person couldn't miss Viktoria Boykov, what with her platinum blonde hair, ice-blue eyes, and delicate features that, Kolya thought, reminded him a great deal of their dead mother. Vik was tall, but not willowy, considering she dressed in such a way that reminded every man around her that she was very much a woman who enjoyed being looked at. Sometimes, it made Kolya want to hurt people ... but again, none of his business. He stayed out of it.

Or tried.

She had started drawing shortly after their mother died. Her childlike scribblings turned into real art, and then drawing eventually turned into tattooing. Although, one wouldn't look at Vik and think, *tattooist*. She didn't have visible ink—but for the cursive B on her index finger for *Boykov*—and Kolya wasn't all that interested in asking if she had ink where someone couldn't see.

Vik knew she had a fucking attitude, too, and was quick to use it whenever someone thought pointing it out might shame her into toning it down. It never did—she just got worse.

She'd smile if someone called her a bitch—proud as fuck. And then gut them with words right after.

Currently, she was standing next to the counter with the cash register sitting on top, and glaring at Sumerki who was *behaving* in his spot next to Maya.

"It's my dog," Kolya said. "He is not a *that*, Vik. Since when do you work in a shop?"

"A friend needed an extra hand. Mind your business, no?" Vik's gaze narrowed into slits when she peered back at her brother. "And that can't be in here. It's against the health code."

"He stays," Kolya returned. "And don't call him *that* again."

"You—"

"There's no one else here, and when I go outside, I will take him with me. I am not leaving him in my fucking Hummer, yeah?"

"He's a health hazard."

"The same could be said for you, Vik, but here you are."

Because she was a fucking health hazard to anyone who got too close to her—the woman was toxic in some ways. Cruel and violent. She got that shit from their father, but given that she looked like their mother, it was hard to see the bad parts of Vik when the pretty covered it up well enough.

"Kolya," Maya admonished, turning blazing eyes on him. "That's *rude*. Apologize."

Vik smiled sly and slow. "Yes, Kolya, apologize to me. As your sister, I'm *very* offended."

"Sure you are. Can we do this, yes? I have other things to do today. You know the rules, Vik. Vadim calls for a tattoo, you're to do it. No questions asked."

His sister scowled, but turned her gaze on Maya. "You said stars when you called."

Kolya nodded once. "To match mine."

"*Vadim* approved."

"Would I be here otherwise? He demanded it."

His sister sighed, but turned her gaze on Maya. "You got a name, or ...?"

Maya glanced back at Kolya and he gave her a soft smile. There wasn't much he could do about Vik or her shitty fucking attitude. And he really needed to get this tattoo done for her, so Vik it was because she trusted Kolya's word about their father's order without question. Someone else might call to check.

"Maya Kozlov," she told his sister. "Nice to meet you, Vik. Kolya hasn't said too much about you, I'm sorry to say."

Viktoria laughed, and smiled. "It's fine. Nothing he has to say about anyone is anything nice."

Kolya cocked a brow and made sure his sister saw him tip his head in Maya's direction. "Except her, yeah? Keep that in mind."

His sister's amusement was quick to fade, then. He waited to see Maya into the back room, and allowed Vik to get her set up before Sumerki started his sniffing. That only meant one thing. Vik seemed all too pleased to tell him he could take the dog outside and keep him there.

"I'll be an hour at most," his sister said, snapping on her gloves and getting her rig set up. "Surely, you can do something with th—the dog—for an hour. Throw a fucking stick, no?"

Kolya decided that before he said something that was really going to hurt his sister, he should probably get the fuck out of there. So, he did just that.

He took his time to walk Sumerki around the quiet city block, and then he grabbed a coffee on the way back after paying a teenager fifty bucks to hold Sumerki in the doorway of the cafe. By the time he got back to the tattoo shop, well over an hour had passed. He stepped back inside the business with Sumerki tucked under his arm—fuck what Vik said—and froze like a statue at the sound of laughter coming from the back room.

He didn't hear the familiar hum of a tattoo machine. Not silence. Not his sister's harsh words or bad attitude. No, just ... *laughter*.

He quickly moved to the back rooms and returned to the one he'd left Maya in. The laughter stopped the moment he darkened the doorway, but it didn't matter. He'd still heard it, and while his sister stopped smiling at the sight of him, Maya did not. She glanced over her shoulder, back bared, and with two new, black-and-white, eight-pointed stars coloring her skin right where he wanted them to be ... she still smiled at him.

"How does it look?" she asked.

Fuck.

Why was his throat so tight?

Why did the sight of his stars—ones that had been designed to be unique for just him—on her body make his dick hard and his heart ache?

Why?

"Kolya?"

Maya's quiet question brought him back to reality with a bang.

"Perfect," he said. "They look perfect, *dushka.*"

Vik was quick to pass her brother a look at the endearment he used so casually that was anything *but* casual. He didn't miss the way his sister's eyes said, *Ah, I get it now.*

He willed her to shut up and stay quiet.

She did.

Mostly.

"Kon called; said you wouldn't pick up your phone," Vik said.

"I need quiet every once in a while."

Vik shrugged. "Whatever—he's at the Compound with Dad. You need to get over there. Her too, apparently."

Great.

What now?

• • •

Kolya might have found Maya's wide-eyed expression amusing, if it were any other time that he had brought her into the Compound. She looked to be experiencing a mixture of amazement and confusion, all at the same time.

"How big is this place?" Maya asked.

"As in square feet?"

Maya nodded.

Kolya shrugged. "Hard to say."

"Huh."

Sumerki trailed behind them at a good pace. Kolya had stopped checking on the dog after they had moved through the main entrance section of the Compound—how was Sumerki going to just do what he needed to do if he constantly needed someone to remind him to do it? That didn't seem like a good way to train an animal to Kolya.

He needed Sumerki to just do because he *knew.*

Simple.

"And you use this place for—"

"Many things," Kolya interjected. "A lot of which are unsavory, and none of which you should ask about."

Maya was quick to nod at that. "Got it."

"Vadim is also here."

His girl frowned, but was quick to hide it by looking away. "So, stay quiet?"

"Please," he murmured.

"Okay."

She said that as though it were okay, but Kolya was not blind or dumb. He could clearly see her discomfort the longer they were inside the walls of the Compound. The place *could* be intimidating but he didn't think it was the Compound that had her nerves acting up—more like his father. He didn't know what to tell her, frankly.

Vadim had that same shitty effect on everyone.

Kolya directed Maya beyond the printing room rather quickly, although he didn't miss how her eyes widened even as they strolled past the wall of money. To her benefit, she kept quiet and asked no questions, even as they entered the elevator that would take them to the upstairs where Konstantin and Kolya's offices were located.

Today, they were going to Konstantin's.

Kolya kept an eye on the camera in the corner of the elevator as they silently rode the floors higher. It wasn't until they were standing just beyond Konstantin's office that Kolya reached out to stroke Maya with two fingers against the back of her neck.

"Quiet, I know," she told him.

He nodded. "Good."

All hell broke loose when they entered the office.

Or rather, Vadim's usually thin patience snapped.

"Where in the hell have you been, no? I called for you *hours* ago!"

Kolya pressed a hand to Maya's back and gestured for her to go sit against the far wall in one of the available chairs. He waited until she was seated, comfortable, and Sumerki had placed himself directly at her feet before turning his attention back on the men. He found Vadim sitting behind Konstantin's desk—certainly an irritation for his brother if Konstantin's scowl was any indication from where he stood just in front of the desk.

"No Grisha?" Kolya asked.

"He has other things to do," Vadim barked.

"Ah. Well, here I am. What do you need?"

Vadim's gaze drifted to Maya, but just as quickly, he went back to Kolya. A good thing, surely. No one—and certainly not Kolya—wanted his father's attention on Maya for too long. Nothing good would come of that.

"What do I *need*?" Vadim asked.

His father let out a sharp, dark laugh.

Konstantin, on the other hand, gave Kolya a look that practically screamed for him to tread lightly. Shit was not good, it seemed. Kolya had missed something.

But what?

Vadim snatched a remote from the corner of the desk and pointed it at the flat screen on the far wall just above Maya's head. "You see what was sent to us this morning, and then tell me what I *need*, Kolya."

Kolya would have responded to his father, but the scene playing out on the television took his attention, and seemed far more interesting. At least, for the moment. Even Maya crooked her head back a bit to watch what was happening.

The first thing to focus on the screen?

A man tied to a chair with a black hood pulled over his head. Other than the boxers the man wore, and the hood, he was naked. There were no defining marks on his body—no tattoos, or scars to say who he was. He struggled against the thick ropes keeping him bound, but he wasn't going anywhere. A knot formed between Kolya's brows as he moved slightly closer to the television in an attempt to make out the surroundings behind the unknown man.

Kolya stopped walking the second a Gashi Albanian came into frame, and moved close to the man tied in the chair. The Albanian captain took his time to fix the suit jacket he wore before pulling a gun from inside, and then smiling coldly at the camera.

Maya was quick to scoot to the edge of her seat; Kolya didn't miss it.

"A message, Vadim," the Albanian said on the camera, "from me and my bosses, so you can rest assured this is all an answer to your recent *gift* of my boss's man being sent to us in pieces, as well as our property you have yet to return in the form of Maya Kozlov. We answer your actions back in blood—we will continue to answer this way until you give us an appropriate apology, and the rest of what belongs to our family. I am sure you don't need me to explain how seriously we Albanians take our blood debts."

The man in the video lifted his gun, racked the weapon, and then tapped it against the struggling man's temple, saying, "Today, we'll start with Alexei Kozlov. Tomorrow, it'll be Sergei Kuznetsov—a captain of yours, I believe. We'll continue to remove one Volkov man until we are satisfied that your debt has been honored."

Behind Kolya, Konstantin murmured, "Sergei was removed from his home this morning by force. His wife was left untouched."

Shit.

"*These deaths are not a suitable repayment,*" the Albanian's voice echoed.

And then gunfire.

Kolya glanced back at the screen in just enough time to see the struggling man in the chair go still before he slumped off to the side, and the camera cut out. The video was silent for less than two seconds before Vadim exploded behind the desk.

"I want them *gone*! I want this mess fucking finished! *Make it happen.*"

Something crashed behind Kolya, but he didn't bother to turn around and check. He was a little distracted by the fear reflecting on Maya's face as she stared at him. He did catch sight of his father leaving the office in a rage.

Konstantin's heavy sigh resounded around him. "Well, that escalated quickly, no?"

11.

MAYA COULD faintly hear Kolya and Konstantin discussing what had just happened, but their voices were only background noise in her head. She was still staring at the blue screen of the television, and trying to make sense of what she had just witnessed. Oh, sure, the video had long since cut off, Vadim had had his temper tantrum, and run out … but she swore even as she stared at the television above her head, she could see the video playing out again and again.

A hooded man dying.

An unknown Albanian speaking.

Again and again.

She should be terrified—and *oh,* she was—but something far more pressing kept poking at the back of Maya's mind like a hot needle that just wouldn't stop. Even as the Albanian's threats whispered in her ears, and that fear slithered around her spine like a cold snake, something else was keeping her from feeling it entirely.

Something else was keeping her quiet.

"Maya."

It was Kolya's voice that dragged her back to reality for the moment—all rough, heavy, and dark in that way of his. *God,* she had come to adore his voice. One could not tell his mood by his tone, unlike most people, but she could.

Right then, she heard anger.

And fear.

Glancing over her shoulder, she found Kolya standing next to his brother. Apparently, the two had moved to stand in the middle of the room together at some point. Probably while she had been stuck staring at the television screen like a foolish girl.

Konstantin quirked an eyebrow high in silent question, but Maya didn't have the first clue about what he might be trying to ask her. Kolya, on the other hand, folded his large arms over his chest.

"I said let's go, *dushka,*" Kolya murmured.

Maya glanced back at the screen. "Would you play it again?"

Konstantin cleared his throat. "Why?"

"No," Kolya interjected. "There's no need—let's go."

Maya shook her head, saying firmer, "Please, play it again."

"Maya, it's unnecessary. You saw what happened."

"It's not that … It's …" Maya stood from the chair, and Sumerki was quick to stumble out from beneath her seat at the same time. Closing her eyes, she faced the screen, and pointed at the spot just below her collarbone. "Right here—he has a jagged scar right here. Except he didn't there, right? Did you see one, because I didn't."

"What is she talking—"

"Who?" Kolya asked, interrupting his brother.

Oh, *now* he was listening.

Maya spun around, and her eyes flew wide, even as she kept her fingers pointing at the spot where she knew that scar should have been on the man who had been killed in the video. That was, *if* he was actually her brother.

"Alexei," Maya said. "He has a jagged scar—maybe two inches long?— right here. He was drunk one night when he came home from a party, and I was maybe fourteen. Got pissed at me for something stupid, and chased me out of the house after he punched me in the face. I threw a beer bottle at him and it cut him right here. *Was there a scar?*"

Kolya's gaze darted to Konstantin, and the younger of the two brothers shook his head subtly. She could see it on Kolya's face before he even confirmed what she already believed. No, she hadn't been the only one— they'd seen it, too.

Or rather, a lack of it.

There was no scar.

"That wasn't my brother," Maya said, her voice fainter than ever.

That fear she'd been holding back started to wrap its way tighter around her spine with every passing second. It reached her chest and grabbed hold of her lungs there, too. Squeezing and draining the air right from her body with every little breath she dared to take.

Even as her panic started to swell, she heard Konstantin and Kolya's voices drifting around her overworked senses.

What did it mean?

Why would they *say* it was Alexei if it wasn't?

Her brother terrified her just about as much as Valbon Gashi did, honestly. The only difference between the two—as their cruelty to her was just about matched in all senses—was the fact that one shared her blood, and the other one simply enjoyed spilling it while he made her scream.

"He's not a *vor*," Konstantin said. "He wouldn't have proper tattoos, if any at all. Nothing to identify him. Maybe he sent someone in pretending to be him—got lucky that the fucker who usually handled business with his father wasn't there to say it wasn't actually him, yeah?"

Kolya made a noise under his breath—dark and bitter. "But *why*? What is the angle there, Konstantin? Why fake his death, or want us to believe he's dead?"

"Eyes are not on him. He can do … other things."

"Other things—say it, asshole. You mean—"

"Maya," Konstantin murmured. "I mean her, yeah. He did put out word on the street after you first took her; she's his sister and he wanted her back. His way of repaying that debt, I guess, to the Albanians. What if he knew they were going to kill him? Maybe he got word ahead of us, and he's smarter than we think he is. It wouldn't be the first time someone outplayed someone else in this business in that kind of way."

"Could he be the one, then?" Kolya asked.

"Which one?"

"The one that attacked you—the second attack, Konstantin. Would that be possible, do you think?"

"But what's the angle?"

"I already asked that, no?"

"You had a point, then," Konstantin countered. "We need to know the angle. At least, for right now, Vadim's attention will be away from Maya for a bit. How long that is going to last will be anyone's guess."

"I did what he wanted—he asks, you tell him that."

"*You* tell him."

"I will, but I'm hoping he doesn't bother."

"We need to figure out that angle, and take care of it," Konstantin murmured.

"You're saying things I'm already aware of. I need you to talk about things I don't know, *brat*."

"You need an attitude adjustment."

"Oh, is that what we're going to call it now?" Kolya asked. "Vadim used to just say I needed the shit beat out of me, and usually did it himself, no? That black belt of his was a particular favorite. I still have scars from that. Those were the good days."

"*Sorry*."

Kolya grunted dismissively under his breath.

Maya was trying to listen to them, and keep up with their conversation, but her fear was saturating everything. She could feel it in her very marrow and taste it on her tongue. It rang in her ears like blood rushing through her veins. Somehow, she was trying to shrink in on herself so that the anxiety lessened even a little bit. A tight ball made it all better—or somewhat.

It was too much.

Too much.

Too fucking much.

"Maya," Kolya snapped.

Her head jerked up at the same time Kolya darted away from his brother's side. Sumerki was at her feet barking as loudly as his little snout could yap for a pup his size. He'd put his paws onto her shoes and kept making noise until someone *heard*.

She only glanced down at Sumerki briefly, and then by the time she looked back up at Kolya's oncoming form, he was already there. One hand reaching around her waist and the other one landing firmly on the back of her neck, right over those newly tattooed stars.

She might have flinched any other time.

Except it didn't hurt.

It just … *grounded* her.

Every towering six feet, six inches of Kolya pulled her in close, and then swept away the fear coloring her mind with a soft kiss against her forehead, and then a searing brush of his lips along the seam of her own.

"It's *fine*," he said.

She didn't think it was.

It was better with him, though.

"It's probably not," she whispered.

Kolya's hold on her became impossibly tighter. "We don't know that."

"Well, it sounds to me like two men—but if we add in your father, that makes *three*—want to either get ahold of me or get rid of me."

"Four," Kolya muttered. "I'm the fourth, but I have you. And besides, let's look at it like this. It makes for an interesting woman when she keeps things entertaining like this. That's all."

Maya couldn't help but laugh, and even felt Kolya's smile curve against her forehead. His shitty attempt at dry humor was really the last thing they needed, but it did make her concentrate on something else for the moment. Like the fact he'd even *tried* to be funny.

"Cute."

In the background, Konstantin chuckled. "Oh, he has *jokes*. When do you ever have fucking jokes?"

Maya found Konstantin's stare as she peeked around the side of Kolya's form even as he ignored his brother.

When he's with me, she thought. *He jokes with me.*

Konstantin tipped his head to the side as though he were studying her and then he nodded.

"It's fine," Kolya said again.

She still didn't think it was.

• • •

"You're being unusually quiet," Kolya said from the driver's seat.

Maya peered over at him, and though he pretended like his attention was only on the road ahead of him, she knew better. It seemed like this man always had at least one eye on her … or a portion of his attention in one way or another. Like now. Sure, he was focused on driving, but every so often, his gaze slid in her direction like he just wanted to check on her or something.

"Am I?"

"Hmm?"

"Being *unusually* quiet," she said.

Kolya nodded, and his grip on the steering wheel tightened. "I think so, yes."

"And that bothers you?"

"A lot of things bother me, *dushka*."

"Yes, but *this*, too, right? This bothers you—thinking I am upset."

Kolya's tongue snaked out to sweep across his lower lip, but he nodded. "I don't like it when you're upset, no? That bothers me."

So she was coming to learn.

Maya was a hot button for Kolya. Her mood or reactions seemed to easily influence his as well. Even when it seemed like he wasn't feeling or thinking a single thing, he still searched her out in a room to gage *her* emotions at any given time. Then, he reacted accordingly.

Like at the Compound.

Maybe that was why Maya decided to be … as he put it … unusually quiet. She was still scared; still too fucking anxious to breathe or think right. Except those feelings weren't going to do anything good for her, but for upsetting Kolya or sending him into a fit. Not that he meant any harm, but when nothing could be done, why bother getting him worked up?

So, no … she forced herself to be calm.

Quiet.

Collected.

Even if inside, she was anything but those things.

"I don't think it's unusual for me to be quiet," Maya said.

Kolya's gaze drifted to her before going back to the road ahead of them. The edge of his mouth curved upward with the *most* sinful smirk before he let out a dark scoff. "Oh, yes it is."

"Not really."

"Maya, if you started vomiting rainbows and glitter, it wouldn't even be a surprise. You're loud even when you think you're being quiet. Do you know you *hum* when you eat? Hum a fucking song, girl. And when you brush your teeth, you do these little dances. They're cute; still, you do them. You walk about like there are clouds under your feet. Are you a *fairy*, yeah? Because you move like it. You smile all the time—rarely ever frown. And you find good things in everything. It's fucking *odd*. So yes, when you are quiet, it is unusual."

Maya blinked, silenced.

Something warm and hot and cloyingly sweet clenched around her heart and took away her words. With it went her breath and any lingering doubts that may have been buried somewhere inside her body about this man. Gone was her rationale, and in its place was an adoration so strong, it could blind her.

"What?" Kolya asked, glancing to the side.

"I didn't say anything."

Did she have to?

Should she?

Didn't he understand that he had just outed the fact that he paid far more attention to her than she even realized? That he apparently knew things about her that she hadn't even knew about herself?

"Yes, but you made a little noise." Kolya tried imitating whatever noise he thought Maya had made, but his sound came off more like a dying mouse. He shook his head and waved a large hand, saying, "You did, though; you made a *noise*."

"I was … just thinking," she said lamely.

Kolya's brow dipped. "About what?"

"You."

"Don't think about me, yeah? I'm a sure thing. It's a waste of time."

Maya smiled and said softly, "Far from it, I think."

"What was that?"

"I said, I was thinking that you shouldn't worry about me being quiet," she lied. "Sometimes, I just want to enjoy the silence."

Kolya chuckled. "That's me, no? Not you."

Maya shrugged. "Turn the tables, then."

His hand left the steering wheel and before Maya knew what happened, his warm palm cupped her cheek with a soft touch. The gentle way he often held or touched her was such a bright contrast to the violent, angry man she knew he could be. His thumb stroked the spot just beneath her eye.

"Nice deflection," he murmured. "But you get a pass on telling me the truth. At least, for now."

Maya didn't bother to ask what he was talking about. His answer came when he pulled off the side of the road and into a parking lot for a rundown apartment complex. Some of the bricks were crumbling and badly faded. The railings needed a good paint and the windows dearly needed to be replaced. There was no grass or greenery. Just cold concrete and a green metal trash bin that was overflowing.

She knew this part of the city a little too well—tried to stay away from the Heights as much as possible given it wasn't exactly the greatest neighborhood around, and all that.

Drugs, gangs, drive-by shootings, and worse were a little too common.

Maya took note of the gathered group of people on the stairs of the apartment building. Some of them sat on the steps and others leaned over the railing. Two toddlers—barely three years old—played on the sidewalk with little trucks. One of the men on the stairs took note of Kolya's Hummer as he pulled into a free spot and gave a nod to the young man on the bottom step.

The kid—he couldn't be more than twelve—was quick to jump up and head over before Kolya could even cut the engine.

"Why are we here?" Maya asked.

Kolya gave her a look. "This is where I live."

Oh.

"Do you want me to stay—"

"No," he was quick to say, and rather sharply. "No one who knows my name around here would touch you anyway, but no. You come with me. *Always.* I'll come around and help you down—leave the pup; he's sleeping."

Maya nodded and waited as Kolya exited the truck. He spoke to the young boy who had patiently waited by the front of the Hummer while they had talked inside. She saw Kolya pass the kid money—how much or for what, she couldn't tell. Then, he came around to her side of the vehicle and opened the door.

His arms were already outstretched for her, and Maya let him lift her down.

"You know, I think you should get some steps for me on this thing," she said.

Kolya pressed a hand to her lower back and directed them toward the building's entrance. "Why would I do that? Then I couldn't get my hands on you every time you needed to get in or out."

"Good point."

He patted her ass, but just as quickly put his hand back to her lower back. "I thought so."

It didn't matter.

He'd done what he'd done.

The hot shot of heat that went straight to her pussy proved that well enough without her needing to say it.

Maya ignored the growing lust as the people on the steps moved to allow them through. None of them looked Maya in the eyes, but the one who had alerted the boy to Kolya's arrival gave him a nod as they passed and greeted Kolya.

"Boykov," the man said.

"Gerald. How's the place?"

"Good."

Kolya pushed against Maya's back to make her walk the last step. "Keep up those payments and that's how it'll stay."

The man nodded again but said nothing more. Once inside the building, Maya was quick to take in the sixties carpet in the hallway that desperately needed replaced, and the faded paper on the walls where she couldn't even make out what the design used to be.

"I think they were lotus flowers," Kolya murmured, noting the way she stared at the wallpaper while they walked down the hallway. "But who knows?"

She said nothing until they had climbed two flights of stairs, Kolya unlocked the apartment that belonged to him, and she was allowed inside. He flicked all the lights on at once, and then left her side for the first time.

It allowed Maya to explore the dank apartment—frankly, *dank* was a nice description. He had very little furniture, and what he did have was worn and severely outdated. The floor was a cracked linoleum that made noise when she walked on it, and in the kitchen, an entire counter of empty vodka bottles littered the space.

She wouldn't say the space was dirty, but it was lonely.

And too empty.

Maya found Kolya in his bedroom—or rather, pulling items from the closet when she walked in. Even here, his bed was nothing more than a mattress and box spring on the floor with a sheet tossed over it, and clothes piled up on the side.

"Why here?"

"Hmm?" he asked over his shoulder.

"Here, this place. Why do you live here?"

And live like this?

She held back from adding that, too.

"I don't follow," Kolya said.

"Well, you have *money*."

And he was a Boykov.

Kolya shrugged, seemingly understanding what she wasn't saying, and turned around to face her. "I didn't even need this place. Just to stay out of the fucking rain is enough for me, yes?"

Maya frowned. "It seems very … lonely."

"That's how I liked it, *dushka*."

"That's a little sad."

Kolya dropped a black duffle bag on the floor, and a few items of clothing inside it as he bent down to rearrange the items. "I never needed anything else."

"But … don't you want a home? Something to come back to at the end of the day?"

He hesitated and then glanced up at her. "I didn't have anything to come home to."

Didn't, she noticed.

Past, not present.

"Okay," she whispered.

Kolya nodded, and went back to his job of packing up whatever clothes he seemed to want to take with him. Maya watched it all in silence—*unusual* silence, as he might tell her.

Because, yes, she was thinking.

Constantly, now.

About him.

• • •

The knocking echoed through the hotel room, and sent Maya flying out of the bathroom to answer the door. She'd ordered room service for lunch when Kolya called to say he wasn't going to get back in time to eat with her, and it was just about the time the food should arrive.

She didn't even think to look through the peephole.

Why should she?

Kolya had a man at the door.

Maya yanked the door open with a smile and then promptly turned in to a block of ice at the sight of the man waiting on the other side.

Well-dressed.

Hair slicked back.

Broad shoulders.

Cold eyes.

Vadim.

The man smiled thinly at the sight of Maya. Behind him, the man Kolya always had watching the door stood with his hands at his back. Well, she supposed given that Vadim was the boss, he didn't have much of a choice but to let him in.

Kind of like me right now.

"You look out of breath, girl," Vadim said. "Did I interrupt something?"

"Is my face painted?"

Vadim arched a brow. "Partially."

"Then, yes, you interrupted me."

"My apologies."

Yeah, he sounded sorry. Maya wasn't exactly the type to be purposely rude to anyone, but Vadim hadn't exactly done very much to make her feel welcome … let alone *safe*. In fact, when she was in his presence, he pretended like she didn't exist, and if he did notice her, he acted like she was trash.

How was that supposed to make her feel?

Vadim gestured at her, and the half-closed door. "Care to let me in, Maya?"

Not particularly.

It didn't look like she had a choice, though.

12.

VADIM DIDN'T give Maya the chance to step back and *allow* him inside the hotel. No, he simply gave her a cold smile before he drifted in the doorway and basically forced her to move, or he would have been the one to move her.

By the time she had closed the door—although not before she saw the man Kolya left to watch her pull a phone from his pocket—and turned around, Vadim had already crossed the room. He made himself right at home beside the wet bar by overturning a crystal glass, and pouring himself a hefty drink of vodka.

His blank, pensive stare drifted over the room, but barely took notice of her as he absorbed the surroundings. All the while, he never said a thing. Not even when Sumerki wandered out of the bathroom, and stopped to sniff his shoes.

Then, finally, Vadim turned that sharp gaze on her. "This is a step up for you, I imagine, no?"

Maya folded her arms over her chest. "The hotel, you mean?"

"My son's wealth."

Get right to the point.

"I don't think your son realizes how wealthy he is, considering the only thing he has to *show* he's got any kind of money is his vehicle and the suits he wears."

Vadim tipped his glass in her direction, saying, "That's fair enough, girl. Kolya never was the type to be ... excessive." His gaze pointedly drifted over the hotel room again. "Except, it seems he's throwing a bit of money around at the moment, isn't he?"

"Not because I want or need him to," Maya returned.

"Money isn't your angle, then?"

It was really hard not to be offended when someone was purposely trying to be offensive. Maya did her best to tamper down the automatic reaction to snap back at Vadim, but only because the two of them were currently alone and she didn't think that would work very well to her favor.

Life had taught her to be wary of men like this.

To be careful.

Tread lightly.

"I've lived this long without having a great deal of money," Maya settled on saying. "I'm not going to break down tomorrow if Kolya decides to, oh, I don't know, cut me off from the funds he *isn't giving me to begin with*."

Vadim's mouth edged upwards in the corners. It was the barest hint of amusement coloring his stone-like features. Maya didn't think Kolya realized it, really, but in this way, he was very much like his father. Cold and inanimate for the most part—like a statue—and only occasionally allowing something real to shine through.

Tipping his glass up for one long drink that emptied the vodka, Vadim then set the cup aside before bending down to get a closer look at Sumerki. He put his hand out as if to offer it to the pup, but the dog didn't move from his spot where he'd decided to sit directly between Maya and Vadim. He didn't move, even when the man teased the dog a bit by bending his fingers as though to coach him.

Vadim glanced upward, saying, "You're quite a dainty little thing."

Maya blinked. "What?"

"Small featured, girl. You look like a *sprite*—a fairy. A good gust of fucking wind would blow you over, yes?"

"Is there a reason you're insulting me? What, you woke up this morning and thought, *yes, that's on my to-do list today; insult Maya because I can*."

Vadim chuckled dryly, but stayed bent down on one knee. "I wasn't insulting you by stating an obvious fact. I also didn't say you aren't beautiful, girl. You obviously are—although for the life of me, I can't see what so many others seem to have found in you. What is it about you, do you think, that has a handful of men willing to go to war to either keep you or have you?"

A lump caught hard in Maya's throat.

"I don't know," she admitted. "I didn't ask for any of that."

She'd simply woken up one day and gone to work like her father told her to do. From that moment forward, her entire life changed. Never once had she asked for this to happen, though.

The man shook his head when the dog still refused to budge from his spot and stood straight again. "I have always said and told my sons, that no woman is worth a war. There have been enough wars fought over women who were not worthy of the men fighting for them; our name does not have to be attached to yet another one."

Maya opened her mouth to speak, although she wasn't sure what exactly she might say in response to that statement, but Vadim held up a hand to stop her. His cold gaze met hers and he gave her a tight-lipped smile that screamed *I am in control here*.

"The pup is endearing, isn't he?" Vadim asks. "Thinks he might protect you. From what, I don't know."

You, she wanted to say.

Maya kept quiet.

"His name?"

"Sumerki," she said.

Vadim nodded. "Nightfall. *Fitting*."

"Kolya thought so."

"Yes and while we're on the topic of him ..." Vadim pointed a finger at Maya as he drifted across the room to stand in front of the large window overlooking the busy city street down below. "How does he treat you—well?"

How did he treat—

"Stop looking at me as though I'm stupid," Vadim barked at her, "and answer my question."

Jesus.

"He treats me how he treats me," Maya settled on saying.

Which, yes, Kolya treated her far better than just "*well*," but no, she was not going to offer that information to Vadim. Something told her that she shouldn't. He had not shown up here to be pleasant or to have a kind conversation with a woman his son was clearly interested in. She didn't take Vadim to be the type, frankly.

"I suppose anything would be a step up from your father and brother." Vadim shrugged one shoulder and turned to stare out the window again. "They didn't treat you well at all, girl. Heavy-handed and sharp-tongued, I think. Your brother's favorite pet name for you was *whore*, and your father, *bitch*. Which, who am I to say, may have been appropriate—I tend to favor my girl over my boys, though. She actually knows how to *listen*."

Something clenched tight around Maya's heart. Painful and swift. It took the damn breath right out of her lungs, but somehow, she managed to keep her calm facade. But that's all it was. A *show*. Inside, her fear was growing.

Vadim knew entirely too much about her. She hadn't even told Kolya those things.

"They weren't kind to me," she said quietly.

Vadim glanced over his shoulder, but there was no sympathy or empathy in his hard stare. "Challenges like those tend to make or break a person—either way, you tend to come out better for it, no? Some even *need* that kind of treatment. Maybe you were one of them."

"I doubt it."

The man only shrugged and went back to staring out the window. The silence dragged on for long enough that Maya considered asking Vadim what in the fuck he wanted with her, but his next statement stopped her from saying anything at all.

"Two of my men are dead and a third is now missing," Vadim said in barely a murmur. She could see the way his shoulders tensed as he talked, but his posture remained rigid. "You know about the other two, don't you?

You were there at the Compound. The third was taken last night, from his favorite club, while his girlfriend was getting him another drink from the bar. The second man who was taken—my Captain—was returned to me … or parts of him."

Maya shuddered.

Vadim continued on unaware of her plight, saying, "Your brother, however, was not returned. I suspect that's because they know I don't give a single fuck about him or his remains. I expect the third will be killed before the night is out because the Albanians don't tend to wait when they have decided on something. Perhaps this time, I'll get more than my man's cock and hands back when they decide to send him to me through the fucking courier."

Oh, God.

That sick feeling growing in Maya's stomach had become progressively heavier, until she felt as though she might lose her lunch. She could have done without the mental visuals now running rampant through her already overactive imagination.

She didn't think Vadim cared.

"I didn't kill those men," Maya said quietly.

She knew better than to mention the little fact that her brother wasn't actually dead. She hadn't been so lost to her panic that day in the Compound that she hadn't heard the conversation between Kolya and Konstantin.

Vadim turned to face Maya, then, and it seemed his face had reverted back to that cold, expressionless wasteland of nothingness. She thought that was even more terrifying than his rage, maybe. One could not tell when he was going to snap like this.

"What does that have to do with me?" Maya asked.

"That's what I am trying to figure out," Vadim said, eyeing her in that unnerving way of his. "You may not be the *exact* reason why this or that happened, but you were a catalyst to it. Think of it as … the man who orders the gun is just as guilty as the one who pulls the trigger."

Maya swallowed hard. "But I didn't order—"

"Mmm, not important. Quiet for a moment and *listen*. I assure you that it will serve you far more than running your pretty mouth. Besides, I only care for a woman's mouth to move when I have ordered it to." Vadim sighed and peered down at Sumerki, who had still yet to move from his spot. "If you get in my way, Maya, with my son, or otherwise … it will not end well for you, girl."

"How could I possibly get in your way with those things?"

She didn't even know him.

Never sought him out.

Vadim laughed darkly. "*Catalyst*, remember?" He pointed a finger at her again as he moved away from the window and crossed the room, only stopping in front of Sumerki. "My son—he has many expectations and rules to follow. Most of which, I don't even think you have the first clue of. While right now, he is behaving ... should that change, then so will my responses to his actions. Do not be the reason that I have to make a choice that will bring you harm and him pain."

Silently, Vadim leaned down just enough to attempt to pet Sumerki. The dog snapped back quickly, and nipped the man's fingers. Vadim was quick to pull his hand back out of harm's way, but not without flinching.

"He's less cute now," Vadim murmured before heading for the door. Over his shoulder, he said to Maya, "And should you be wondering where Kolya is today, or why he isn't back, or why he *won't* be back until at least tomorrow ... it's because I have sent him on a wild goose chase. See, there is really only one person in this world who pulls Kolya's strings, girl, and I promise it isn't you. I am always the one in control, even if you may think differently. Remember it."

• • •

Maya blinked awake at the sound of a door clicking shut. The noise was quiet, but not quiet enough for a woman who had been on edge ever since a certain man's father had left her hotel room. How she'd even managed to fall asleep—although it was closing in on two in the morning before she finally did—was anyone's fucking guess.

The haze lingering from her sleep was quickly blinked away as she sat up in the hotel bed and tried to find where the unknown noise had come from. Soon enough, Maya realized it was the bathroom door.

She'd opened it before bed. It was now closed and a small sliver of light spilled out from the crack at the bottom of the door. If that wasn't a good enough clue, the fact that Sumerki had climbed down from the bed—a feat he was still scared of doing alone—and had now perched himself in front of the bathroom door would have done the trick for her.

Kolya was back.

Finally.

Maya rolled over and checked the clock on the bedside table. It told her it was only five in the morning, which explained why she was still so goddamn tired. The time also meant Kolya had been gone for an entire day—or just about. He'd left the morning before after getting a phone call, and had told her practically nothing.

Vadim had given her more information, frankly.

Maya climbed out of the bed when she heard a low curse come from inside the bathroom. The water turned on before she even reached the door. She rapped two knuckles against the wood as she glanced down at Sumerki, who was staring up at her like he was two seconds away from falling over and going back to sleep.

Poor dog.

He really had missed his human.

"What?" came the angry grumble from inside the bathroom.

Maya frowned. "Can I come in?"

"No."

"Kolya—"

"Go back to sleep—it's too early for you, *dushka*."

Maya huffed. "It's been a whole day. You didn't even *call*. The least you could do is let me come in and see you."

Silence echoed for a whole three seconds before she heard heavy footsteps cross the bathroom. Then the door was abruptly swung wide open with no warning. Kolya stood just beyond the threshold in nothing but black slacks. Even his feet were bare. Behind him, she saw a puddle of ruined, bloody clothing on the floor.

She might have overlooked those things, but she couldn't pretend like his raw, sore-looking knuckles weren't a cause for concern. Never mind his hostile disposition.

Maya blinked. "What happened?"

"Nothing."

Her gaze darted back to him. "Is *nothing* also why your knuckles are bruised and bloody?"

Kolya didn't even try to hide his hands at her question. "Possibly."

"*Kolya.*"

He sighed. "I got angry, yeah? Bad things happen when I get angry."

Like the fucking Hulk, or something.

"Do you know—"

"That my father sent me on a fucking impossible task *just* to keep me away from you for an entire day, and then proceeded to taunt me with it until I was able to get back here? Yes, I know."

Maya's shoulders dropped. "Oh."

Kolya jerked his chin upward. "Go to bed. I want to clean off and then I'll join you."

"I don't think so."

Now that he was here—back with her where she needed and wanted him to be—the very last thing she wanted to do was let him out of her sights again. She really just wanted to touch him; to hold him, and hide away from the rest of the world for a few moments. Because when it was just her and Kolya, nothing and no one else seemed to matter. Nothing could break through that wall he was able to put up to barricade them from reality.

He was her safe place.

Or so she was learning.

Yeah, she just wanted to be close to him.

Hug him.

Something.

"Maya, please don't argue with me. I had a long day, and a worse night. I only want to be here with you, and—"

That was all she needed to hear.

Maya lurched forward and slammed into Kolya without thinking about it. Her arms wrapped around him as much as they could—which wasn't even enough to circle his entire frame, but fuck her if she didn't *try*. Kolya let out a quiet sound when her body impacted with his, and it took him a beat or two in time before he reacted to her sudden move.

But when he did …

God, when he did, it was wonderful. He rested one large arm across the back of her shoulders and his other hand came to tangle in her hair. She felt his head dip down so that he could press a kiss to the top of her forehead that lingered and sent shivers cascading over every part of her that it could reach.

She stayed right there.

Just like that.

Holding on so damn tight to him.

He didn't make her move, either.

Quietly, Kolya murmured against the top of her head, "Everything will be *fine.*"

"Will it?"

Her words were muffled against his bare chest, but he still seemed to hear it all the same.

"*Da.* There's nothing to be worried about. I'll handle it."

"He threatened me, you know. Your father, I mean. Maybe not in so many words, but what he didn't say … it felt just as important as the things he did. And nothing he said was very well-intended."

She felt him stiffen, but still, he said, "It'll be fine."

"I don't think it will be."

Something inside just told her … this would not end well.

"Maya—"

"How can you keep me safe—*really* safe? And it's not just about me; it's you, too. It's *you,* too, Kolya."

In a blink, he'd pulled away from her. He dropped to his knees right there, though his hands grabbed tight to either side of her face and stared up at her. Although, he didn't have to look up very far like this.

She was so fucking short.

Him, way too tall.

"I will *always* keep you safe," he murmured. "I don't have a choice. I did not wait this long to find you just to let you go. It's not about me, Maya. Nothing—not even myself—will ever be as important to me as you are. Not now."

His words were not exactly *I love you.*

They were, however, the closest thing to it without actually saying the words and maybe ... she thought ... even better than it, too. For now, anyway.

Just this was enough to terrify her and overwhelm her all at the same time. If this was his idea of baby steps when it came to falling in love with a woman, then his strides were quite wide.

Not that she didn't *like* it. She did. Probably too much. That was also part of the problem.

"You don't even know me," she whispered.

Kolya shrugged. "I know all the things that matter to me; I will learn the rest, yes?" When she didn't respond right away, he grinned and raised his brows. Asking again, "Yes? It's always *your* choice, Maya."

He was right there.

Next to taking her—which in the end, had probably been the very best thing to ever happen to her—every choice between them was always left for her to decide. He never stepped in to force something on her, or make her do anything she didn't actually want to do.

She adored him for that, really.

Amongst many things.

Maya drew in a shaky breath and nodded. "Yes."

"Good—that's my *dushka*, hmm?"

"According to you."

Kolya chuckled. "And I'm sorry."

"For what?"

"Scaring you yesterday—last night, I imagine."

Maya's first inclination was to deny it, *simply* because she didn't want him to be upset over the fact she had been upset. She settled on the truth instead. "It did scare me."

"It won't happen again."

She doubted that.

He was who he was.

This life was what it was.

She fully believed it would happen again—she simply hoped he would apologize each time it happened. Therein lied the difference.

Kolya was quick to rise from the floor, but not before he pressed a fast and fleeting kiss to her lips on the way up with one of his sexy winks. It was not nearly enough for Maya. It felt more like he'd dangled the promise of something more in front of her very eyes, and then taken it away before she could even try to reach for it.

Maya couldn't have that.

She fast closed the distance between them and kissed him in a way she hoped made it clear what she wanted—*him*—and when she wanted it—*now*. Kolya didn't hesitate to kiss her back, and if his husky laughter were any indication, he got her unspoken demand well enough.

The bathroom door was slammed shut a second before Kolya shoved her against it. The force was enough to make her spine ache. Yet, she barely felt it at all. How could she, when her attention was spread thin between the way he was kissing her, his hand slipping between her thighs? His palm cupped and stroke her sex, and his other hand that had thrust its way into her hair grabbed tight.

"Fucking made this easy on me, didn't you?" he asked as his mouth grazed along her chin, letting the pressure of his palm and the tips of his fingers tease her. "Wearing my shirt and no panties. *Easy.*"

Maya gasped, and tipped her head back to the door when that teasing mouth of his traveled over her throat. He always found the right spots— *tasted, bit,* and *drove her so fucking crazy* with just his fingers and mouth alone.

She was hot all over.

Burning up already.

Wanting more.

And entirely unashamed about it.

Her pussy made a wet sucking sound when his fingers finally—*finally*— slipped inside. Kolya grunted out a low curse in Russian against her throat. He curled his fingers hard against her inner walls in a fast, sure way that had her shaking in just a few strokes.

"So fucking wet, *dushka,*" she heard him say. "Tell me what you want from me—use your words."

How was she supposed to talk like this?

How?

All it took was Kolya's hand sliding down from her hair to circle her throat. He squeezed just enough to make her breath catch, and forced her gaze up to his. The words slipped out easy then—it was hard for her to deny him anything when he looked at her like this.

"I want to come," she whispered, "and then I want you to fuck me."

Something burned in his gaze.

Something violent, and vicious, and *cold.*

Something unique to Kolya that only came out to play, she thought, when his control was all but gone.

It should scare her.

It only turned her on.

Because even when he looked lost, he was never truly gone with her. She knew that much—it was the only thing she was sure of.

"Please," Maya added quietly.

That did it.

Kolya's mouth slammed down on hers with a brutal kiss—one that showed her no mercy, even when her lungs screamed for air and her bottom lip stung when his teeth cut into the soft flesh. If nothing else, it was a promise of what was yet to come.

And good God … she couldn't wait.

The sensations mixing together of his kiss, his hand on her throat, and the one working between her thighs were just all too much. It came together in a tidal wave of bliss and crashed down on her quickly. She couldn't breathe when she was being dragged under the current of an orgasm that all but blinded her, but she couldn't find it in herself to care.

His fingers were still stuffed in her pussy.

His lips still on hers.

A hand on her throat.

What did the rest matter?

His hands only left her body long enough for her to hear the snap of a button and the hiss of a zipper. She didn't even hear his slacks shuffle before she found herself lifted against the door. One of his hands was back on her throat at the same time she felt him heavy between her thighs. And *fuck*, when he finally slid inside her, the world went black for a brief moment.

All senses gone.

All rationale disappeared.

The world looked a little different like this.

She was stretched full of him and aching because of it. He squeezed her throat a little bit harder as he worked his cock into her tight cunt. Those fingers of his that had been stuffed into her pussy pressed against her lips, and Maya didn't even think twice about opening her mouth for his unspoken request.

On his skin, her come tasted tart and heady.

She sucked his fingers clean as his hips flexed forward and he started a punishing beat that had the fucking door shaking against her back. Rough and harsh … that ache between her thighs settled deeper, but it only made her want more.

"Fuck," Kolya uttered when his fingers slipped from her mouth to leave a wet trail over her lips. "You're going to kill me squeezing my dick like that, Maya."

Was she clenching?

She hadn't even realized it.

She couldn't fucking control it.

Every thrust of his cock dragged along her nerves like they were exposed—each one brought her closer and *higher*.

Breathless and shaking.

"I'm gonna—"

"Come," he said roughly, "*yes*, that's what I want. *Give it to me.*"

She did.

So hard.

But he wasn't even close to being done.

It seemed he had entirely forgotten about his shower and the bloody pile of clothes on the floor. Especially when he bent her over the sink, fisted her hair, and fucked her hard from behind until she'd shouted his name loud enough that her throat turned raw.

Her throat felt better, though.

After she sucked him dry.

Nothing looked better than Kolya watching her swallow his dick.

Maya would bet her life on it.

13.

VADIM MAY have *thought* Kolya was a stupid man, but he was far from it. And he certainly wasn't so distracted with everything happening in his life that he didn't notice how his father did everything in his power to divert or deflect Kolya.

For an entire week, ever since Vadim cornered Maya in the hotel room, everything from Kolya's calls to requests for meetings had either gone unanswered, or an excuse had been given. Never from Vadim directly, but rather, whoever Kolya tried to go through to get *to* his father.

No, he was not stupid.

Vadim clearly thought he was, though.

Kolya was getting sick of this shit.

Currently, it was Grisha attempting to deflect Kolya's attempt to get a meeting with his father. Actually, Grisha had been the one who'd done most of the diverting this past week. He was, essentially, Vadim's right-hand man.

"Where is he, then?" Kolya demanded.

"I told you—busy," Grisha replied tiredly.

"Or you could just tell me the truth and say he's trying to keep me away until he thinks I've calmed down after his show with Maya."

Grisha made a noise in the back of his throat. "If you know, why ask?"

"So that *is* what it is, yes?"

"Kolya—"

"Vadim is not so busy that he can't see his oldest son for five fucking *minutes*."

"He doesn't want to see you. He doesn't give a shit if you're calm or not. That's never mattered to Vadim; it doesn't matter now, no?"

"Great. Then, you should have no fucking problem setting a meeting up between him and I. *Soon*."

"I do have a problem with it, yes. I told you—he doesn't want to see you."

"And I don't give a shit."

Whatever control Grisha had on his thin patience snapped with that statement. Really, Kolya was surprised the man lasted this long. Usually, he just hung up by now, but not before telling Kolya to *go play in traffic*. That was Grisha's nice way of telling someone to fuck off.

"You're under some sort of impression that just because you demand something, I must immediately jump through hoops to give you what you want, Kolya. That's your first mistake—try not to make another. I answer to one man and you are not that man."

Testy.

He almost laughed.

Almost.

Except Kolya couldn't laugh at all when he was so goddamn pissed about this whole thing. One entire *week* of this garbage, to be exact.

Kolya's jaw clenched so tightly, his molars ached. Grisha was lucky he was speaking to Kolya through a goddamn phone and not face to face. This little chat would not have ended well for the older man otherwise. Kolya was not in the mood for this nonsense.

"Yet," Kolya uttered.

"Excuse me?"

"You heard me—*yet*, Grisha. You do not answer to me yet." Kolya smiled when the man's breathing slowed on the other end of the call. "Because you *will* answer to me eventually. Vadim made sure of it; the cross on my chest says so, yes? Don't you forget *that*. Because I sure as fuck won't forget this."

Kolya didn't give the man a chance to respond. He hung up the phone and slipped the device into his pocket before he could consider smashing it into the ground at his feet. That might have made him feel better in the moment but it would also be selfish.

It was the only number Maya knew to call—other than Konstantin's— should she need something. Plus, she'd been texting him pictures all day on her trip out of the hotel, wanting opinions that he didn't think he had any place to give. He did it anyway, knowing she probably smiled for each one.

He didn't need it hanging over his head if one of her texts went unanswered because he was a prick who broke his phone.

Kolya didn't miss the way Konstantin's brow lifted as he entered his brother's office at the Compound.

"What was that all about?" Konstantin asked.

"Hmm, what?"

"Your phone call. I heard it."

Kolya gave his brother a side eye. "Spying is a bad habit, no? Quit before someone breaks you of it."

"I wasn't spying. You were talking loud enough for the devil to hear."

"Same difference."

Konstantin's gaze narrowed. "Oh, you're in one of *those* moods again."

Jesus Christ.

"I'm not in a mood. This is how I am."

And it would do *everyone* well if they would just figure that out, and quickly. Kolya was getting tired of explaining it again and again.

"Sure." Konstantin nodded. "What, didn't get to forget your own name from being buried in pussy this morning?"

Actually, he had.

And he'd done so happily.

Not that it was his brother's business.

Kolya gave Konstantin another look; this one promising violence if he didn't shut the fuck up, and *fast*. Konstantin only rolled his eyes in response. He swore the two of them had the strangest relationship—everything was always a competition to Konstantin when it came to Kolya. From business to their father, and even little things like challenging Kolya's threats in a way no one else would dare.

Oh, sure, he respected his brother for it. How could he not? That didn't mean he knew what to make of it, or why Konstantin felt the need to rise to every occasion where Kolya was concerned. It *was* the only way they actually got along, though, so Kolya indulged it.

He liked Konstantin well enough. Might even use the word *love,* although that felt a little strong.

He loved one thing—one woman—he had come to find, and nothing else felt the same in that regard. It was too heavy of a word to throw around, especially considering Kolya had no idea how he'd fallen in love, and he had yet to even utter the words outside of his head.

Konstantin moved onto something else, thankfully. "Since when do you throw your position in people's faces like that? It isn't like you to use that against someone—especially *Grisha.*"

Konstantin wasn't lying.

It wasn't like Kolya to use his position as his father's heir to scare a man or set him straight. Mostly because Kolya didn't want that fucking position to begin with. He never had, and he never would. It also wasn't his choice to make; or so the story went.

"It just slipped out, yeah? Stop asking questions."

"Fine. You should really take up a class on social skills and how to conversate with someone else, Kolya. It might help with … things, no?"

"But *why?*"

"Never mind," Konstantin muttered, his gaze drifting past Kolya to the space behind him. "No puppy or woman today?"

"Sumerki is with Maya."

"Playing fetch?"

"I'm going to break your face, Konstantin."

Konstantin shrugged. "Probably someday. I figured you'd bring her in, since it's your first day back working at the Compound."

"She has other things to do."

"Like what? She stays hidden in a hotel."

Kolya chucked dryly. "Not today. She's looking at penthouses in the city, and properties in the suburbs, actually."

His brother turned into a statue behind the desk. "It's *that* serious, yeah?"

"Don't say it like that."

"Tell me where I was wrong."

Kolya sighed. "We've come to an understanding that she would like to stay with me, and not in a hotel, but also not in my dump of an apartment. So yes, she has taken Sumerki to look for places today. I have someone keeping an eye on her and the realtor she's with, but from a safe distance. *And* it's someone Vadim doesn't know. Are you satisfied with prying into my personal life, now, or no?"

Konstantin grinned and leaned back in his chair like a smug fucker. Had it been another day, when Kolya had been just a little bit more pissed off, he might have made it his first and last mission to wipe the smirk off his brother's face.

He couldn't even be bothered today.

"Yeah, I'm done," Konstantin said.

"Good. Do *you* know where Vadim is?"

"Avoiding us."

Yeah, he figured.

Fuck.

"He can only avoid us for so long—tribute is next week, right? You could just let the incident with Maya and the hotel go," Konstantin suggested. "You know how Vadim is. He's dominant, aggressive, and has a tendency to piss on anything he considers his territory."

A lot like them, too, Kolya thought.

He didn't say it out loud.

"And if he meant to hurt your thing," Konstantin continued, "he would have."

"Don't call her that. She isn't a *thing*, Konstantin. It's bad enough Vadim wants to label her property. Don't diminish her like he does."

"She is yours, though, isn't she?"

Well, that was a whole other story.

"Moving on," Kolya said gruffly. "Any news on the Albanian front this week?"

Konstantin shook his head. "Nothing. They've been quiet."

And that was seriously concerning.

Why?

The debt wasn't paid.

They'd made that clear.

"Then, they're probably just about due for another incident, aren't they?" Kolya asked.

"Likely."

But who would the Albanians take this time?

Which Boykov *vor* would it be?

• • •

Vadim was rarely the first person to show up at tribute. In fact, he was often the last man to grace everyone with his presence. Boss's right, Kolya supposed. That was exactly why he wasn't at all surprised to find his father hadn't even arrived at the meeting of the Boykov men by the time Kolya got there.

Konstantin had arrived first, it seemed. Tucked away in the corner of the room with his back facing the row of bookshelves, his brother was able to see everyone around him, and didn't put himself at risk in the same breath.

Boykov men were all the same.

Kolya included.

Despite not wanting to chat—and Konstantin was so fucking *chatty* lately—Konstantin was far easier on Kolya's head than anyone else in that goddamn room. He headed his brother's way and didn't give anyone else a second look. Not that any of them would expect anything different from Kolya.

They were all quite accustomed to his moods.

"Maya find a house yet?" Konstantin asked.

See, chatty.

"She's very picky," Kolya admitted.

And she was … *Jesus.*

She wanted privacy, but not so much so that she felt shut off from the rest of the world. Frankly, Kolya would have liked that just fine. She also wanted grass and maybe a fence. Hardwood floors and natural crown molding. Four bedrooms and an equal number of bathrooms. For visitors' sake, she explained.

What difference did it make?

He didn't have the first clue.

All Kolya knew was that Maya had settled in—she quite liked her place with him and whatever it was that they were doing together. He liked having her there, too. He wasn't about to fuck that up, or make her unhappy, by opening his moody ass mouth and making a comment about the kinds of floors she wanted or the number of bathrooms being ridiculous.

"Could always *build*," Konstantin suggested as though he could read his brother's mind. "You've got the money for that."

More than actually.

"I could," Kolya agreed. "She still might find something."

His brother glanced over at him with curious eyes. "Is living with a woman really as difficult as everyone says?"

"What?"

Konstantin shrugged. "Difficult, yeah? Fickle, even. I wouldn't know. I'm curious."

No, Kolya supposed Konstantin *wouldn't* know much about living with a woman beyond their sister Viktoria, and that had only been as long as he'd been required to live under the same roof. It wasn't like Konstantin made much time for women beyond busting a nut—not that Kolya had been any different, so he didn't have much to say there.

"It's not … she's good," Kolya settled on saying. "A ray of fucking sunshine in the morning."

Quite literally.

The woman woke up smiling.

Konstantin made a face. "I think you just lucked out, no? That doesn't seem to be the norm."

Possibly.

Kolya didn't respond. He couldn't, when his father just walked into the room, and everyone else went quiet. Konstantin was quick to notice Vadim, too, and reverted back to his previous stillness. Grisha trailed two steps behind Vadim, as usual.

It'd been two weeks since the hotel incident. Two weeks of Vadim ignoring Kolya and refusing to see his son. Two weeks of fucking *nonsense.*

And yet, his father smiled when he laid eyes on him. Vadim passed a couple of his men who had stood from the long table to greet him without as much as a hello in their direction. He came to the end of the table where Kolya and Konstantin stood against the bookshelves. Directly behind the chair their father liked to sit in.

They were the only men Vadim would turn his back on, after all.

Funny how that worked.

"I haven't seen you two around in a while," Vadim said. "Working hard, I assume."

Kolya's teeth ground in an effort to stay quiet. Konstantin saved him the trouble of finding a suitable reply that didn't include telling Vadim to go fuck himself with a metal spike. That would not have ended well.

"We're always busy," Konstantin said. "That's what you like, isn't it?"

The backhanded question probably seemed like it flew right over Vadim's head to anyone else in the room. Kolya wasn't as gullible, nor was Konstantin. They didn't miss the familiar flash of annoyance in their father's gaze.

But.

Money was on the table.

In envelopes, that was.

Several.

That changed everything.

Vadim nodded. "I do like it when you keep busy. You're right. You stay the fuck out of my hair that way. Let's begin tribute. Grisha?"

At the call of the man's name, Grisha was quick to move around the table and scoop up the waiting envelopes from the men. Vadim, on the other hand, took his seat and didn't pay his son's any more attention for the moment.

Tribute went on as normal.

Money was paid.

Issues discussed.

Nothing new.

Kolya was only there to pay his dividends alongside his brother, watch Vadim make a show about tribute as he'd done for every single one before this, and then get the hell out as fast as he could. He would deal with his issues regarding Vadim another time.

Tonight was not the night.

It was the soft vibrating of Kolya's phone in his pocket that had him moving away from the bookshelves, and a few steps from his father. Vadim didn't seem to notice, considering he was attempting to calm the questions about the Albanians being thrown at him left and right.

That was the thing about being the boss—you were expected to have all the answers, even when you knew very little.

Kolya didn't bother to check the caller ID as he slipped from the private board room his father rented just for the purpose of tribute. He put the phone to his ear with a gruff, "*What?*"

"Hey," came a soft, familiar voice.

Soft, yes.

But *fearful.*

"Maya?" Kolya asked.

"Yeah, hey, sorry. I'm just trying to figure out where I am?"

Rustling sounded in the background of the call, but Kolya was already moving down the hall. He heard footsteps echoing behind him but didn't pay it any mind.

"I need your help," Maya said.

"Where are—"

"You know that bakery in Melrose? The one with the big cupcake painted on the window? That's where I am. Come get me? *Please.*"

Kolya blinked.

That bakery—he knew which one she was talking about. It had been closed down for at least a couple of years. Why was she even in Melrose at this time of fucking night?

"Maya—"

The phone call clicked off.

Kolya pulled the device in front of him and stared at the screen. The number staring back at him wasn't the one that belonged to Maya's burner phone. Nothing felt right about that call, and yet, when Kolya tried to call Maya's actual phone … no one picked up.

That switch he had—the one Maya controlled without knowing it? The one that went on or off depending on what the situation called for?

Yeah, it was all the way off.

"What's up?" he heard Konstantin ask from behind.

"Something's wrong," Kolya muttered.

"With Maya?"

"I need to get to Melrose."

Konstantin strolled ahead of his brother. "Well, fuck, I've got the faster car. Also, tribute is a *bore*."

• • •

Kolya was quick to jump out of Konstantin's car before his brother even cut the engine. He stayed on the passenger side of the car and stared at the bakery just on the other side of the vehicle. The rundown building looked like he suspected—as though the owner had given up on the place ages ago, and hadn't gone back.

The FOR SALE sign he remembered being in the window was gone, though.

Konstantin rolled down the passenger window and called out to his brother from the driver's seat, "What are we here for?"

Yeah.

He'd forgotten to explain.

"Maya called," Kolya said. "She was here."

Except … she clearly wasn't.

He pulled out his phone to call Maya's burner again, but before he could, another call was ringing through. This time, it was the same number that had interrupted tribute.

Kolya didn't even think about answering it.

"Where the fuck is she?" he demanded.

A man chuckled on the other end. "Did you like my little trick, Kolya? Cute, no? See, my sister called me once … stupid teenage shit; stayed out too late and got scared. I wouldn't pick up the phone for her, so she left a message. I saved that damn thing just because. It worked well for me, yeah?"

Kolya's jaw ached from how fiercely he clenched it. "Alexei, is it?"

"It is. Fucking shame we haven't met."

"I wouldn't call it a *shame*," Kolya returned.

Konstantin had gotten out of the car, and he came around to Kolya's side without a word. No, like a smart man, he simply *listened*. Kolya put the phone on speaker and waved a finger at Konstantin as if to say, *Fuck*.

"Why did you trick the Albanians into thinking they had killed you?" Kolya asked. "What purpose did that serve?"

"Clearly, they didn't. I'm alive."

"Yes, but *why*."

"You ask stupid questions," Alexei returned. "And now I'm bored. You see, we just need to get you and your kin out of the way, and smooth shit over with the Albanians. It won't be long now."

Kolya scowled. "Shit *you* caused."

"Mmm, no. You took the bitch, didn't you?"

He stiffened all over, a threat already forming on his tongue.

Alexei beat him to it, saying, "I think we'll start by getting rid of you, Kolya. Have a good evening. I'm sure it'll be a blast."

The second those words left Alexie's lips, the bakery behind them blew up. The bang was incredible—a deafening noise and sharp pressure that sent both Boykov brothers slamming into the ground. Kolya felt his skull crack against the pavement, and swore he heard Konstantin hit the car.

The car . . .

It was the only thing that might have saved them. The glass and debris peppered the vehicle, but mostly left them untouched.

Kolya's head rang.

His ears ached.

Was he bleeding?

It didn't matter.

That phone call hadn't clicked off.

In the background of the noise, he could hear screams coming from the speaker.

Feminine screams.

Maya's screams.

14.

IT TOOK entirely *too fucking long* for Kolya and Konstantin to get back to the hotel where Maya was supposed to be safe and sound like he had left her with a guard to keep watch on her door. Konstantin's car was completely totaled on the one side—there was no way in hell they were driving that goddamn thing back. Instead, they'd had to stumble down the block to make sure they weren't in front of the blown-up building when the cops got there, and then wait for a Boykov man to come and pick them up.

Like idiots.

Like a couple of cocksuckers who were running out of time with every single second they had to wait to be *picked up*. The longer he had to wait, the darker his mind turned and the worse his mood became.

Konstantin was not missing it for a second. Apparently, his brother thought it would be worth the risk to talk right then. Frankly, Kolya was liable to bust anyone's damn mouth at the moment.

His brother should have known that.

"Kolya, relax, yeah?" Konstantin said quietly. "Slow down a bit."

He barely heard his brother—his mind was a total fucking mess at the moment. Chaotic, and *crazy*. Running through every single mistake he had made, playing them back again and again. Taunting him with them. It was like needles had slipped into his veins and were now traveling all over his body to prick and stab him with every movement.

Because he knew …

He just *knew*.

This was bad.

It was only going to get worse.

Kolya didn't manage this sort of thing well. He liked disappearing into his already-lost mind, and letting instinct and emotion take over. He'd wake up after it was all over and done with, while standing in pile of carnage all around him. He'd feel better then. He always did.

It was enticing.

That was Kolya.

Not today.

This was … *Maya*.

"Kolya—"

"Shut up," Kolya snapped at his brother.

His head was still pounding and that damned ringing in his ears hadn't left since his head had cracked off the pavement. He was sure he had a fucking concussion. No doubt. What difference did it make? He suspected he wouldn't be sleeping for a while ... that's all the doctors would tell him to do, too.

Kolya bypassed the bank of elevators altogether and pushed open the doorway for the stairwell. He could climb five flights faster than that elevator could take him up. He took the steps three at a time, with Konstantin right on his heels. All the while, his brother kept telling him to relax and whatever else.

Don't go to the worst place possible first, Kolya.

That was the thing about Konstantin and Kolya. It was where they differed the most, he thought. Konstantin was willing to objectively look at even the worst situations and find a reason to think everything was going to be okay. Kolya, on the other hand, saw shit for exactly what it was.

And this was bad.

Before long, Kolya had slipped into the hallway leading to his hotel room. He could already see from way down the fucking hall that something was wrong. For one thing, the guard tasked with watching Maya for the evening wasn't at his position. Kolya knew the man would likely never be seen from again, as that's just how this shit usually went down. The closer he came to the dark-stained door with the brass number in the middle, the quicker his suspicions became confirmed.

A single crack in the door where it had been left open. Probably because the door couldn't close properly. It looked like someone had kicked the goddamn door open near the knob. Splintered wood littered the threshold of the doorway.

Kolya's chest tightened, and pain coursed through his system as he reached forward to put his palm against the door. He took one quick breath—despite the way it ached—before pushing open the door.

A damn mess welcomed him.

The hotel room had been entirely trashed. Blankets torn off the bed, and the curtains ripped down from the windows. Crystal from the glasses on the wet bar had been shattered across the floor. A chair at the table had been overturned, and what was left of the sandwich on the plate was flipped down the table.

She did *not* go without a fight. That much was fucking obvious. Kolya wanted to take comfort in that fact. In knowing that his girl, who had been so quiet and seemed far too fragile for her own good when he'd first taken her, had decided to shed that bit of meekness.

A huge part of him hoped she kept that up until he could get her back. Because he *was* going to get her back—there was no doubt about that. And then the asshole who took her was going to wish he had never heard the name Kolya Boykov. But until that point … Kolya needed Maya to keep fighting.

Taking a step into the hotel room, his gaze scanned the place and the mess again. It was everything he knew he was going to see, but not what he wanted to face. Those were two entirely different things.

Maybe a part of him was like Konstantin and had been hoping for something different. Maybe because it was Maya … he just *hoped*.

Jesus Christ.

He hated when he was right.

Hope was for the goddamn weak. Hope did nothing but fucking *wreck* a man when it was ripped right out of his bleeding hands.

"Fuck," Konstantin cursed under his breath. He stepped in behind Kolya, and then walked farther in. Kolya said nothing as he watched his brother tip the chair back onto four legs. Konstantin scanned the room with a wary eye before his gaze drifted back to Kolya hesitantly. "It's bad, no?"

"*Da.*"

Konstantin's mouth tipped down into a frown at the quiet darkness that edged along with Kolya's tone. He was *barely* keeping himself contained. He had more self-control than he realized.

"Beyond bad," Kolya muttered.

Konstantin cleared his throat and shifted on his feet. "We have to call—"

Whimpering interrupted his brother from saying more. That sound was quick to make Kolya move to find where it was coming from. Kolya was down on the messy floor in a blink as a back ball of fur peeked out from beneath the bed.

Sumerki's big yellow eyes reflected terror, even at the sight of Kolya stretched out on the floor and reaching for him. The pup crouched lower and scurried back a few inches just out of Kolya's reach.

And then whimpered *again*.

Kolya didn't miss how Sumerki refused to put weight down on one paw, and how his panting seemed heavier than normal. Had whoever come into the hotel room to get Maya hurt the pup? He was *little*. An *animal*.

Practically defenseless.

"Come here," Kolya demanded low. "Let me look at you now."

The dog refused.

Fine, then.

"*Priyekhat'.* Right now."

Sumerki hesitated, but not for long. He'd test an English command if he thought he could get away with it, but never when Kolya spoke in Russian. Even if he had said *exactly* the same thing he'd told him in English, for fuck's sake.

Far too slowly for Kolya's liking, Sumerki worked his way out from beneath the bed. Even being small, the bed was low to the floor, and Sumerki was a tight fit under there. He must have been terrified to smoosh his body under the bed like that.

The second Kolya had the pup in his hands, he stood up and checked the dog out. Just touching the side of his furry body had the dog whimpering again before he let out an even bigger yelp.

That meant *one* thing ...

Kolya's jaw ticked from how fiercely he was clenching his jaw. "Someone kicked him."

And he needed to see a vet. Make sure he didn't have any broken ribs, or worse, internal damage. He would have to get a man to take Sumerki into the emergency vet because he couldn't afford the time that was going to take for him to personally do it.

Already, he was *far too many minutes* behind Maya's brother. Who knew where in the fuck the man planned on taking her? Never mind what he planned to do with her once he got her there. The thought was enough to make Kolya—

"Let me see him, yeah?" Konstantin slipped the dog from Kolya's hands with a cautious look. "You're going to hold him too tight."

Fuck.

"Call someone for him," Kolya said.

"Before or after we call Vadim?" Konstantin asked back. "Better *we* call him and let him know what happened, rather than he finds out from someone else, and he calls *us*. Don't be fucking stupid right now."

Like he needed to be told. Shit, maybe he did need to be told.

Right then, all he wanted to do was find Maya, drink, rage, and kill someone. It did *not* have to be in that order either, as long as he found Maya first.

"Well?" Konstantin demanded.

"Fucking call the bastard, then," Kolya uttered.

He wouldn't be doing it, though.

All it meant was more seconds lost, and more time for Alexei to get far away from him. *With* Maya.

Fuck his whole life.

• • •

How could one tell that a situation was serious when it came to Vadim? Was it when the man was so silent that he seemed statue-like? Or when he raged so violently that anyone in his pathway was in serious danger of being caught in the crossfire?

No, none of those.

It was when Vadim called in *everyone*.

Not every man, no.

Every person in his direct *family*.

Including Viktoria.

Kolya eyed his quiet sister sitting on the other side of the table as Konstantin *again* went over what had happened earlier in the night. Viktoria, out of all of them, was by far their father's favorite. He was still trying to figure out why, but that wasn't important right now. Kolya couldn't figure out why his father had called her in for this, though.

Pointless, really.

"You left your car there?" Vadim asked, dangerously calm.

The drink in his hand swayed back and forth between loose fingertips. Kolya kept one eye on that glass and another on Konstantin. His brother wasn't fucking stupid—he was watching that glass, too.

"What choice did I have?"

"*Make a call*," Vadim barked, his icy gaze turning on his youngest son. "Make a fucking call and get it removed. You do that before you do anything else, Konstantin. We have rules in place, and people at the ready, for this exact fucking reason. You know this, yes?"

"We had other places to be, Vadim."

Vadim turned on Kolya, then. "Yes, the *girl*. You had to chase after her, even knowing she was already taken. That's what Konstantin said. Instead of making sure *nothing* would be left at the bombing for the officials to tie to us—his goddamn *car*—you left it right there because you had to chase after a fucking ghost who was already gone, Kolya. Stupid boy."

That insult might have pissed Kolya off at any other time, but right then, he had far too many other things to be angry about. Vadim was nothing more than a fucking blip on his radar when it came right down to it.

Unfortunately, when Kolya didn't give his father the reaction Vadim was clearly looking for … the man exploded. In typical Vadim fashion, too. That glass he'd been keeping a loose grip on went flying in the next breath. It exploded against the wall right beside Kolya's head in a mess of glass and liquor flying everywhere.

Kolya didn't even flinch. Instead, he let his gaze drift to his now red-faced father as Vadim stood slowly from his seat and never once looked away from Kolya.

Konstantin was a lot like Kolya in that moment—unmoved and unsurprised. Viktoria, on the other hand, hid her discomfort and fear by keeping quiet and staring down at the table. It was easier for the woman to ignore the kind of bastard their father could be to his sons when she didn't have to *watch* it happen, he supposed.

So was the way of their entire fucking lives.

Nothing was soon to change.

"Risking us for a *woman*," Vadim spat. "Again."

Kolya was still entirely unaffected by Vadim, his anger, and whatever the hell he wanted to say. There were other things to handle. More important than this would ever be. He was sick and fucking tired of wasting time.

"If you're done, I have other places to be," Kolya murmured.

"*Why?*"

The volume of Vadim's shout might have busted ear drums or broken glass. Who fucking knew? To Kolya, it just felt like a dull background noise in his already screaming mind. Funny, how that worked.

"Why, *what*, yeah? Be specific, Vadim," Kolya said, entirely over pretending to behave for his father. "I can't read your fucking mind despite how many times you've kicked the shit out of me for not being able to do exactly that."

An uncomfortable shift moved down the table—touching each one of his siblings, but seemingly bypassing Vadim altogether. That was the thing about his father. The abuse Vadim inflicted on his sons was never really *abuse* to him, but rather, lessons for them to take into becoming *vory* and being his children. Nothing more, and nothing less.

"*Why*," his father asked, "if the Albanians took the woman they wanted, did they turn around and also take Grisha's son tonight?"

Kolya stiffened in his seat. Konstantin grew just as still across the table next to Viktoria.

Shit.

Grisha had one child—one adult son.

"*Talk!*" Vadim barked. "They should have got what they wanted, Kolya! Why take another man—my closest man's son? *Talk before I make you speak.*"

Now or never, he supposed. After this, it would be impossible to hide from Vadim that there was more than one person coming after them and their organization. It just wouldn't make sense to his father if the Albanians kept coming at them, even if they supposedly had what they wanted.

"The Albanians didn't take Maya," Kolya said, keeping his tone level. "Or at the very least, the men who have been ordering the hits on our men didn't make the call for her to be taken. They probably don't even know about it right now."

Vadim eyed his son in that deathly still way of his. "Then who did take her?"

"Her brother."

"He's dead. We saw him be killed in the video the Albanians—"

"That was faked … or at the very least, it was faked for *our* benefit. Maya knew that wasn't her brother."

Vadim's fist rhythmically clenched and unfurled over and over at his side. "How on earth would the Albanians *not* know that wasn't Alexei? The man who wants Maya was the one who did business transactions with *my* brigadier, Kolya. They started with Alexei because of that. The Albanians *ordered* the hit on Alexei to start this whole thing. He was the first. He was specifically called out by them because of *who* he was."

"But did *they* know who was under the hood?" Kolya asked back. "Or did they simply trust the word of Valbon, who said that's who it was under the hood?"

"What are you suggesting?"

"Perhaps because there's more going on than what it seems like. Maybe we're not the only ones being fucked around here, no?"

Vadim turned slightly to edge around the corner of the table. It brought him closer to Kolya than he was comfortable with, but there wasn't much he could do except sit there and stare up at his father.

This was Vadim's favorite place to be. *Above* them. Looking down on them. It gave him all the power and left them weak beneath him.

"What I hear you saying to me is that *you* knew Alexei was not actually killed by the Albanians, but you allowed *me* to believe that was the case, yes?"

Kolya opened his mouth to speak, but Vadim was quick to stop him with a raised hand, adding then, "What I understand from your words is that *you* believed there was a second issue coming for us but you had no issue with allowing *me* to believe we only had the main problem with the Albanians to concern ourselves with, correct?"

"You don't actually want me to answer, Vadim. You know the answer."

Fire and furry flashed in his father's gaze as the man murmured, "You knew someone else was attacking us—*me*—and chose not to tell me. That's what you did."

There was a warning lingering heavily in his father's tone. The promise of swift violence if Kolya didn't give Vadim the answer he wanted. The problem was—there was no way for him to lie or hide this anymore.

It was there.

His father *knew*.

It meant betrayal. It meant Kolya had purposely betrayed his father by proxy. Not by outright acting against his father and the Boykovs, but by willingly omitting details that would have affected the way Vadim chose to handle his business.

And Maya.

But that was the thing, right?

Kolya was never going to do anything that put her in danger, and that included Vadim and whatever he fucking wanted.

"When did you suspect this was the case?" Vadim asked quietly.

That violent gleam had yet to leave his father's eye. Vadim continued standing as still as a statue but for the way he kept clenching his fist. The thin thread of control his father was hanging on was just about to snap.

Kolya figured he should get out of the way, but what was the point? If not today, then his father would act against him another day.

It was inevitable.

Kolya wouldn't be able to escape it.

"*When?*" his father asked again.

Kolya's gaze darted to Konstantin, and though his brother wouldn't care or even *ask* for him to do it, he offered the truth in a way that suggested he was the only one who knew. "When Konstantin was attacked in his car—I started looking into things on my own and put two and two together. It made sense."

"*That long?*"

Kolya chose not to answer. His father didn't actually want him to. He expected Vadim to strike out at him, but surprisingly, his father's hand cracked down hard enough on the table to make everyone's glasses jump.

"You betrayed me—*your father*—for a woman. You chose to spit on the legacy I am willing to pass onto you for *that?* Do you even know what you've done?"

Not particularly, but he figured Vadim would be quick to correct that ignorance and teach him. So was his father's ways.

"*Fine,*" his father spat, "you get the woman, Kolya. She's what you want; what you're so willing to fucking ruin everything I've given you for, yeah? Get her, then. But know, absolutely *everything* you take from me has a price. This will not be different and you will pay accordingly. How dare you, Kolya."

It was not even a question.

His father stormed from the kitchen, leaving the three of them sitting in silence.

Konstantin spoke up first—unsurprisingly. "Bad things are coming for us, *brat.* From Vadim, bad things are coming."

No doubt.

He just didn't care.

He needed to get Maya back.

15.

If there was ever a face Maya never wanted to see again, it was Alexei's. His face—although, far less pudgy—reminded her of their father's. Sharp lines and eyes that were so cold they burned when he chose to look at her. It was almost better when he wasn't looking at her—when he was pretending she didn't exist at all. Just like their papa. That alone was more than enough to turn her fucking stomach into a mess of knots.

And *not* the good kind.

"Move," Alexei barked.

His hand hit the spot between her shoulder blades with a rough smack. Maya hadn't been expecting it and stumbled over her own two feet. *Barely* missing a crack in the tarmac that easily would have sent her flying into the pavement.

Even knowing it might encourage her brother's rage to come out and play again—her cheek was already stinging from the incident in the car—Maya glared at him. Alexei's cold gaze simply drifted over her as though she were a nuisance to his life at the moment. Not like *he* had broken down the door of her hotel room and dragged her out kicking and screaming.

He walked ahead of her, then, like he wasn't the slightest bit concerned she might take off. It wasn't really possible, given when she looked over her shoulder, a bull of a man was still standing next to the car that had driven them here. He was bigger than even Kolya, but she didn't think he was nastier.

Probably the same.

Except ... Kolya was never nasty to her.

It didn't matter.

Between Alexei and that guy, there was nowhere for Maya to run. And even if she did, it wouldn't take them very much time to fucking catch up with her. She had to figure out something different if she planned to get out of this alive.

"Hurry up, lazy bitch," Alexei snarled over his shoulder. "Or I will drag your ass inside the plane if I have to. Don't test me tonight. You've done that more than enough for my liking."

"Like you didn't deserve it, no?"

"What was that?"

Maya narrowed her gaze on her brother but refused to speak again. It would only earn her another slap or punch. Hadn't she earned enough of those today?

She'd given him a hell of a fight, sure. That hadn't really made a difference when, in the end, Alexei pulled a gun on her, pointed it right at her temple, and racked the gun with that fucking wild gleam in his eye.

That cold, mean gleam that was *just like their father's*. It brought back a rush of memories that made her want to lose her lunch in an instant. *Years'* worth of abuse and neglect from her own blood because she was just another mouth to feed and an extra body in the house to take care of. She wasn't useful or wanted at all. Not by them.

She had never been.

So, why did he fucking want her *now?*

Maya didn't have time to think about it. Besides, as she eyed the private jet waiting with the stairs already extended and a pilot at the top, she figured there would be lots of time for her to overthink and *plan*.

After all, it wasn't over yet.

"Don't make me tell you again, *suka*."

Huffing under her breath—you would think after all these years, she would be used to the insults and abuse—Maya picked up speed to catch up with her brother simply to avoid another issue. She hated even thinking of him like that; he wasn't *anything* that a family should be. He never had been.

Alexei kept his gaze on the jet, even as Maya slipped into step beside him. At the stairs of the plane, it was then that he grabbed her and forced her to stop. His fingers dug painfully into the delicate skin and muscle of her arm, promising to leave bruises behind from the force alone. With a rough yank on her elbow, he made her look at him.

Maya hated what stared back—features that reflected hers, and blue eyes that were like mirrors of her own. They even had the same dark flecks of navy-blue swirling in the sky-colored irises.

The difference?

Alexei held no warmth in his gaze like Maya did. He felt nothing for anyone except himself. He was only kind when he thought it might benefit him, and it would last as long as it took to get whatever he wanted. His kindness could *not* be trusted.

Right now, though, he wasn't even pretending to be kind.

Her brother had a vicious streak that couldn't be contained—it shone brightly like a promise in his gaze. *That's* what frightened Maya the most. The possibility of what he might do if given the chance.

Not because it was part of his plans—whatever those were—or even because she earned herself something violent, but simply because he fucking wanted to hurt her and would get some kind of sick enjoyment out of it. He'd proven this time and time again over the years.

"You're going to get on that plane and *behave*," her brother told her, never once breaking their staring contest. "You're not going to cause me troubles between here and where we're going. You will *listen* when I tell you something, and you won't make me tell you things more than once. In return, I won't have to beat your ass so badly that you'll need to be carried out of the plane when we land. Do you understand me, Maya?"

Fuck him.

"Haven't you beat the hell out of me enough over the years?" she asked him.

Maya was proud that her voice didn't waver and her tone didn't lower. Her whole life had been spent *cowering* under this man and her father. Hiding away and pretending like she wasn't there at all. Keeping extra quiet because she didn't want to remind them how unwanted and unneeded she was in their daily lives.

Alexei's lips stretched into a cruel smirk. "Well, if you don't want that again, yeah, then you'll behave." He let her go and gestured at the stairs. "Ladies first, no?"

What choice did she have?

Maya tossed one last look over her shoulder before she climbed the stairs of the plane. There was no one coming to save her—no car racing into the private airstrip to save the day. She had to wonder if Kolya even knew she was gone yet.

A cold shiver raced up her spine. It was intense enough to make her hands ball into tight fists at her sides, and it had her breath catching hard in her chest. It was the same feeling she felt whenever she caught Kolya looking at her when he thought she didn't notice.

Like her soul was whispering to her, *Oh, girl, he knows.*

Maya peered over at her brother.

She could have warned him, but he didn't deserve a warning. Besides, she had to figure out how to stay alive.

One thing at a time ...

• • •

Maya stood near the closed door of the plane and waited for it to be opened. The entire flight had consisted of her *trying* to ignore her brother, and not irk Alexei's ire. For now, she still considered that the smart way to go.

"Right then," she heard Alexei muttered, "don't fight too much. I'm not in the mood."

Maya turned to ask her brother what in the hell he meant, but she didn't even get the chance to do that. Alexei came up behind her like a fast snake—appropriate, considering he couldn't be trusted—and slipped a black hood over her head.

Her first instinct was to put her hands up and try to rip the hood off. Alexei was quick to answer that back by tightening a cord around her neck that all but choked her air off completely. Maya *panicked*. She tried to drag in another breath as she pulled on the hood and spun around. Her hip hit something, and she cracked her wrist on something else. The pain was enough to make her want to fall over, but she didn't care.

She couldn't see.

She couldn't *breathe*.

Amused, cold chuckles echoed all around her. It was like her brother got a sick sense of enjoyment out of watching her struggle. Her fear made him happy, the bastard.

That didn't last too long.

Alexei quickly got bored, and before Maya knew what happened, she felt her back hit the floor of the plane as her brother kicked her to the ground. His boots hit her right in the ribs, and his hand fisted into the top of the hood on her head. He yanked on her hair and the goddamn hood as his boot pressed into her stomach to keep her on the ground like she was some kind of animal for him to abuse.

No matter how hard she tried to keep it in, a small cry escaped her lips. She tried to strike out at him, but with little air, fear filling up her mind, and pain echoing through her body … it was entirely pointless. She landed a hit, but she was sure it barely hurt him at all.

In fact, the asshole just laughed at her again.

"I hope this was a good lesson," Alexei said, dragging her up to her feet by the hood and her hair. "You're testing my patience tonight, yeah? *Quit it*."

"What *patience?*"

Even though the words were mumbled behind the hood, her brother still heard them.

"Fair point. Doesn't matter. I need you to behave for the next few minutes. I told him you were pliant and easily controlled. Do *not* prove me wrong, *suka*, or you will not like what happens to you. No one is coming to help. Stop behaving like someone is."

So he thinks.

Maya heard the pressure release in the cabin a second before her brother yanked her along with him. This time, by her arm, thankfully. He didn't direct her where to walk or help her along. She almost stumbled down the steps one too many times, despite how careful she tried to be.

God knew she couldn't run with a broken leg, for fuck's sake.

Maya had no idea where she was with the hood pulled over her head. The place was quiet, and a breeze slipped over her exposed skin. The air smelled like her own breath, and the thick cotton of the hood.

She was distracted by trying to figure out where in the hell she was when a new voice dragged her out of her thoughts.

"I was starting to get tired of waiting, comrade," the unknown male voice said.

His tone was dark and unfamiliar. Smooth, though, and relaxed even. Certainly not like he was staring at a scared, hooded woman in front of him. Or maybe he was used to these kinds of sights—who knew what kind of humans her brother was associating himself with now?

Alexei's grip on Maya's arm tightened to a painful point. "I can't make the flight go any faster, boss."

"Mmm. She's a sprite, no? Tiny thing."

"Yeah, well, for whatever reason … she seems to be something they enjoy looking at, yeah? Between the Albanian and Kolya Boykov, they can't fucking get enough."

The unknown man chuckled. "So it seems, yes. Once we're done ruining the Boykovs in Chicago through the sons, she will be a good bargaining chip to smooth things out with the Albanians and calm their rage. Just what I needed. Well done, Alexei. But you didn't need me to tell you that."

"I do enjoy praise, occasionally."

A scoff answered her brother back. "You won't get much of that from me—don't expect to. How long are we going to stand out here on this tarmac? I have better places to be and good vodka to drink. I think I deserve one after all this. We're almost at the end."

"Do you think this plan of ours is going to work?"

Maya heard the condescending smile in the unknown man's voice when he replied, "It has no reason *not* to work, yes? And once it does, I'll absorb Chicago into my own organization. The entire east coast operation will be mainly controlled by me. And all because someone wanted a *woman*. It'd be funny if it weren't so fucking disgusting. These *boys* have yet to learn that women are very rarely worth this kind of effort." A sigh echoed before the man added, "Are we going, or not? I hate standing around."

"Anytime, boss."

The man muttered something in Russian, too low for Maya to understand what he was saying, before she was dragged along again. She'd figured staying quiet and listening was the better option.

She still had to plan a way out of this, after all.

• • •

It was disconcerting to be shuffled around from place to place like a sack of potatoes. Disorienting might be a better word. Alexei and the other man barely spoke a word to Maya as she was put in one car and then another. They said nothing during the drive except for the occasional order to who she suspected was a driver.

But it was hard to say.

The longer Maya had been forced to keep that hood over her head, the better she dealt with it. It wasn't so claustrophobic and she actually started to feel like she could breathe. She was just getting accustomed to the darkness when she was shuffled from another car and walked for what felt like *forever* before the unknown man spoke.

"Make her comfortable," he said.

"She doesn't give a shit about *comfort*, yeah?"

The man sighed. "I didn't realize that was a suggestion, Alexei."

Her brother grunted under his breath before his hand was back on her arm and his fingers dug into her muscles painfully again. He made no effort to carefully or kindly move her across the room before a chair scraped along the floor, and then he was barking at her.

"*Sit*, Maya."

Like she was a dog or something.

Maya bristled, and had a good mind to tell him to go fuck himself. Her fists clenched in front of her—they'd slipped zip ties around her wrists during one of the drives because apparently, she couldn't be trusted. Not that she had done anything to warrant that kind of treatment.

She chose to sit without a fight, but only because she was tired. Maya wasn't sure how long she had been up for now, but it had to be closing in on twenty-four hours. Getting a second to sit down in something that wasn't moving seemed like a good choice, all things considered.

The second she did sit down, that hood was finally ripped from her head. Maya blinked when bright lights instantly blinded her. It took more than a couple of seconds for her to get used to the change and recognize what she was staring at.

Not fucking much.

A room in a house, it looked like. Nothing spectacular to look at, and it certainly didn't look lived in, so to speak. There were no curtains on the windows, and not a lot of furniture. Alexei was quick to move behind her to loom there like a threat on her back that she couldn't possibly forget.

All the while, her gaze landed on the man sitting across the room from her in the only other chair except for hers. His large, high-back leather chair with curved arms looked a hell of a lot more comfortable than her hard, plastic one. Next to his seat was a small table with a crystal dispenser of what looked like liquor, and he held a matching crystal goblet filled with the same colored liquid.

She took in his older features as he lifted the glass and sipped on his drink while he watched her like she was an animal that might bolt. He appraised her with his gaze, not even bothering to hide the way he lingered on her features, and then traveled down her body.

Maya didn't have time to feel uncomfortable, when she was mostly confused. Who in the hell was this man, and what did he want from *her*?

"Maya, is it?" the man asked.

"That's what my mother called me."

"A good-for-nothing whore," Alexei muttered behind her.

Maya didn't even react to that. She'd heard it time and time again in her life. It wasn't anything new and it barely even stung. She hadn't known her mother—she didn't know if the things her brother and father said were true or not. She didn't care to defend a woman she didn't know.

The unknown man's cold, blue gaze drifted from her to her brother, and then back to Maya again like something had just interested him. What it was, she didn't know. Maya didn't care to ask, either.

"You are a pretty thing, no?" the man across the room asked. He didn't wait for a reply from Maya before adding, "Not *my* preference, but I can see why someone might find you interesting to look at. Some ground rules, then?"

Maya blinked. "What?"

He gestured at her with a hand lined in various golden rings. "While you are here, I do not want to hear or see you unless you're told otherwise. You're to *behave*, and do what is demanded of you. Be pleasant and your stay will be less traumatic."

A thick ball of emotion lodged in her throat. "Just how long am I going to be staying here?"

And who the fuck are you?

The man smiled coldly. "As long as it takes. Now, I have a gift for you, if you're interested. Do keep quiet, and act like a good girl—I am sure you know how to do just that."

Maya had no idea what the man was talking about, but he pulled a phone out of his pocket, and waved it at her. He pressed a button on the screen, and then another before sitting it on the arm of the chair as the sound of a call ringing through started to echo from the speakers.

Her brow furrowed as the call clicked through. Before whoever was on the other end of the line could even greet the caller, the man sitting in the chair said, "She's here, if you'd like to say hello. Keep it short, yeah? My patience for today is already shot."

"Apologies, old friend."

Maya was stuck between the fear coursing through her body all of the sudden at the sound of Valbon Gashi's voice filtering through the phone, and the way the man across the room rolled his eyes at being called *friend*.

She didn't know which one to deal with, not that it mattered. Valbon was speaking this time, but instead of directing his conversation to the man, he was talking to *her*.

"Maya, I've missed you. Beautiful girl, it's been too long. Not too much longer now before you'll be back where you belong."

She sucked in a sharp breath, and it ached in her lungs. On her lap, her tied hands balled into fists all over again, and her fingernails cut into her palms. The pain was enough to keep her fear under control, but she wasn't sure how long it would last.

"I couldn't seem to get my fill of you," Valbon murmured, "not since that first taste, anyhow. So much so, that I even found more ways to indebt your father to me just so I could keep coming back."

His following laughter made Maya *sick*.

She barely held back the vomit.

"I certainly hope the Russian hasn't ruined you for me," Valbon said darkly, "but we will find out soon enough, won't we? Be a good girl, Maya."

The phone call clicked off, and Maya's gaze flew to the man across the room, who picked the device up and slipped it back into his jacket pocket. He seemed entirely unbothered by the fact Maya had no color left to her cheeks and was struggling to take in a decent breath.

Valbon *terrified* her. He took great enjoyment in taking from her in whatever way he could—as though her body were not her own, and she didn't get to choose. When she was in his sights, there was no escaping that fucking man.

If she had a monster, Valbon was it. He was the demon who had latched onto her life, and refused to *die*.

How many times was she going to be put at the feet of that man for his taking before someone showed her mercy?

"Well, that was interesting," the man across the room said.

Maya could only swallow back her fear.

He smiled at her again. "Welcome to New York, Maya. Shame you won't get to see the sights, no?"

16.

KOLYA ITCHED to move. Eyeing those around him who took their sweet fucking time strapping protective gear onto their bodies, he had to beat down the urge to snap at every single one of them to hurry the fuck up and get a move on.

What did they need Kevlar for, anyway?

Didn't they know—

A vest was slammed against Kolya's chest, taking his attention away from the handful of men prepping for their next move. He met his brother's gaze, but he could tell just by the hard set of Konstantin's jaw that his brother was *not* in the mood for an argument from Kolya.

He wondered if his brother was up for a punch in the mouth.

"Put a vest on, *brat*," Konstantin demanded.

The corner of his lip twitched—a slight provocation of a smile, although he was sure it would come out bitter, and dark. "Since when do you care, yeah?"

Konstantin gave him a look. "Put the fucking vest on."

His brother hit him with the vest again and let it go. Kolya caught it before it could drop to the ground. Shit, if putting on the Kevlar meant they were going to get out of this alley quicker and start the show, then he didn't mind doing that.

As it was, Kolya was too numb.

Too *quiet*.

There was a *very* real possibility that if he got Valbon Gashi in his sights tonight—or any fucking Albanian—then things would end badly. He'd been on this train of thought for *three fucking days*.

Too many days, really.

All he was allowed to do while information was gathered to make this move against the Albanians was fucking *think*. Stay stuck inside his head and imagine the worst possible things a man like him could conjure up in his messed-up mind.

If she was hurt …

If she was in any worse condition than he'd left her …

Bad things were coming.

Bad things had a name—it was Kolya.

Konstantin pulled out a rifle from the back of someone's trunk—an AR-15 by the looks of it. The trunk was full of them. He passed the gun to a waiting man, and then gave Kolya another look while he finally strapped on that vest. Maybe a little too tightly, given the way the Velcro bit into his shoulders, but he didn't care.

Everything was an afterthought right now—pain, *care*, and life. Nothing mattered, and he could do without it. If he could forget to breathe until this was over, that'd be fucking perfect. Who needed air, anyhow?

"*What?*" he barked at his brother.

Konstantin straightened with a new rifle in his hands, which he offered to Kolya. He yanked the gun out of his brother's hands while Konstantin murmured, "Nothing. You just look … distraught. That's the right word, yeah? Hopeless."

Kolya's eye twitched and he switched to Russian when he said quietly, "Don't say that."

"The truth?"

"My weakness."

Because Maya was exactly that for Kolya. He was too fucking good at hiding *everything*. The world and people around him knew nothing of Kolya except for what he showed them. How was he ever going to protect Maya when he couldn't hide how he felt about her? How could he protect himself when it was obvious what would be the easiest thing to use to get at him?

For the first time in his life, Kolya felt a genuine fear that wasn't a byproduct of being a boy and hearing heavy footsteps coming after him. A fear that was not a result of someone beating it into him.

He did not know what to do with it.

Konstantin cleared his throat and was quick to look away. "*Prosti.*"

"Let's just go, yeah?"

"Ready whenever—"

It was the sight of a black car pulling up to the mouth of the alleyway that quieted the brothers and the chatter of the other waiting men. All heads turned in that direction as Vadim stepped out of the back of the car. Kolya didn't miss how his father's gaze drifted over each of the men but him—he didn't exist to Vadim at all.

Kolya wasn't sure if he should be concerned about that or not.

"Are we ready?" Vadim asked.

Konstantin arched a brow. "*We?*"

Vadim nodded. "You didn't think you would get anywhere but a war with the Albanians if you went in on them at their main meeting hub without your *Pakhan*, did you?"

"We have reason to—"

"Get killed, yes. Quite aware, Konstantin. I'll come in once you've cleared the place to sit down with Saban. The Albanian leader is not going to take kindly to this action against him, but perhaps I could ease him into less violence once it's said and done, no?"

Vadim didn't care about what happened after this. Of that, Kolya was most sure. But who in the fuck was he to speak against his father's choices? He'd done that enough lately. No need to go poking that monster more than he already had.

"Fine," Kolya uttered, moving away from Konstantin's side, "then let's get this shit show started."

And find Maya.

Vadim once again acted as though Kolya hadn't spoken at all, but he wasn't concerned about that. He had other things on his mind to focus on now—*violent* things. His fingers twitched and itched with the need to get hot, sticky blood coating his skin, while the sound of pain echoed in his eardrums.

Next to getting Maya back, *that* was going to do wonders for his mood. Kolya was sure of it.

Kolya slipped into the black car that he was using for the night and gunned the engine when Konstantin stopped to chat with Vadim for a moment. He didn't have time for this fucking shit. His brother passed him a warning look, but Kolya gunned the engine again.

His silent order to *move*.

Konstantin gave one last nod to Vadim—who knew what the two were talking about—before he joined Kolya in the car. The two-block drive to a dive bar owned by the Albanians passed in silence. The Albanians used the business for all their organization meetings and as a main hub for most other things. Konstantin said nothing and barely moved at all except to resituate his and Kolya's rifles.

Less talking was better.

Talking only pissed Kolya off.

While Konstantin and Kolya drove, the others had to *walk*. That way, it would seem like the Boykovs weren't actually prepared at all to storm the bar. The Albanians would be distracted by their presence and wouldn't notice the ten other men slipping through the front, side, and rear entrances before it was too late.

"All right, let's get to it, yeah?" Konstantin muttered as Kolya parked. "Try to rein in the crazy until we actually get some usable info or we're all going to be fucked, *brat*. Including *her*."

Konstantin didn't give Kolya a chance to respond—to tell him to fuck off; he already knew that—before he pushed open the door and stepped out. Kolya didn't even bother to cut the engine before he got out, too. The leather of his gloves tightened around his hands as he gripped the rifle tighter. Standing slightly shadowed by the corner of a neighboring building with a streetlight busted out above their heads, the Albanian watching the door of the bar couldn't see them until it was too late, and they'd stepped out of the shadows.

Kolya already had his rifle aimed and his finger wrapped the trigger. It was Konstantin's voice drifting through his violent thoughts that stopped him from pulling the trigger back.

"Don't earn us another blood debt, yeah?"

Ah, fuck.

Why did Konstantin always have to make the smart choices?

The Albanian stumbled back against the door.

"*Run,*" Kolya snarled. "Or we're all going to get to see what your brains look like when they paint a fucking door after coming out the back of your skull. *Run.*"

The man did just that.

"See, you could do that more often," Konstantin muttered as they opened the bar's front door. "Scare people, I mean. You don't have to go straight to violence first."

"Says who?"

Because Kolya *liked* violence.

It worked for him.

The brothers didn't waste time once they were inside the bar. A few thousand dollars into the right hands had given them floor plans and all the information they'd needed as to what the inside of this place looked like, and where the important shit went down. It was a Friday night—Fridays always meant Saban's men showed up to pay their dues while he sipped on expensive liquor in a private section of the bar.

Kolya was the first of the two brothers to enter the main floor of the bar. He pulled back the trigger on his rifle in quick succession and let bullets pepper a wall, bottles on shelves behind the bar, and even the ceiling. The noise and surprise attack sent several people to the floor to protect what they could—fucking predictable.

With the few extra seconds that gave them, Kolya and Konstantin quickly slipped through the bar to the back rooms. Kolya kept his AR aimed at *anyone* who looked like they might shoot back.

"*Fuck,*" Konstantin muttered as they rounded a corner.

There, at the end of the hallway, two Albanians stood with their own weapons already aimed and ready to fire. They'd expected this to happen, but Konstantin always liked to have hope that shit would be easier than it was. He was the optimist—Kolya was the fucking realist.

There they stood like a bunch of fucking idiots with guns aimed at the Albanians while they stared down their fucking guns, too.

"There's no exit out of that room you're trying to protect," Kolya told the men, "so how about you step the fuck aside, and let us go talk to Saban, yeah?"

The one on the left spat something at them in a language Kolya couldn't understand. Already, he was sick and tired of this shit. Entirely over it and ready to draw some blood.

"Relax," Konstantin murmured.

"*Stop pointing it out*," he barked back.

His brother rolled his eyes. He was seriously going to punch Konstantin for this shit.

They didn't have to play chicken for very long with the two fools. The backup they'd been waiting for stormed the bar with bullets flying. Kolya smirked a bit as Russians started to fill up the hallway behind him.

Not all ten, no.

A few had to stay on the floor.

It was still enough to well outnumber the two down the hall.

Then, Vadim came, too. The men separated for their Pakhan to walk through without a word. Including Konstantin and Kolya. Vadim didn't pass them a look, but he came without a weapon in his hands and no Kevlar strapped to his chest like the rest of the men.

Maybe his way of being so fucking arrogant it was ridiculous, but it was more likely his way of offering a hand of trust to the Albanians.

Or both.

Likely both.

Vadim smiled. "Tell Saban he has a meeting with Vadim Boykov, and I don't like to wait."

His father offered those words to the waiting men but said them more than loud enough for whoever was inside the private room to hear. It took all of ten seconds for one of the Albanian's head to turn to glance inside the room before he came back to Vadim with a nod.

Wordlessly, they stepped aside.

Kolya almost let out a sigh of relief. There really was no other way this could have ended, what with their plans, but sometimes, people got fucking cocky. One could never prepare enough and trust that *everything* would go exactly as planned.

Vadim gestured with one hand for the men to go ahead of him. Kolya went first, with Konstantin and the rest following behind. Guns lifted and aimed. Ready to shoot the first thing that moved.

The men inside the room sitting around various couches and chairs were not an unexpected sight. Given this was the night Saban's men came to pay him, they expected Albanians. A lot of them.

Hoped for it, really.

There was only one Kolya really gave a fuck about. The moment he laid eyes on him in the corner—Valbon Gashi—that's where he went. Kolya dropped the pretenses; he no longer cared about the fucking *plan*.

The barrel of his rifle met Valbon's head so hard that the man's skull cracked against the plaster of the wall behind him. Kolya was sure his gaze burned with iciness as the Albanian stared up at him.

"*Where the fuck is she?*" Kolya demanded.

Valbon smiled. "Who, Russian?"

Oh, his fucking finger twitched on the trigger. But if he killed this dumb fuck right *now*, he wouldn't get what he wanted.

"Step back from my cousin," came the accented voice across the room. *Saban.*

Kolya didn't move an inch. In fact, he pushed the barrel against the man's forehead again. "Where is Maya?"

Valbon laughed lowly. "I don't know—"

"Do you understand that I will pull out your insides and let you hold them while you're still alive, just because I think it'd be a good lesson for you?" Kolya asked. "Keep fucking with me, Valbon. Test me."

"Kolya, that's quite enough."

He still didn't move, but the voice of his father did quiet his threats. He refused to put the gun down, though.

A sigh echoed.

Vadim.

Again.

"As you can see, Saban," Vadim murmured, "my son has taken issue with your man."

Saban laughed bitterly. "Shouldn't it be the other way around, old friend? Did your son not take something that belonged to Valbon? I hope you know you're going to have to answer for this show, here."

Vadim hummed quietly. "I think not. What do you know about the first Russian from my organization that you killed? Alexei Kozlov, hmm."

Koyla didn't miss how Valbon's gaze darted away from him and the man stiffened. He didn't move too much though. He still had that gun pressing against his forehead, after all.

"He seemed like the best one to start with, as he was directly related to the issue at hand," Saban stated. "As I am sure you're aware, yes?"

"Because Valbon gave you that information," Vadim stated.

"Who else would I have gotten it from?"

Vadim made a noise under his breath and then someone shuffled in the room before a familiar video—one that Kolya had watched far too many times over the last day—began to play. The sound was all Kolya could hear, but he knew what was playing on the screen for Saban to see.

Alexei forcing Maya out of the hotel just a couple of days ago.

"As you can see," Vadim murmured when the video was done, "Alexei is very much alive, and apparently quite well."

"He is not—"

"He is alive," Vadim countered before Saban could refuse it. "But Valbon said the man you killed was Alexei, correct? How could—or *why* would—he be mistaken? He was the one making the deals with Ivan Kozlov—he'd *know* who was whom within the Kozlovs. He wouldn't be *mistaken*, would he? Would he have *any reason at all* to want Alexei to remain alive while you assumed he was dead?"

Saban was quiet for a moment. "I'm not following where this is going, Vadim."

"Did he lie, Saban? Did he tell you that was Alexei?"

"Why would he—"

Valbon jerked forward a bit like he wanted to stand and speak, but Kolya was pressing that rifle against his forehead so hard that the man was pinned where he sat. It would have been almost fucking amusing, if Kolya weren't itching to beat the life out of this asshole for all the things he had done to Maya. Was still doing.

The man's need to move and attempt at it wasn't missed by the others in the room if the way their answering silence was any indication.

"Did you know that Maya had been removed from my son's possession?" Vadim asked.

Kolya swore he heard teeth crunch across the room.

"I was unaware—we took another man for that reason," Saban murmured.

"Yes, my right hand's son. Is he …?"

"Quite dead, I'm afraid."

Vadim's exhale echoed. "Well, then."

"The logical explanation you're offering to me is that Valbon is working with Alexei, then?" Saban asked.

"It is always the most obvious explanation that is usually correct," Vadim returned.

"Valbon?" Saban asked.

"I don't know what he's suggesting," Valbon muttered through gritted teeth. "Why would I do something like that?"

"*Valbon*," Saban said darker, a threatening edge coating the man's name.

"I don't know—"

"The better question is *why*," Vadim interjected quietly, "your own family would be willing to risk being caught by you for lying and likely killed for a woman … doesn't seem reasonable to me, all things considered. Something else to *sweeten* the deal, perhaps? We have reason to believe there is someone else involved in this with Alexei and Valbon, only because that makes the most sense. Together, they have nothing to gain. If someone else was funding this or moving their pieces, then we could correct everything that has happened. I was hoping *you* might be able to help me with that, no?"

Saban was quiet for a moment, and Kolya glanced over his shoulder to find the Albanian boss was nailing Valbon to the wall with his burning gaze. "It seems you already know quite a bit, Vadim. What can I possibly help you with?"

"The other evening—when the girl was taken—a business blew up. My sons were in front of it."

Kolya didn't miss the narrowing of Saban's eyes.

Vadim continued on. "Seems that shop is owned by Valbon, but he isn't known for his bombs, is he?"

"He isn't. And he *owned* that—it is no longer his, as of a few weeks ago."

Kolya stiffened.

Like Valbon.

And Vadim.

"Who does it belong to?" Vadim asked, a genuine curiosity lighting up his tone. "I am sure you, like me, know all of your men's business in that sense, even if *they* don't know you know it. So, who?"

They figured—if they found who set the bomb, they would be one step closer to whoever was working with Valbon. It was another piece of the puzzle, that was all.

"Don't," Valbon uttered to his cousin, a pleading gleam in his eyes. "Saban, you don't understand—"

"You *lied* to me," Saban said back without emotion before he told Vadim, "Vasily Markovic bought the business a short while ago while in Chicago. As far as I know, the papers have not been finalized, which is why it will still be showing as Valbon's."

Kolya's grip on his gun loosened slightly.

No fucking way.

Vadim, on the other hand, had turned into stone. "Is that so?"

"Yes. I was assured any deals made with Vasily would be *to our benefit*, according to Valbon. I'm wondering now why that is."

"As you should," Vadim murmured. "Please, keep Valbon alive for now. He may be useful. I would appreciate it."

Saban was quiet for a spell before he replied, "My apologies to your men—we will rectify what has happened, Vadim."

"I'm concerned it may be a bit late."

"I certainly hope not." Saban shifted in his chair. "What else can I do for you tonight, to begin correcting this process?"

Vadim gestured at the man Kolya was still holding hostage. "You can make him tell us everything we need to know to retrieve the woman."

"Fuck you, you—"

"*Shut up!*" Saban barked at Valbon.

Vadim continued on like the exchange hadn't even happened. "He clearly has information—we need it."

Saban stood from his chair, and Kolya saw from the corner of his eye as the man opened a hand up to the Albanian beside him. A knife was handed over. "Give me an hour, then."

• • •

Kolya gazed over the flickering lights on the tarmac just outside the port windows of the plane as the wheels finally touched down. New York was not *unfamiliar* to him in a sense of what and where it was. As a place he enjoyed being, though? That sentiment couldn't be further from the truth.

The jet's wheels bounced on landing, which made a few people sitting around him shift in their seats, clearly uncomfortable.

Kolya didn't care. He had other things on his mind. He was so fucking close to Maya now that he could practically feel it thrumming in his heart. A solid, steady beat that threatened to entirely throw him off his game if he didn't *focus*.

"Saban was sure?" he heard Vadim ask from the next row over.

"Positive."

His father grunted something indecipherable. Saban had needed *less* than an hour, actually, to draw all the information he wanted to get out of Valbon. Including how he'd agreed to work with Vasily through Alexei because he figured it would be better for the Gashi organization in Chicago once the Markovic bastard took over the Boykov faction.

Kolya wished he could be surprised that Vasily Markovic was involved, and basically the brains of this whole operation. He couldn't be too shocked, though, because snakes were always going to be snakes at the end of the day.

God knew Vasily had a hard fucking nut for Chicago—always had, too. Some things never changed, and nothing was as it appeared in this business.

The only good thing about this whole shitshow?

Kazimir wasn't involved.

He might be the *only* Markovic man next to his brother who would come out of this unscathed once Vadim was done with all of them. But that really depended on a hell of a lot of things, too.

And Vadim was fickle.

The plane taxied to the end of the runway, but Kolya was already unsnapping his belt and getting up to walk to the front. He didn't feel the need to wait, even as the one flight attendant on the private jet asked him to sit back down until the plane stopped moving. He simply brushed her off with a wave of his hand, and a glare.

Vadim spoke as Kolya waited near the front of the plane. "You may take one man with you to help with getting the woman back."

Kolya passed his father a look. *One man?* What good would one man do for him? "Why did we bring a small army, then?"

Not really a small army—about ten Boykov men who were willing and capable of doing something like this. Storming a warehouse, and removing something—or in this case, *someone*—from within before disappearing without a sign that they were there to begin with other than the carnage they left behind.

Vadim tipped his chin up as arrogant as ever. "They are here for *me*."

Ah.

Once again, Kolya was unsurprised.

"One man," his father repeated. "Pick one."

Kolya quickly ran through the men on the plane, and which ones had the skills that might be most useful to him in this moment.

Konstantin was quick to speak up. "I would like to go with him, then. I will go as a third."

Vadim didn't even pass his youngest son a look before he flicked a wrist at him. "No, you will stay."

"But—"

"Repeating myself is not required. I gave my answer."

Konstantin met Kolya's gaze, and a genuine concern reflected back. He didn't know what the point of this was with Vadim, but he was sure it would become clearer over time. So was Vadim's ways.

"Besides," Vadim added, "Vasily expects an army, I am sure. Why send what he wants? And frankly, Kolya, you are not worth very much to me now, not after all you've done. Why would I risk those who do matter for the whims of one who doesn't?"

Kolya stared, unaffected, at his father. "So be it."

He would do this alone.

He *could*.

And he would not fail; he couldn't.

"It's okay," he told Konstantin when it looked like his brother was going to speak up again. "It's fine, yeah?"

But it wasn't.

It couldn't be.

• • •

Kolya stared down at the information on his phone—a single text from Konstantin that confirmed everything he had been wondering about but hadn't had the time to check in or ask for himself.

Sumerki is doing well—cracked rib; he'll be fine for pick up tomorrow.

Following that message had been a second confirmation of the address to the warehouse in Little Odessa where Maya had supposedly been moved to over the last couple of days. Originally, according to a *very* broken Valbon, she'd first been placed in a house outside of the city limits. Vasily moved her after she'd thrown a glass at him when he'd invited her to eat with him.

That's my girl.

Slipping the phone into his pocket, Kolya leaned against the back of a rental as the one man he'd been allowed to bring along readied his gear. Strapping on Kevlar and pulling out what few weapons they actually had.

None of it was going to help.

Kolya knew it.

"The warehouse is what, three blocks down, yeah?" Roman asked.

Kolya nodded. "About that, from the info I have."

"Be better to sneak in from a side door or something, wouldn't it?"

Probably.

What did it matter as long as they *got in*?

When Kolya didn't answer the man, Roman passed him a look. "Are you not suiting up?"

"I don't see the point."

He had one goal here—to get Maya *out*. Or at the very least, lay eyes on her before it all went to shit. Then, at least she would know somebody fucking gave a shit about her. Somebody cared enough to *try* and save her.

Hadn't she been forgotten enough in her life? Hadn't she been the afterthought for too long? She was none of those things to Kolya.

"This is a suicide mission," Roman muttered.

Kolya pulled his favorite leather gloves out of his pocket and slid them onto his hands with firm tugs. *Time to get to work.* "Can't think of a better place to die, no?"

Or rather, he couldn't think of anyone other than Maya that he would die for at the end of the day. Besides, he'd been ready to die the moment Vadim put that fucking thieves cross on his chest—it seemed appropriate that he was probably going to die for the very woman he betrayed that cross for.

Yeah, why the fuck not?

17.

MILDEW HAD a distinct smell. Musty and wet. Maya could handle the smell of mildew without it turning her stomach if it was for a passing moment—*two days*, though? Her empty stomach was rolling. Add that onto the cold, damp pavement that had been her bed and her body was screaming for some kind of relief.

She would get none.

Her hands had been bound at her back, and her legs tied at the ankles. Not to mention, a gag put in her mouth because Vasily had gotten *tired of hearing you make noise with that hole in your face*. That was part of the reason she was in this stupid warehouse to begin with. Because she wouldn't shut up and she pissed him off.

That wasn't the only reason.

Far from it.

Maya's gaze slid to the corner of the room and landed on *it*. A bomb the size of a small chest. A man she didn't recognize had wheeled it into the room on a fucking cart that morning. Vasily followed behind with a grin that would rival the devil's when Maya started shouting behind her gag.

The only thing he'd said?

"It starts counting down when the door opens. Let's see how Vadim does when I take out a good portion of his men at once."

He hadn't lingered after that to listen to Maya hurl insults at him behind his gag. It wasn't even Vadim that she gave a shit about. It was *Kolya*. Vasily's words implied someone was coming for her and he knew it. He acted accordingly with the bomb because he expected people to show up *here*.

One of them would be Kolya.

Of course, it would.

Maya felt useless. She couldn't warn anyone like this, but certainly not Kolya. She knew exactly why Vadim had put two minutes on the timer—it took far more than two minutes to get to where she was in this huge warehouse.

It was a *maze*.

There was no way they were getting out.

Maya rolled from her back to her knees, ignoring the way her wrists protested from having been pinned between her back and the cement for so long. She wasn't sure how long she'd stared up at the cracking, peeling paint on the ceiling but she needed to do something—anything—different.

On her knees, she was practically eye-level with the bomb across the room. The small screen resting on top of the main components blinked with red numbers. *2:00.* It wasn't even counting down yet and already, it was taunting her.

And there was absolutely nothing she could do.

Nothing but pray.

• • •

Maya was in and out of a semi-state of consciousness when the noise started somewhere outside of the room that had become her cell. Despite not wanting to sleep, her body gave in after days of being awake nonstop. Not that it was restful, far from it. The slightest noise in the room or outside of it would have her jerking wide awake all over again.

She was more tired than ever.

But these new sounds ...

Shouting.

Banging.

Russian.

"Maya! *Govorit', dushka!*"

It took her a second and then two. Another shout of *him* calling her name and asking where she was. Sure, she heard another man's voice alongside his, but she didn't care about that one. The only person she cared about was Kolya.

Because *fuck*, he was there.

He was *there.*

And they were going to die.

Somehow, Maya managed to get her aching body back to her knees. Carefully balancing on shaky legs, she got up to her feet, too. Her mouth started working before her brain could catch up to speed with the rest of her. Because as much as she wanted to see him, maybe she could save him. If not herself, then at least he would be okay.

"Don't come in here, Kolya!"

As soon as the words passed her lips, she heard the first kick hit the door. Not that he would have been able to understand anything she said with the gag in her mouth. Every word was muffled and garbled coming out. Fuck. *No.* He couldn't come in here—he *couldn't.*

"*Don't!*"

A sob ripped past Maya's dry, cracked lips even as the door broke from Kolya's second kick, and he stormed the room. Substantial in size, shadowed by the dark hallway despite the dim light in the room, and looking straight at her. The gun in his hand was tossed to the side as he came forward.

Maya felt the hot tears slip down her cheeks the second his hands were on her face. His hard gaze drifted over her for a quick second before he pulled that gag out of her mouth and tossed it aside.

"Kolya—"

"Shh."

That was all he said before his lips were on hers. A harsh kiss that ached and stung at the same time. For a moment, that was all that mattered. His kiss in a room that she wanted to disappear from. His kiss in a world that was soon to end for them.

This took it all away.

His thumbs stroked her cheekbones.

"I'm sorry," he murmured.

Maya shook her head wildly. "We have to *go*."

"We are." He let out a heavy breath as his hands slid down to feel the zip ties at her wrists, and his gaze found the ones on her ankle. "Let's get you untied first."

"But—"

"*Maya*."

"The *bomb*, Kolya!"

At her exclamation, a new voice at the doorway muttered, "Holy shit. It's counting down.*"

Maya followed Kolya's gaze to find the bomb still waiting in the corner. Only now, there were twenty seconds gone from the timer. And a low beeping had started to echo from the device.

"That's big enough to flatten this place, yeah," the man said faintly.

"Get out," Kolya uttered.

"*What?*"

Deathly calm, and with a grip on Maya that *hurt*, Kolya's words slipped out again with that same coldness. "Get the fuck out. Run."

"Kolya—"

"*Go!*"

A cold spike of dread slammed into Maya's spine. Kolya still hadn't looked away from that bomb, and she had no idea what was running through his mind. Usually, she could find what she needed to see in his eyes, but even there, he just looked dead.

"There's not enough time to get—"

"Then jump out a fucking *window!*" Kolya snarled.

The man in the doorway didn't need to be told again. He spun on his heel and bolted away. Kolya worked fast, then, too. Maya didn't even get the chance to see where he pulled a knife from before he was bending down and dragging the blade through the binds at her ankles. A rough hand turned her around before he did the same thing to her wrists.

She felt how close he was to her back when he murmured in her ear, "Can you run, *dushka?*"

Maya's gaze drifted to the bomb again. *One minute, thirty seconds left.* She nodded.

"Run straight, hit the stairs. *Go.*"

His hand hit her back and Maya ran. She didn't know where she was going. In her panic at being dragged inside this place, she hadn't thought she would need to memorize the layout. All she remembered was that it was full of hallways, and rooms. Like a goddamn maze. She simply did what Kolya said.

Run straight. Hit the stairs.

Though she wanted to look behind her and make sure Kolya was coming, she didn't. She could hear his heavy steps echoing behind her anyway.

Maya was halfway down the stairwell when Kolya's voice shouted out behind her, "Keep going down!"

Maya tried to remember how many fucking stairs she had climbed before they dragged her down that last hallway. Three, maybe?

It didn't matter.

She flew down the stairs, and almost stumbled on the way. A strong hand was there to catch her by the back of her shirt and set her back to her feet again with another shove for her to keep going.

Maya pushed open the heavy metal door at the very bottom of the stairs and came to a sight she did remember. A large, open section of the bottom floor that still wasn't anywhere *near* the front of the warehouse. Maybe the middle? It was full of junk and shit. Like someone had used this space as their own personal dumping grounds for *everything* over the years. Everything from taped up boxes, to leftover furniture. There were even metal and plastic barrels in one corner, and an iron claw foot tub resting against another wall.

"Oh, my God," she mumbled at the sight.

How long did they have, now?

Thirty seconds?

Less?

It was impossible. They were never going to get out in time.

"There's no way—"

Maya didn't even get to finish her sentence before Kolya's arm wrapped around her middle, and her feet left the cold cement floor. Her vision swam from how fast he moved, then.

"You stay *down,*" he uttered.

"What—"

"Stay down—stay under me. You stay like that *no matter what*, yeah?"

Maya blinked through the curtain of her hair covering her face. She couldn't ask him what in the hell he was talking about because he set her to the floor again. Maya turned in just enough time to see Kolya grab the edge of that iron claw foot tub and flip it over with a bang that echoed through the warehouse. He lifted it up and jerked his head toward the tub.

"Get under there, now."

This man was *crazy*.

Maybe it was her that made him like this—totally unbidden, and willing to do the more insane shit because it was *her*, and he was willing to take that chance. Who knew?

Maya stared at him. "Kolya …"

"*Get under it.*"

There was no point in arguing, but she had serious fucking doubts this was going to save them. But what did it matter? If they died under a fucking tub or running for an exit that wouldn't come … it didn't make a difference.

They were still going to die.

But at least they would die together.

Maya got down on all fours and crawled under the tub. All over again, cold cement met her back, and scraped against her already tender skin. She couldn't find it in herself to care—what would the pain and discomfort matter in a few short seconds, anyway?

Kolya was quick to slip under the tub and let it go at the same time. The heavy weight of the iron coming down hit Kolya against the back and sent him sprawling over Maya. His body practically suffocated her as his arms wrapped around her head, and he pulled her as tightly as he could get her against his chest.

Even in their last moments, he protected *her*. He used his body to shield her. He was willing to take the hit on the off chance she might be okay.

Maya shivered.

Cried.

How many seconds left?

Ten?

Five?

"Kolya—"

"It's okay," he murmured against her hair, his lips moving fast but soft. It wasn't okay.

And this was *not* the best time.

"I love you," Maya said. "I *do*."

She did—more than anything else in the world. How could she not?

Kolya stiffened. "*Dushka*, I have—"

The noise was deafening.

The pressure, *painful*.

The bomb blew.

And the world went dark.

• • •

Something heavy—*way* too heavy—pinned Maya to a hard, flat surface. Her back ached, and no matter how much she tried, she couldn't get whatever was on top of her to get off. Even as she forced her eyes open, a bright glare burned her irises. She couldn't focus enough to see what was on top of her, never mind where she was.

Blinking and blinking and *blinking* … she willed her mind and body to cooperate. Disoriented didn't come close to describing what she felt in those first few seconds. Her head pounded. A deep, constant pain in the base of her skull that just wouldn't let up.

"*Help*," she gasped. "*Someone, help me.*"

No one answered her back, and the heavy weight keeping her pinned down didn't move, either. Maya turned her head to the side to find … nothing staring back at her. Well, not nothing really. But a confusing mess of a space.

She could feel a breeze and see the sun above her. Smoke curled from the blackened masses around her, and ash drifted down like snowflakes in the air. With every breath she sucked in, more of that smoky ash filled her lungs.

Was she outside?

How had—

Maya's gaze caught sight of a misshapen, blackened tub just ten feet away. Overturned so that it was sitting on its claw feet—although two were broken, now—she *remembered*.

She remembered everything.

The warehouse was gone—flattened to the ground. A smoldering lump of blackened ruins in the middle of … God knew where.

"Kolya," Maya breathed. "*Kolya!*"

That's what—or rather, who—was on her, she realized. It was still his body keeping her pinned to the ground in an attempt to add an extra level of protection from the blast.

Finally, Maya forced her head up. Kolya hadn't moved all that much except lower. No longer was her head tucked against his chest, but instead, exposed to the air and breeze. Only one of his arms were still wrapped around her body, but his other was extended straight out, and … bleeding.

Maya blinked again.

She struggled to get her arms free from under his weight just so that she could touch him. She ran shaking fingers through his hair, and over the sides of his slackened, dirty face. Ash that littered his hair, and a streak of it muddied his cheek. She couldn't see him well enough to discern much more, but she could feel by the way his back moved that his breaths were shallow, and far too fast.

"Kolya, get up," Maya mumbled. "*Wake up.*"

Nothing.

"Kolya!"

Pain saturated her body, and something gripped her heart far too tightly.

"*Kolya, wake up!*"

Why wouldn't he wake up?

Maya hit his back with her fists and couldn't stop the sob from slipping past her lips. She needed him to wake up. "Please wake up."

In the background of her screaming thoughts and panic, Maya heard two things. Sirens, and a garbled ringing. Blood rushed her ears and her fear climbed impossibly higher. She struggled to find where the ringing was coming from, even as voices started yelling all around her.

First responders?

Cops?

Maya found the ringing phone in Kolya's pocket. It took all of her exhausted strength to pull the device out and hit the answer button. She couldn't, however, get the phone back over Kolya's large arm to bring it to her ear. She could see the screen, though, and despite it being half blacked out with a crack, she saw enough of a name.

Kon.

"Konstantin," Maya mumbled hoping to God it was loud enough for the man on the other end of the call to hear. "Help us. *Please help us.*"

• • •

There was something uncomfortable about hospitals, although Maya couldn't quite put her finger on exactly what it was that made her feel that way. Maybe it was the fact that they all smelled the same, and in a way, looked similar, too. Never mind the fact that it was never a good thing when someone was *stuck* in a hospital.

Maya tried to offer Konstantin a thankful smile when he dropped a blanket around her shoulders, and then his hands squeezed her gently before he sat down in the chair next to hers. The first thing she noticed about the blanket was the fact it was warm—and hospital issued. After all, it was the same style as the ones the nurses had tucked around Kolya earlier.

You know, right before they'd asked her to leave his room.

"Thanks," Maya whispered.

She didn't have much of a choice but to whisper, really. Her throat was raw from smoke inhalation, crying, and shouting. Not to mention the two-hour long interview with detectives that ended the same way it began: with Maya saying she couldn't remember anything while a lawyer hired by Vadim stood at her back with beady eyes trained on her.

"No worries, yeah?" Konstantin gave her a smile. "Stole it from a cart down the hall."

Maya laughed. "That's for the *patients*, Konstantin."

"Like you shouldn't fucking *be* one?"

Fair point.

Maya only shrugged and grew quiet again. Konstantin didn't seem to mind joining her in that, but she wasn't surprised. From the moment he walked into the hospital, he'd stuck to her side like fucking glue. The only time he'd had to leave her on her own was when the detectives came into play.

But even as his father stood across the family waiting room—stoic, silent, and foreboding—Konstantin didn't leave Maya. She wondered, if the way Vadim kept glancing their way with that cold, furious expression of his, if Konstantin was making some kind of silent statement to his father.

She didn't know.

It wasn't the time to ask.

"He's going to be fine, by the way," Konstantin said quietly. "Once he wakes up."

"*If* he wakes up," she countered.

Konstantin shook his head and chuckled darkly. "Kolya wouldn't go out this easily. He's just taking a break, that's all."

Maya dragged in a painful breath and *hoped* Konstantin was right. But she didn't know if he was, and that's what killed her the most. She said those words—three little words that might seem insignificant to some people, though *not* to her—and Kolya didn't even get the chance to say them back.

Would he?

Did he love her?

Maya caught the stiffening of Vadim across the room as his gaze left her and Konstantin, and drifted to the doorway of the private family waiting room. *Stunned* did not do her current feelings justice when she found who was standing there in the doorway.

Vasily Markovic.

The men who had filled the chairs earlier all stood quickly. Vadim, on the other hand, simply straightened to his full height, and tipped his chin up as if to look down on Vasily. The other man gave a sly smile.

"He survived then, comrade?" Vasily asked, sounding entirely too smug for his own good.

Vadim's jaw flexed. "Seems so."

"Lucky man. Shame the other man didn't make it." Vasily sighed and passed a glance to Maya before going back to Vadim just as fast. "I expected more to be in the warehouse than what was there. Why choose that move, Vadim? Why risk sending your son up against ... whatever I had waiting practically alone?"

"You think I didn't *know* what you had planned for him in there?" Vadim countered just as fast. This time, it was his turn to smile. "You think Valbon didn't tell us you had a kill switch if it all went bad—the *bomb*? You're a snake, but unlike Valbon who didn't know that, I do, Vasily. You can never turn your back on a snake. Not like Valbon did, because snakes like you are quick to bite then. You were never going to give him the girl— the kill switch would have been your default, no matter what."

Maya heard what Vadim said and what it meant.

She heard him and it killed her.

"It was never about the Albanians or the girl," Vadim continued on, unaffected and cold, "it was always just about Chicago, and me. The *Boykovs*. The thing you've always wanted but can't have. Tell me I'm wrong. Go on, do it."

"You were willing to kill your son, then, *knowing*," Vasily murmured.

"Better you kill him than what I will do to him when he wakes up," Vadim returned softly.

Konstantin stiffened beside Maya.

What did that mean?

What did that fucking mean?

Vasily smiled again and nodded. "Until next time, no?"

"Next time, I will slaughter you, Vasily."

"You can certainly try, Vadim."

Vasily was quick to turn and leave then. Maya figured … it was smart of him, too. Vadim looked about three seconds away from ripping someone's face right from their skull. The second the man was gone, Vadim gestured with a hand at the rest of the people in the room.

"Everyone out, yes, but her. Go."

Konstantin stayed sitting.

Vadim gave him a look. "Even *you*."

"She's—"

"Fine," Vadim interjected sharply. "She will be fine."

Men started to filter out of the room as Konstantin stood. He passed Maya a glance, and then followed suit. He closed the door behind him, leaving her alone with Vadim.

The older man sat in the chair across from her and stared at her for longer than she was comfortable. He crossed one ankle over his knee and surveyed her with his forefinger and thumb resting on his jaw like she was the most boring thing in the world he had ever laid eyes on.

"I imagine you hate me," he said.

Why lie?

"Hate isn't a good enough word," she whispered.

A hint of a smile graced Vadim's lips. "You're quite a defiant thing for

… well, whatever you seem like. You're going to need that, Maya."

"Fascinating."

Something flashed in his gaze—annoyance, maybe.

She wished she cared.

Vadim tipped his head back and nodded once. "It *was* better he died in that warehouse with the thing he was so willing to die for, rather than face the consequences of his actions against me."

Maya's brow furrowed. "What are you talking about?"

"More than you or he knows," Vadim murmured. "You see, even when my son thinks I don't know something, I still eventually find out. On your back … may I see your brand, please?"

He posed that as though she had a choice, but Maya knew better. There was no choice. She was grateful that Konstantin had closed the door because it allowed her some privacy as she stood and shrugged off the warm hospital blanket.

Turning around, she lifted her shirt up high enough to show off the two eight-pointed stars just below her neckline.

"He is smart, but he is also stupid. That is not the brand you were to have, girl."

"They're his stars."

"I am quite aware of that, and what they mean for me." Vadim made a quiet noise. "You may sit back down, Maya."

She did, and quickly tucked herself back into the blanket.

"A final line between him and I. That's what those stars mean to me. Whatever ties were between the two of us are gone—irreparably fractured. He may find it worth it today, but it is tomorrow that he will understand the price he must pay for this." Vadim stood from his own chair, then. "Regardless of what happens now, trust that *you* will be okay. Kolya, however … well, he survived the first round, yes? For now, he gets to keep you. Let's see if he can survive what happens next."

Maya was too scared to ask what that meant.

18.

THE NURSE gave Maya a sweet smile as she gestured toward the open doorway with a nod of her head. "Go ahead; he's been asking for you."

Maya wrung her hands, and glanced between the doorway, and the nurse. "Yeah?"

Two days of her asking time and time again to see Kolya had been refused. He wasn't awake, they kept saying. And then when he was, he was disoriented and angry. Maya had laughed when they'd told her *that*.

They didn't know Kolya *at all*.

He was angry anyway.

That's just what he was.

"Yep, go on," the woman said.

Maya didn't need to be told again. She darted forward and slipped past the dimly lit threshold of the room. A curtain had been pulled all the way around Kolya's hospital bed so she couldn't see him at all when she first entered.

He must have heard footsteps, though, because his first words were, "I swear to fucking God if someone came in here to poke me again or *talk*, and it isn't Maya, we're going to have a problem."

The nurses were right. He did sound pissed. Not any more than usual, though. This sounded like typical Kolya on one of his good days.

But fuck what everybody else thought, because she *loved* typical Kolya. She would take him any way she could have him.

"And what if it *is* Maya?" she asked, grinning.

Silence echoed back before the bed creaked, and then the curtain was ripped back faster than Maya could blink.

The first thing she thought?

Oh, good, he'd gotten to shower.

It was a stupid thought to have, considering all they had been through. A thought that really didn't matter in the grander scheme, but apparently, this was the way her mind was choosing to deal with all of this shit.

For a long while, the two of them stared at one another and didn't move. Maya, at the end of the bed. And him, sitting with his legs thrown over the other side.

"Someone got you pants?" she asked.

Kolya *smiled*. "Konstantin snuck a pair in."

"And he didn't tell me."

She tried *really damn hard* not to sound petty right then. It was good for Konstantin that he had managed to get through the barricades the police had thrown at them over the past couple of days as they'd tried to talk to Kolya. But at the same time, it still irked her that *he* had gotten in to see his brother while she had needed to wait.

The pants were only one thing she noticed. The other bit was the burn that had been wrapped on his arm, and that spot she thought was an ash mark on his face? Was actually a badly blackened *bruise*.

Kolya didn't miss the way Maya was looking him over, if his fading smile was any indication. "It's fine, *dushka*."

Maya sniffed and tried to ignore the way her eyes prickled with the threat of tears. "It's *okay*, really?"

"Here we are, Maya."

How black and white he saw things.

How simple things were for him.

"Barely," she whispered. "We are *barely* alive."

Kolya nodded. "Maybe so, but we're alive nonetheless."

Maya's mind flashed back to those last few seconds in the warehouse. How everything had seemed entirely fucking impossible, and she was staring at the end. She always thought when the end of her life came, she would see what everyone else always talked about.

Flashes of her life.

The important moments.

Things—people—she loved.

That's not what had happened for her at all. She hadn't drifted into memories or remembered all the good times in her life. Instead, she had been so sharply *present* that she hadn't thought of anything else at all. She didn't even have to wonder why that was, either.

Her life had just *been* before Kolya. A thing she was doing, and not something she particularly wanted to be doing, she supposed. She went through the motions because she was alive and breathing, and wasn't that what you were supposed to do?

And then there he was—angry, and confusing, and *beautiful*. A soul so unlike hers, but one that fit hers, nonetheless.

Why would she want to remember the rest of her life when she hadn't even been living it before him?

"You're too quiet," Kolya murmured, tipping his head sideways a bit to survey her. "I don't like it. Come here."

Maya didn't need to be told again. She quickly rounded the bottom of the bed and found the arms that were already outstretched and waiting for her. She briefly thought to ask Kolya if he was in pain or to tell him to be careful, for the sake of his head and bandaged arm, but he didn't give her a chance.

He grabbed hold of her, wrapped her in his bar-like embrace, and that was it. Her feet left the floor as he tucked her into his lap, her head found his shoulder, and her face tucked close into the side of his neck. Silence coated the room and if anything, his arms locked around her even tighter.

Maya kissed the side of his neck. "You are *crazy*."

Kolya's chuckles rocked them both. "Am I?"

"Completely insane."

"That's not news, no?"

She almost rolled her eyes but managed to just shake her head instead. "We hid under a *tub*, Kolya."

"But did it work?"

"Fair," she returned.

Kolya sighed. "It scared you."

"Didn't it scare *you*?"

She knew better than to ask that question. She figured nothing in life scared Kolya. It was as though he perpetually walked around, expecting death to eventually catch up to him, and he simply waited with open arms to welcome it like the familiar friend it was to him. Maya didn't know whether or not to be terrified of that fact or resigned to it.

"The only thing that scares me is not having you," Kolya murmured against the top of her head. "And when I feel like that, nothing else matters. Just this very strong need to make whatever is threatening you go away. A switch goes off in my head—I do what needs to be done, then."

Was that what it was?

Huh.

"*Dushka*," Kolya said quietly.

Maya pulled back just enough to look up at him. His lips had curved into the smallest, softest of smiles. One she hadn't seen on him before, and it made her heart speed up a bit. Just enough to thunder in her chest and make the blood race in her veins.

No big deal or anything.

"Yeah?"

Kolya tipped his head down, and his mouth brushed against hers. A gentle kiss, at first. Soft and sweet. Like he was reminding himself in those moments that she was still very much there and alive with him. If anything, she felt him relax in her hold the longer he kissed her. Her heart thundered impossibly faster, too.

Maya stroked his cheek with her fingertips, and then let them drift through his short-cropped hair, too. It was only when his arm tightened around her waist, and his tongue teased at the seam of her lips that the softness was gone, and something far more sinful took its place.

Oh, she loved the familiarity of their kiss. The way that even like this, he had to control and own her entirely.

All too soon for her liking, he was pulling away. Maya still smiled.

"What was that for?" she dared to ask.

Kolya laughed low. "A lot of things. Do I need a specific reason?"

"Maybe I like hearing them."

"Ah. Well, because here you are."

Maya grinned, and whispered, "Here I am."

"And because I love you, yes?"

Her gaze found his, then, and she found life staring back. More life than she'd ever found in his gaze before. It was all for her, too.

"That word—*love*—seems strange to me," Kolya said, reaching up to stroke her cheek with a large palm. "It doesn't seem like the best *fit*. I feel much more than something as simple as love when it comes to you. I have since the moment you looked at me across the bar. It took me this long to figure it out because I am … not good at this *thing*. Whatever we are, I am not very good at it, Maya. I'm sorry."

Maya sucked in a sharp breath. "You are perfect for me."

And wasn't that the only thing that mattered at the end of the day? She thought so.

"And I want you just as you are, Kolya," she added.

He gave her a nod before pulling her in for another one of those burning kisses that set her mind on *fire*. Yeah, the rest would never matter, as long as this remained the same at the end of every day.

It was the clearing of a throat that caused the two to break apart. Kolya shifted Maya from his lap to the bed beside him with one arm like she didn't weigh a thing. There was no missing the darkness in his eyes at having been interrupted when he turned to find who was waiting for them in the doorway.

He only relaxed slightly when he saw it was his brother.

"Konstantin," Kolya said.

Konstantin smirked. "He *lives*."

Kolya chuckled dryly. "You knew that."

"I know, but it's still fun to say it."

Maya pressed her lips together to keep from smiling. These two brothers—who always seemed to be balancing on a very sharp line where each other were concerned—were not simple or easy to figure out. Their relationship seemed tainted by the life they lived, and the father hovering over their shoulders. Competitive and problematic on their best days, sure.

And then there were moments like now, and for the last two days, when all of that disappeared and all that was left was a raw bareness of love. Maybe the only kind of love they really knew how to show one another, but it was there, nonetheless.

"Try not to do that again, yeah?" Konstantin muttered.

Kolya nodded. "That's the plan."

"I think it's worse when I'm not there to rein you in."

"Well, who's fault was that, no?"

Konstantin's jaw flexed. "Speaking of Vadim …"

Maya didn't miss the way Kolya tensed, but all it took was her hand stroking the side of his bare arm for him to calm again.

"What about the bastard?"

Konstantin sighed, and glanced at the clock on the wall. "He knew what was going to happen. In the warehouse, yeah? He knew and sent you in."

Maya didn't even bother to simply *touch* Kolya that time. Before he could react, her hand was curving around the back of his neck. Soft fingers lying flat to his skin and holding tight. She could feel the way his blood pulsed at this pressure point, and the way his skin jumped.

"Is that so?" Kolya uttered.

"Sorry, *brat*."

Kolya didn't respond.

Konstantin then added, "And he's left to go back to Chicago. The morning after you were admitted, actually."

"I should probably thank him for not staying long enough to visit."

"Or run," Konstantin returned.

Kolya met his brother's gaze, unafraid. "I'm not running from that man."

"You know he's going to—"

"Punish me for this, and her, and all the rest? Quite aware, yes. I'm still not running."

"Then you are crazier than I thought."

"Or I'm just tired of this, Konstantin," Kolya murmured. "I have been tired of being this man for him for a long time. Between the two of us, we both know I am not the better fit, no?"

Konstantin's jaw ticked once but he nodded. "When do you want to get out of here and go home?"

"Any time would be great."

"You got it."

Konstantin was quick to leave the room then, leaving Maya alone with Kolya once again. She wasn't quite sure what she wanted to say, but her first thoughts slipped out of her mouth before she could think better of them.

"I don't want you to be punished for me, Kolya."

His gaze never left the doorway. "As long as it's always *me*, and never you, *dushka*. I will always take it."

And that was why, she knew.

Why he'd given her *those* stars—his stars.

He'd made her untouchable.

And in the process, ruined himself.

• • •

"*Blyad*," Maya heard Kolya curse the second she walked back into the hotel suite. "Stupid fucking *thing*."

Yeah, they were back here—although, a *new* and bigger suite with more rooms and space—for a spell. She was hoping it wouldn't be too long. She set Sumerki down and undid the straps on his ThunderShirt. It was supposed to help the pup with the pain of his cracked rib, apparently. All she knew was that he *hated* it.

"Stay," she told the dog.

Sumerki gave her a look with those big yellow eyes of his and then wandered off toward the bedroom where his bowls of food and water were set up. Not to mention, his bed. Really, she thought the pup was just happy to have Kolya back.

Maya found Kolya in the small kitchenette of the hotel suite. It was attached to a much larger dining room. With a kit of bandages and creams set up on the counter, Kolya bent over the edge to rest as he attempted to clean his arm.

Three times a day, that bandage needed to be changed. Each time, he refused to let her help for whatever reason. Maya had been fine with letting him grit his teeth and curse his way through it before, but not so much now.

This was ridiculous.

Kolya didn't even notice Maya was in the room with him until she slid in beside him and took the cold cloth right from his hands. Those blazing eyes of his turned on her, and had it been someone else, they might have shrunk under the weight of his anger. She, on the other hand, stared back unbothered.

"Let me do it," she said, "you *hate* doing it, anyway."

Kolya sighed. "You don't need to do it, *dushka*."

"But I want to, so …'"

He said nothing then, but he also didn't argue. Turning his back to the counter, Kolya offered his arm to her wordlessly. He didn't even like looking at the burn, really. He stared at the decorative clock that covered one entire wall behind the large dining table.

The second Maya pressed that cold cloth to his arm, she didn't miss the way he flinched, and air hissed between his teeth.

"Sorry," she whispered.

Kolya shook his head subtly, and his gaze went back to clock like he was waiting for the time to get to a certain number. "It's fine, no?"

Three days they had been back in Chicago, and this was how it had been the entire time. Kolya … waiting. For what, Maya wasn't sure, but she could see it in his eyes. He was waiting for something. The other shoe to drop, maybe.

But he wasn't telling her.

Maya set the cloth aside and grabbed the cream that needed to be applied to the burn three times a day with every bandage change. She knew why Kolya didn't want her doing this—he didn't want her bothered by the sight of the burn, but that was honestly the last thought on her mind as she applied the cream.

She was pissed it'd happened at all.

Fucking crazy.

But goddammit, she loved him.

Still, she didn't miss the way Kolya flinched again when she started wrapping the bandages around the burn. She thought maybe she could distract him …

"You know, before New York …"

His gaze drifted to her. "Thought we agreed to not talk about *that*."

Well, he did.

She just agreed.

"Not New York, Kolya, *before*," Maya said.

"What about it?"

"I found a house I really liked, actually. I never got the chance to show you. It's perfect—six bedrooms, four bathrooms, three floors, and a three-door, attached garage. Indoor pool in the back, with a small guest house. Huge backyard for a certain you know who … ten-foot high fence."

Kolya made a noise. "I do like *that*. It's not white, is it?"

Maya smiled, but hid it by glancing down. "The fence?"

"Exactly that."

"I suppose you're not the type for the white picket fence, and two-point-five kids, are you?"

She'd just finished securing the bandages with medical tape at her question, which freed Kolya's arm. He used that to his advantage to wrap it around Maya's trim waist and yank her into him. Without a word, he slipped a hand under her jaw, tipped her head back, and kissed her hard. His tongue snuck into her mouth to tangle with hers, and quiet all those chaotic thoughts that seemed to constantly color up her mind.

Pulling away, but not going too far, Kolya murmured, "I am yours, *dushka*."

Maya winked. "I know."

"I am whatever *you* need."

"But the fence is dark-stained wood."

"*Good.*"

Maya laughed. "We probably *should* fill those bedrooms, though."

Kolya arched an eyebrow high. "Not yet, though."

"Not yet," she agreed.

This was a give and take, after all.

She was fine with that.

"Did the realtor put an offer in?" he asked.

"Not yet. *Things* happened."

Kolya scowled. "Fucking New York."

Maya reached up to press the pad of her thumb right into the spot between his eyebrows to smooth out the knot there. "I can call the realtor tomorrow."

"Do that."

"I will."

In the next breath, Kolya's hands found Maya's waist and gripped tight. He picked her right up from the floor, and three steps later, her backside met the smooth surface of the dining table. There was something about the way his palms skimmed beneath the skirt of her flimsy dress that had her shivering. He leaned in close enough for his lips to graze hers as his body fitted tightly between her widening thighs. There was no missing the hard ridge of his erection pressing against her core.

"I don't think you're in *any* shape to be doing this, Kolya Boykov," Maya warned him.

She had to give him some kind of warning. All too soon, she knew her warnings wouldn't matter at all. He'd start kissing her and then his fucking touches would start, too. Then, he'd be buried deep in her cunt, and she wouldn't care at all that he was probably in pain, all because he wanted to fuck her.

"Sorry," he replied, "I don't remember asking what you thought, no?"

Maya gasped. "That's *mean!*"

He kissed her gently, and then the tip of her nose, too, with a chuckle. "Do you like me when I'm *nice?*"

"Yes!"

"Right now, yeah?"

Maya pressed her lips together. "I plead the fifth."

"This isn't a courtroom, *dushka*. This is me and you. A man and a woman. A man who would like to get a taste of your pussy before I fill it full—maybe if you're good and ask nicely once I'm done, I'll bend you over, do it again, and spank your ass. And a woman who would *greatly* like to beg for exactly that, yes? There is no easy way out."

God.

Why did he have to be so right?

"Good."

She didn't want a way out, anyway.

"Is that a yes, then?" he asked.

Maya didn't even hesitate to say, "It's always *yes*, Kolya."

That was all he needed, it seemed. Those teasing, sinful hands of his skimmed higher under her skirt until he was able to fist the waistband of her panties. She only helped him by lifting a bit from the table to let him pull the lace down her thighs. Once that scrap of fabric was gone, he spread her thighs wider with fingers digging deliciously into her thighs and bent down.

That first contact of his mouth against her cunt was a tease. Nothing more than his lips kissing her folds and then his tongue flicking out to *taste*. And still, *already*, Maya found her hands curving around the edge of the table to hold on as tight as she could because she knew what was coming once he got his fill of making her crazy.

She was morphine.

He was addicted.

And yet, it was always her who was left feeling *far* too high from him.

"*Christ*, I love this pussy of yours, Maya. Always sweet, and pretty, and *ready*."

She shivered and sucked in another ragged breath when his tongue flattened against the entrance of her cunt. She didn't have to wait very long for him to give her exactly what she wanted. Two of his fingers buried deep in her pussy, and his tongue on her clit. A direct shock to her G-spot, and a constant beat against her clit to make her shake.

Even though the noise of her own bliss, she could hear the sounds *he* made. The hums and his grunts. Appreciative and pleased, every single time she clenched or jerked for him. She was nothing more than an instrument for him to play, and he knew it so well. He knew this song like the back of his hand, and soon, the crescendo would come to leave her breathless, trembling, and wanting so much more.

"*Please, please, please …*"

The chant left her lips fast and slurred. High, and entirely airless.

And when the control she had been holding onto slowly slipped away, nothing had ever felt better. Pleasure raged through her body, and like the ocean with an uncontrollable tide, she was happy to let it drown her.

Maya hadn't even finished coming down from that high before Kolya was standing and leaning over her again. His mouth found hers as he shuffled his pants down. Before she knew it, he was exactly where she wanted him.

Hard, thick, and heavy between her thighs. Stretching her open and filling her full in a way only he could. His teeth cut into her bottom lip the second he was seated deep in her cunt. She was so slick and shaking again. Her gaze locked on his as his lips drifted over hers, and down her chin.

That first thrust was bliss.

The second, *heaven*.

"Get those fucking legs of yours around me," he demanded.

She did and held him close. It was better when he was closer, anyway. So fucking deep, and keeping her nerves snapping like live wires.

"What do you want, yeah?" he asked, another hard thrust punctuating his words.

He knew.

He always knew.

"For you to fuck me," Maya breathed.

His hand splayed out at her back, while another yanked her dress down to show off a bare chest—some dresses just looked better with nothing underneath.

"And love me," she added.

"No one else ever will."

Not like he did.

19.

KOLYA STARED up at the white ceiling of an unfamiliar bedroom. Wide awake, despite the fact it was closer to three in the morning than he was comfortable with admitting. His body wasn't even tired, let alone his mind. How could he be tired when all he could do was wait for the other shoe to finally drop? When his father finally decided to act against him like he promised to?

He wasn't an easily frightened man.

He *was* getting tired of waiting.

Tipping his head to the side, Kolya found the sight that helped to make everything better. Maya slept peacefully in a new bed—one she picked for their bedroom because the headboard was a cushioned white leather that reminded her of clouds.

Fucking clouds.

Like the soft white bedding she chose to match. And the half of a dozen pillows, most of which were not even functional for sleeping on. Not to mention the large rug that had to be placed just right in the room so that the bed could sit properly on it, but also showed it off.

But he didn't really give a shit about any of that. It wasn't his thing, but he was happy to let Maya go on and do whatever she wanted. Whatever made her happy at the end of the day. Then, he got to see her enjoying all these things she'd never had. He was able to turn in the bed and watch her sleep every single night in a new house he never would have considered buying for himself because as long as he didn't get rained on, he didn't give a single fuck.

She loved it, though.

And so, he did, too.

Maya didn't stir when he reached over and pushed back the wisps of black hair that had fallen over her face in her sleep. With her head resting on top of one of her hands, she smiled even in her sleep.

When the world wasn't out to get this woman, she was something else. Bubbly and perpetually happy. Bouncy on her feet and sweet to her very core.

The world wasn't out to get *her* anymore. He'd made sure of that. The Albanians backed off after the Valbon and New York thing. According to the tape they'd sent over about a week after Kolya returned to Chicago,

Valbon was officially dead. He'd considered letting Maya see it just so she too could watch Valbon die and *know.*

Konstantin thought that might be a bad idea.

Why traumatize her more?

His brother was probably right. Kolya simply told her instead.

Why anyone in the world would want to hurt her, he didn't know. But he was willing to kill any fucker who thought to try it again. There was still her brother left, after all, but that was simply a matter of time before Alexei showed up again somewhere. Snakes did tend to prefer other snakes, and Kolya had people looking in the best spots to find a fucking serpent.

It was the whining at the doorway that finally drew Kolya's attention away from a sleeping Maya. He found Sumerki pacing just outside the bedroom. He swore the pup—despite having his own bed to sleep in that was just one room over—just needed to come and check on Kolya multiple times in a night. And because Kolya wasn't sleeping at all, Sumerki decided every time he came to check, that it was time to go outside.

Kolya slipped from the bed when Sumerki's whining started up again. At the sight of Kolya coming his way, the black ball of fur ran a circle just outside the door, and then proceeded to trip over his big ass paws.

It was amusing.

According to the vet, when Sumerki was full grown, he'd be well over a hundred pounds, and tipping closer to one-fifty. But right now, he was still a pup. Still too big for his paws and learning what those teeth in his mouth could do when he put his mind to something.

Lately, his mind had been on the chair legs of the new table set Maya had picked for the kitchen. She never said a word, though, just laughed and took the dog away from the tables.

Kolya slipped on the slacks and white T-shirt he'd discarded the evening before and headed out of the bedroom. Sumerki was fast on his heels the whole time. It was only once they were in the large fenced backyard of their new home that Sumerki finally darted away from Kolya out onto the damp grass. He waited for the dog to run off his energy and do his business. All the while, he stared at the inky sky over his head.

"I wondered why nobody answered the fucking door."

Kolya didn't jump at the new voice—even though he recognized it was Konstantin—but it was still a shock to have someone sneak up on him, nonetheless. Konstantin wore his smug-as-fuck smile that said he knew exactly what he'd done as he came around the side of the house.

"How did you get through the gate on the side of the house?" Kolya demanded. "It's *locked.*"

Konstantin quirked a brow. "It's locked, really? When has a shitty little lock ever stopped me?"

"Stop trying to break into my house."

Because this was not even the first time Konstantin had pulled this shit since Kolya closed on the house. More like the *tenth*. Konstantin got some kind of sick enjoyment out of finding all the weak spots in a house. Windows, backdoors … *roofs*.

"You need to put a better system in, no?"

Kolya rolled his eyes. "Next week."

Konstantin rubbed his hands together and looked all too fucking gleeful at that statement. "Good, something new to try."

"I'm serious, yeah? Stop trying to break into my house."

"I didn't come here for that anyway," his brother said quieter.

Maybe it was the tone of Konstantin's voice, or the way it faded a bit at the end. Maybe it was the way Konstantin tried to deliver the statement with little emotion, and yet failed still. Or maybe it was the fact it was early morning and Kolya knew his brother would rather be *anywhere else* but here at this time.

"What is it?" Kolya asked.

A muscle worked in Konstantin's jaw as he looked over the backyard, and his gaze landed on a still-playing Sumerki. "Vadim called. He demanded someone bring you into the Compound. Tonight."

An icy sensation slid down Kolya's spine.

Finally, he supposed.

It was *finally* time to finish this.

"Better I delivered the news and had you go in, than someone forced you," Konstantin added after a moment. "He didn't specify how he wanted you brought in, yeah?"

Kolya scowled. "Hmm."

"Sorry, *brat*."

"Don't be. I did this."

And Kolya knew it would be better if he faced his father's punishment— whatever it was—head-on, and just got it over with. The longer he tried to avoid Vadim, the worse this would be in the end. Once this was done, he could finally move on. He could begin this thing called life that he hadn't even been living before Maya. He was actually looking forward to really *living*.

"Stay here, yes?" Kolya asked. "Maya likes someone to talk to in the morning."

Konstantin smiled a bit. "Oh?"

His request was partly for Maya, but also for his brother, too. Konstantin and Kolya were a lot of things, but he knew his brother at the end of the day. There was no way Konstantin would be able to stand back and *watch* a punishment against Kolya without saying something or at least, wanting to.

Kolya figured he could just take that option away altogether.

He shrugged. "You always did talk too much for your own good."

Konstantin rolled his eyes. "I do not."

"A little. But she likes that about you."

With that statement, Kolya turned to head back into the house. The quicker he got to the Compound, the faster this would be over. It was the sharp bark behind him and the pattering of paws against the ground that made him hesitate.

Over his shoulder, he called to Sumerki, "You stay."

Konstantin chuckled when Sumerki still kept coming. "He doesn't listen well, yeah?"

Kolya frowned. "Not when he thinks I am leaving without him, no."

"I'll take him—you go."

Konstantin went to grab the pup, but Sumerki was quick to slide out of the man's way as he darted up the stairs and came to stop at Kolya's feet. Looking up at his master, he waited with his big eyes.

A silent, *Please.*

Kolya sighed. "I'll take him. Vadim won't touch him. Otherwise, he'll whine all night and wake Maya up."

But really, he just wanted his dog. If he couldn't have Maya, then Sumerki would help a great deal to give Kolya something to focus on.

Not that he would admit it to anyone.

"Your call," Konstantin said.

It always had been.

• • •

Zhatka—Reaper—was waiting the moment Kolya pulled into the Compound. He thought that was the first time he'd ever seen the man outside of the chambers he managed beneath the Compound, but Kolya knew that couldn't actually be the case. He didn't even know the man's name, but Zhatka *had* to have a life outside of this hell that Vadim created.

Or did he?

Who knew?

Vadim might very well own the fucking soul of this man. No one really knew anything about Zhatka but Vadim.

Stepping out of his Hummer, Kolya tucked Sumerki under his arm. He could feel the dog's tail wagging against his back, even as he crossed the grounds to the entrance where Zhatka stood dressed in all black.

The man's gaze drifted to the dog, and a slight amusement lit up his eyes. The first sign of real life Kolya had ever seen him show.

"Cute," the man said in Russian, "but he won't be cute for long before he's very *big*, comrade."

Kolya nodded. "That's the idea."

"You should leave him in the car."

His shoulders tensed. "And how long will he have to stay there alone?"

Zhatka sighed a bit. He probably understood Kolya's question as it stood, and the fact that it wasn't so much a direct question for the benefit of the dog, but Kolya trying to ask for *himself*.

"Better you bring him in, then. At least, he'll be with you. I will walk you down."

Kolya nodded.

What else could he do?

The long walk through the Compound felt impossibly longer when a man didn't know what he was walking toward. Zhatka stayed quiet the entire time, and it was only when they were outside one of the chamber's metal doors that he finally turned to Kolya again, but only waved his hand as if to tell the man to go in first.

Kolya set Sumerki to the floor first. "Be *good*. Find a spot and *stay*. Your spot—you *stay*."

The pup's tail finally stopped wagging and his yellow eyes darted from the door to Kolya.

Fuck.

He should have made Konstantin keep him instead.

Too late now.

Kolya pushed the heavy metal door open and stepped inside the chamber. Sumerki snuck in beneath his feet, and Zhatka followed behind. Zhatka guarded the door when it shut with a bang that echoed.

How it echoed with so many men filling up the chamber would always be a mystery to Kolya after that night. And he would remember *that* the very most. Above the burning of his skin, and the words his father spoke to him as he forcibly removed a tattoo and a legacy Kolya had never wanted to begin with, he would remember the eyes of Boykov men who couldn't meet his stare as he entered the room.

No, the only man who stared back was Vadim.

"Your last gift from me," Vadim murmured, gesturing at a table beside him.

There, Kolya found Alexei tied, gagged, and gutted like a fucking pig. The dead eyes of Maya's brother stared up at the damp, cement ceiling of the chamber while blood still dripped from the sides of the table. Wet and sticky, he bet. The man's mouth was stretched open in a grotesque scream of death, but Kolya only felt peace realizing the one thing that might threaten Maya was now gone.

He'd have liked to be the one who did it, but this was fine too. As long as the head was cut from the snake, what did it matter about *who* did it?

Still warm, by the looks of it.

"I heard you had Konstantin looking for the man," Vadim said, "and he is still a threat to *her*, isn't he?"

Vadim really did know everything, Kolya realized. They may have thought they were doing things their father couldn't possibly know, but Vadim knew fucking *everything*.

"You could have saved him for me, no?"

Vadim chuckled. "Well, that would have been *too much* of a gift. And I don't owe you anything now. You, however, owe *me*, Kolya."

Kolya nodded. "Take your payment, then."

Vadim smiled grimly. "How ready you are, Kolya."

It kind of felt like he'd been waiting for this moment his whole life. Wasn't it time to finally get it over with?

The men who couldn't even look Kolya in the eye were quick to move then when Vadim waved a hand. All of them came at Kolya—he didn't know if that's because they expected him to fight, and they thought all hands on deck would make him compliant or what.

He had news for them.

Kolya didn't fight.

What would be the point?

He was forced down. His knees cracked against the cement and a grunt left his lips at the way the sharpness echoed through his bones. The shirt he'd tossed on was cut away, exposing the tattoos that colored his chest and shoulders. Hands tightened on his body to keep him still, but never once did he move to give them a reason to grab him tight enough to hurt.

Someone's hand was in the back of his hair; another on top. Pinning his arms down and grabbing his throat. All the while, he watched Vadim. He watched as knives were heated by a blowtorch and readied to do the exact thing to him that he'd done to Maya's father just a few months ago.

"Everyone has a choice to make," Vadim said, coming closer with knives that glowed a morbid red, "and you made yours. You made choices against *me*, Kolya. That was how you chose to repay me for the life I gave you, and the future waiting for you to take. So, this is how I repay you—by stripping you of those things I gave you."

He could have done without the speech. He didn't really need it.

"Every tattoo but the cross will stay," Vadim said. "I'll even leave your Latin as a reminder, Kolya. Remember, you will die. You felt it so necessary to have that above your cross. You think I didn't know *why* you had it done? It'll be good for you to keep, even alongside your stars, now. Because that's all you are—*vor*, but a worthless one at that. One simply waiting for death that will inevitably come, yes?"

Vadim kneeled down and stared Kolya in the face at eye-level. "She was not worth this, Kolya."

The last words he chose to speak to his father in that chamber slipped from his lips easily, and honestly. "Yes, she absolutely was."

It probably wasn't the right thing to say. If anything, it likely pissed his father off more. But Kolya refused to bend to Vadim more than he already was. He was on his fucking knees, a burning hot knife dangerously close to his chest, and that was *enough*.

He would not give more.

The first burn of the knife coming down against Kolya's thieves' cross was enough to make him open his mouth to shout. Somehow, he forced that urge to scream back. He tensed, sure, his arms and body straining with the need to fight back against those who held him down. But he didn't say a goddamn *thing*.

To make noise was to be *weak*.

To beg was certain death.

He would do none of it.

But the *pain*. The pain was blinding—searing. A shock to his system that nearly sent him straight to his feet even with all the hands keeping him down on his knees. With the second knife, Kolya swore he *felt* the way a strip of his skin melted under the hot blade of the knife, and then how it was ripped away from his body when the weapon was lifted and tossed to the side.

Vadim didn't let up, and he didn't give Kolya a break. Not even when one of the men let Kolya go to stumble off to the side and vomit in a corner. His father only spoke when he was ready to demand another knife be handed over so he could begin the process once more.

Over and over and over again.

Until sweat dripped down his skin and he'd clenched his teeth so hard to keep from crying out that he was sure he'd cracked his molars. Until his fingernails broke through the skin of his palms, and he could taste blood in his mouth.

Until he *wanted* to sob, but the pain had crossed a threshold of no return. Where he was more numb than he was in agony, and he just wished it was over.

And still, he kept quiet.

Still, he didn't fight.

Kolya wasn't sure when it ended—he'd blinked out at some point. The agony touched a level where his body decided to shut down, and all he saw was black. His chest was no doubt a raw mess of burns, and the last thing he needed to do was rest on a dirty, wet cement floor. That was exactly what he did when the hands finally left his body.

The last thing he heard as his body rested against cold cement was the whimpering of a puppy, and the whisper of a man he hated.

"Leave him," Vadim said.

The door banged shut again.

If there was a hell, this was surely it.

• • •

Pain.

That's what Kolya felt when he tried to force his eyes open. It seemed like no matter what he did, his eyelids were determined to stay shut. Or they were *glued* that way. Numbness touched his fingertips and toes.

It was the only place that was numb.

The rest of his body was a war zone. Each movement caused agony to rip through every single one of his nerves.

Fuck.

He couldn't even breathe.

Yet, he needed to.

It was not lost on him that every time he blinked in and out of consciousness, his breaths seemed to come harder and shorter. That every time he woke up again like this on the cold, wet cement, it became harder to open his eyes and take air into his lungs.

His body was a fire.

Warm to the touch and only getting hotter. Yet, he *shivered*. His teeth chattered. He sweated even through the chills. He knew what that meant without someone else telling him.

Inflammation.

Infection.

Kolya needed to get up—he needed to get the hell out of that chamber, or he was never going to leave it. He was going to fucking die there on the cement from a raging infection. It didn't matter, though, because he couldn't do anything.

No matter how hard he tried.

He could barely make a noise, but in his head, he was screaming for help. And then when his struggles to just wake up came to a head and he started blinking out again, he would hear the noise in the background.

The whimpers of a puppy getting louder. Low whines whispering along his cheek, and the huff of a pup who didn't understand, and wanted him to *move*. Soft fur sliding along his skin. A wet, rough, *warm* tongue lapping at the most painful spots on his chest.

Sumerki.

And when the pain became too much to handle all over again, Kolya finally found the ability to move. Just enough to turn his head and vomit all over the cement.

His breaths came even harder.

His mind went black again.

• • •

Kolya didn't know what woke him up again—the murmurings of voices just beyond a doorway, or the barking dog that seemed entirely too loud and way too close to his ringing ears.

"Sumerki, *stop*," Kolya said.

Or, he thought he did.

It was entirely possible that the raspy croak he heard was his own voice, but who knew? He didn't know anything anymore. Kolya wasn't even sure how many days he had been on this fucking floor now. He couldn't tell by time passing. There was no window for him to feel or see the heat of the sun rising and lowering.

He knew *nothing*.

Sumerki kept barking.

Sharp and anxious.

Kolya knew that bark.

Outside, the voices got louder. Had the metal door been opened at some point?

"Let me go in, Zhatka."

Konstantin.

"I cannot," Zhatka murmured. "Vadim was clear. Not you."

"It's been *five fucking days*," Konstantin snarled. "That's what he said. Five days and then we can remove him. Dead or alive."

"*She* may go in and check," Zhatka returned. "And if he is alive, then you may remove him. I follow the orders I am given, Konstantin. That is all I do."

"Then let me go in. Move and let me *go*."

That voice.

That sweet, lovely *voice*.

Maya.

If nothing else could make Kolya wish he could call out or get up from the fucking floor … her voice was it. And yet, he still couldn't move.

If the door was open, why wasn't Sumerki running out? If it had been five days, the dog *had* to be thirsty, hungry, and terrified. Yet, Kolya felt the warmth of his pup tucked in close to his neck, and the barks continued to get sharper and impossibly louder.

He found his spot, Kolya realized.

Sumerki *stayed*.

Jesus fucking Christ.

"Not you," Konstantin was quick to say. "Maya, you don't know what he looks like or—"

"*Let me go in!*"

"She can go," Zhatka said dryly. "Let her go, Konstantin."

"That's cruel, Zhatka. That's Vadim being a *cocksucker*, yeah? Like he didn't do enough—this is the salt in the wound, once it's all said and done. I could go in there first; he would never know."

"I follow orders."

The argument continued but soft footsteps echoed closer. Kolya felt her in the room before she even made a sound. He felt her presence like the saving grace she truly was in his life.

Her ragged inhale echoed and those footsteps picked up until he felt her kneel beside him. Soft hands—God, he loved her hands—found his face, and turned his head with a gentle touch. And still, the pain reverberated.

It was too much.

He knew what she was seeing.

Vomit on the floor.

Kolya in a pool of his own mess.

Infected wounds.

Death in her hands.

"Kolya," Maya whispered. "Kolya, look at me. *Please, look at me.*"

Her hands were shaking.

Or was that him shivering again?

"Kolya!"

His eyes cracked open, but barely. Just enough of a slit to see a black-haired, blue-eyed angel above him. The bare lightbulb above her created a hazing halo around Maya. The second she realized he was looking at her, and *responding*, she let out an aching sob.

"I'm so sorry," she mumbled.

God, for *what?*

This wasn't her.

"He's alive," she called out through tears and tremors. "Konstantin, he's alive!"

Kolya blacked out again.

20.

A WEEK could do a lot for a person. It could change a lot. Maya knew that better than anyone. But even a week after dragging Kolya out of that fucking awful cement room, she wasn't sure if he was getting better … or making things worse.

"Take the IV *out*," Kolya growled.

"No," the doctor replied simply.

The man moved around the bedroom and prepped a syringe of pain medication. Maya was getting used to the different vials littering the beautiful vanity Kolya had said would match the bed she picked out.

"I can take pills instead of this goddamn IV. It keeps me in bed *all day*. Do I need to be in bed all day? I think *not*."

"I cannot pump your body full of antibiotics through pills," the doctor replied dryly. "Because, as I have explained to you far more than once, Kolya, it is the quickest way to shut down your kidneys and liver."

"And the IV won't do—"

"Different antibiotic. You also need the fluids."

"Just take the fucking IV out."

"No, and if you do it, that sweet girl over in the corner who's currently glaring at you is going to call me right away and let me know. Do you know how bad that infection was, Kolya? Into your *arms*. You are lucky you didn't lose one."

That quieted Kolya.

Mostly.

He grunted unhappily under his breath and scowled at the wall. This was Kolya in a nutshell. Never mind the way he bitched every single time those bandages on his chest needed changed. What he really fucking needed was a goddamn skin graft for the size of the burn—a permanent stay in the hospital until he was fully healed.

Here they were.

In their house.

Their bed.

A doctor on call.

Maya was trying really hard not to be pissed off, but it was getting difficult. Kolya was making it difficult. He needed to get better, but his way of doing that did not align with the medical care he needed.

That was the problem.

"Last orders for today," the doctor said, turning to give Maya a kind smile. The man *was* quite nice, all things considered. "Make sure the nurse soaks the burns and removes any dead skin again today. IV stays *in*."

Kolya grunted under his breath again, but this time, it sounded more like a curse. Maya figured, at least he stayed quiet once he finished. That was something.

"No ... strenuous activity," the doctor told Maya, "regardless of what he tries to say or do. Don't let him. *Rest* is best."

Maya nodded. "I'm on it."

The doctor held up the syringe he filled. "And the nurse showed you how to inject this into the IV, yes?"

"She did."

"If he gets too much to handle, just give him it. It's the pain making him snappy and moody."

"No, it isn't," Maya countered. "That's just Kolya."

Kolya sighed *loudly*.

But where was the lie?

Once the doctor was gone, Maya still didn't move from her spot against the wall. She folded her arms over her chest and stared at Kolya where he was resting in the middle of the bed propped up by pillows. His chest was exposed but for the special bandages that were made just for burn victims. He couldn't even wear a shirt or cover up with a blanket. She sure as hell couldn't touch him other than to rest beside him at night and throughout the day.

"Stop looking at me like that," Kolya grumbled.

"Like you're being a child?"

"I am *not*. The IV is pointless, no? Pills would work just—"

"No, they won't. And also, the IV keeps you resting, Kolya. It's also easier to give you meds this way. Stop behaving like this is news to you."

He scowled again. "I don't want the narcotics."

Maya's gaze drifted to the prepared syringe the doctor had left on her vanity *just in case*. "How much pain are you in?"

"Is there a scale?"

"One to ten, say."

Kolya didn't even have to think about it. "Fifteen."

Yikes.

"The narcotics would help a bit," she pointed out.

"They'll make me high, Maya. They won't actually help, yes?"

Another thing she wasn't supposed to do was upset or argue with him. Which was difficult on a good day because for the most part, that was just how Kolya communicated with those around him. Even her.

"Come here," he murmured.

Maya didn't move from her spot. "Not until you agree to drop the IV thing and take the narcotics for the pain."

Kolya sighed in *that* way again. "*Dushka—*"

"Unless your next words are, 'Yes, Maya, whatever you say, Maya,' then I don't want to hear it."

"You're impossible," he muttered.

"No, I *love* you, even when you make it difficult."

Kolya made a noise under his breath. "That's enough of that. Come here now."

Fine.

She padded softly across the room and came to stand next to the bed. She figured he just wanted her closer because lately, that's how his moods flipped. He wanted no one near him, and then sometimes, all he wanted was her.

This time, he grabbed her wrist with one hand, and yanked her into the bed. Maya tried her hardest not to land *on* him, but her hand still came dangerously close to his large bandages.

"Kolya!"

"Quiet," he rumbled, tucking her against him before kissing the top of her head. "Enough of this, *dushka*. It's over."

Maya let out a shaky breath.

It *was* over.

She was still pissed, but not at him. Not really.

There was nothing she could do about it, either.

She knew he was still in pain. She could feel it in the way a tremor skipped over his skin with every movement he made. And still, he dragged her closer to his side, and held her there with one arm like he wasn't ever going to let her go.

"The IV stays," he said.

"Good."

"No narcotics."

Maya sighed.

Win some, lose some.

She had a feeling that was going to be the story of her life with this man.

• • •

Ballet.

That was the first thing Kolya wanted to do when he was given the okay to leave their house for the first time in a month. Maya was stuck between being concerned because he was nowhere near being healed, and also adoring him *so fucking much* because it was obvious he hated ballet, but he saw her reading a review of one in the *Tribune*.

In the private booth, the rest of the crowd watching the ballet couldn't see them. Maya wasn't concerned about them and she wasn't even watching the show anymore, either. She was a little distracted by the man next to her.

Kolya hid it well, but she could see it. Beneath the fitted tux he wore, he was in pain. Maybe from sitting up so long. Maybe from the tight fit of his shirt. It could have been a lot of things, but he was hurting.

"You know," Maya said, "I think when the doctor gave you the okay, it was with the intention of getting you out for a walk, and out of bed."

The edge of Kolya's lips quirked upward. "You think?"

"One to ten?"

Kolya didn't even ask what she meant. "Eight right now."

At least he was below ten.

That was good.

Maya still sighed. "I knew this was going to be too much."

For a whole month, all he'd done was stay in bed and rest. The longest walk he'd made was to the goddamn bathroom and back. He'd gone downstairs once, and almost passed out after getting so winded from the pain.

But they weren't supposed to talk about that.

"*Dushka*," he murmured.

Maya tipped her head sideways to stare at him. "What?"

"I'm fine."

"You're not actually, but maybe if you say it enough, we'll all start to believe it, Kolya."

"*Woman.*"

His growl whispered over her skin and Maya shivered. Like sin and lust had come to wrap around her body simply because he made a sound she liked. That was another thing that had been off the table for longer than she liked—not that it was something they could control.

Sex, that was.

"You wanted to see the ballet," Kolya said, "and so we came, yes?"

"We could have waited."

"This ballet would have been over."

"Kolya."

He gave her a blank look and Maya just ended up shaking her head. He was something else. Even being in pain—she knew he was, regardless of what he tried to say—he was still going to sit right there and let her enjoy this stupid ballet.

It was not worth his discomfort.

"We can go anytime," Maya said, smiling a little. "I miss Sumerki, anyway."

Kolya's hand that had been resting on her thigh squeezed tightly over the skirt of the evening dress. "I bet he's chewed a whole chair leg off by now."

"Probably."

"We are fine to stay."

"I would rather go."

She could watch a ballet *any day*.

It didn't have to be this day.

Or night, rather.

"Lady's choice," Kolya said, standing from the chair with a slow grace she had come to learn meant he was trying very hard not to show how uncomfortable he was. It only pissed her off more that someone who should have loved him had done this to him. Kolya didn't miss the darkening of her expression, if the way he reached out to slip a hand around her neck was any indication. Silently, he dragged her closer. Close enough that he could tip her head back and drop a soft kiss to her mouth. "It's over, yeah?"

He kept saying that.

He kept promising that.

She wished it was over in her heart.

Maya was never going to forgive Vadim for what he had done. *Ever.*

"Come on," Kolya said, tucking her into his side.

He kept her close through the long walk out of the theater. Maya could have easily opened her own door and climbed into the high Hummer. Kolya still opened the door for her and lifted her into the passenger seat like he'd done every other time.

It was only once Kolya was in the driver's seat and they were driving through the city to head back home did she finally see him relax a bit.

The rest of the world was gone.

It was just them again … as it should be.

Maya reached over, and stroked Kolya's jaw with her palm. She saw him smile before he said, "I love you, Maya. Your nagging worrying, and all."

Fucking man.

"I know you do. And I love you."

Kolya quirked a brow. "Good thing."

"Why is that?"

"I don't think anyone else would."

"Their loss."

Kolya chuckled. "No, you're just crazy enough to have me, *dushka.*"

Or that.

• • •

"Oh, my God," Maya gasped. "A *walk*. That's what you're allowed to do, not fuck me first thing in the morn—"

A hot kiss quieted her words instantly. Kolya's kiss was punctuated by his hips thrusting against her core again. It was a little late for her to be backing out of this now, though. You know, considering he was already fucking her, and she was *this damn close* to coming.

It was also hard to deny this man when he woke her up already kneeling between her thighs and looking up at her like he'd just found his favorite meal. But when had she ever been able to deny Kolya? When he wanted something, he got it.

End of story.

"Fuck," Kolya muttered against her lips.

His hands were holding her so fucking tight. Keeping her locked against the bed as he took her slow, and sweet. All things Kolya was most certainly *not*. And yet, she loved this just as much. Flames licked at her skin, and her breaths came a little faster with each flex of his hips.

"Come for me, yes?" he murmured in her ear. "Let me *feel* it, *dushka*."

She had to keep semi-aware of her actions. Like the way her fingernails dragged down his back, and how her legs tightened around his waist. If she hurt him like this, then he wasn't getting fucked again for *months*.

Not until he was good again, anyway.

She just let him have control.

Do what he wanted.

God knew she was loving it anyway.

Kolya's dark, husky chuckles echoed in Maya's ear when she finally jumped from the edge of that cliff. Or hell, maybe he was the one who threw her from it. Either way, she was still left breathless and shaking from the fall.

"There it is," she heard him say.

Maya barely blinked, and he was pulling away. She found herself flipped over on the bed so that she was on fours. He filled her full all over again and pounded into her harder from behind than before. The aftershocks of her orgasm were only made that much better like this, and he probably knew it, too.

A fist found her hair, and his mouth landed on the back of her neck. She was just gasping her way through a second orgasm when a phone started ringing somewhere. Kolya didn't hear it, though. He was too focused.

Almost there, she knew.

He could feel it in the tremor rocking his hands, and the tenseness of his body. She felt him pull out and paint her back with his cum as her name fell from his lips in a strangled moan.

Nothing sounded better than that.

"*Fuck*," he mumbled against her skin.

Maya shivered, chilled from the air and yet warm from him. "Mmm, still not supposed to be doing that."

"Fuck the doctor."

She only rolled her eyes and laughed again.

Then, quieter, he said, "We need to get married."

Maya blinked, unsure she had even heard him right. "What?"

"Married. Rings. That ... bit, yeah?"

"Married," she echoed.

"If you want to," he said, kissing her skin again.

"Is that a proposal?"

She didn't even care that *this* was how he asked. Just that he had.

"I think it is," Kolya said.

Maya turned her head just enough to catch his kiss with her own before she whispered against his mouth, "Then that's a yes."

If only that could have been how the rest of their morning was spent. Instead, the phone started ringing again and Kolya pulled away. He left the bed with a slowness that told her he was sore, and that morning fuck hadn't helped.

She didn't have time to think on it for long before he found his phone. Just by the cold expression that drifted over his face before he answered the call, she knew it wasn't going to be good.

"Vadim," Kolya greeted. "What can I do for you today?"

A month and a day.

That was all Vadim gave Kolya to recover.

One month.

And one single day.

"I'll be at the Compound in an hour, then," Kolya said.

Maya knew better than to ask him to stay, or to point out that he wasn't close to being ready to go back to work for his father. She knew better, because this was his life and he'd chosen it.

She chose him.

"Blue is your favorite color, isn't it?" he asked as he headed for the walk-in closet. He came back out with a suit in hand and a pair of shoes. "Is that what you'd prefer?"

Maya tucked the sheet close to her chest and sat up in the bed properly. "For what?"

"An engagement ring."

How could she not smile?

Even though she was *worried* ...

Even though she was *angry* ...

Even hoping he would be okay ...

She smiled for him when he looked her way. She was going to make sure that her smile was the first and last thing he saw every time he left their home or came back. It was the one thing she could promise he would always have when everyone else just wanted to take from him.

She would give.

Maya would always be the one who gave.

Of course, he was going to be okay. It was Kolya, and when everything was going to hell around him, he was just fine.

"I will love any kind of ring," Maya said softly, "because it came from you."

Kolya drifted her way again and leaned over the bed to kiss her once more. He lingered a little longer than he usually would before pulling away. "Start planning the wedding, then. I don't intend to wait."

If that's what he wanted … then that's exactly what he would get.

Maya would make sure of it.

Reaching out, she grabbed onto his wrist, and tugged softly. "Come home, yes?"

Come home so I can smile at you again.

Kolya nodded. "I will, *dushka*. Nothing on this earth can keep me away from you."

He wasn't lying.

That was probably the most frightening, and wonderful, part of all.

This was *them*.

They were perfect.

ABOUT THE AUTHOR

Bethany-Kris is a Canadian author, lover of much, and mother to four young sons, three cats, and four dogs. A small town in Eastern Canada where she was born and raised is where she has always called home. With her boys under her feet, a snuggling cat, barking dogs, and a spouse calling over his shoulder, she is nearly always writing something ... when she can find the time.

Find Bethany-Kris at:

www.bethanykris.com

OTHER BOOKS

Boykov Bratva

Fractured Ties
Essence of Fear

The Guzzi Legacy

Corrado
Alessio
Chris
Beni
Bene
Marcus

Renzo + Lucia

Privilege
Harbor
Contempt
Forever

Andino + Haven

Duty
Vow
Andino + Haven: The Complete Duet
One Last Time

John + Siena

Loyalty
Disgrace
John + Siena: The Complete Duet
John + Siena: Extended

Cross + Catherine

Always
Revere
Unruly
The Companion
Naz & Roz

Guzzi Duet

Unraveled, Book One
Entangled, Book Two
Cara & Gian: The Complete Duet

DeLuca Duet

Waste of Worth: Part One
Worth of Waste: Part Two

Standalone Titles

Pink
Pretty Lies
Dirty Pool
Effortless
Inflict
Cozen
Captivated
Dishonored

Donati Bloodlines

Thin Lies
Thin Lines
Thin Lives
Behind the Bloodlines
The Complete Trilogy

Filthy Marcellos

Antony
Lucian
Giovanni
Dante
Legacy
A Very Marcello Christmas
The Complete Collection

Seasons of Betrayal

Where the Sun Hides
Where the Snow Falls
Where the Wind Whispers
Seasons: The Complete Seasons of Betrayal Series

Gun Moll Trilogy

Gun Moll
Gangster Moll
Madame Moll

The Chicago War

Deathless & Divided
Reckless & Ruined
Scarless & Sacred
Breathless & Bloodstained
The Complete Series
Maldives & Mistletoe

The Russian Guns

The Arrangement
The Life
The Score
Demyan & Ana
Shattered
The Jersey Vignettes

FANTASY ROMANCE BY BETHANY-KRIS

The Hunted: A 9INE REALMS Novel

Find more on Bethany-Kris's website at www.bethanykris.com.